Felicity turned and stared as Nathan strode into the room.

The candlelight, which she had thought so beneficial moments ago, now seemed far too glaring. There were no concealing shadows that she could step into.

'So. It *is* you.'

Fear tingled down her spine as she saw the glitter in Nathan's eyes.

'Nathan, listen to me, please. When I left Corunna I had no thought of ever seeing you again.'

'Until I became an earl!' he bit out. 'You had no wish to be the wife of a poor army officer, but a countess—no doubt you find the title irresistible.'

'That is not true!' She stepped away, trying to ignore the sheer animal power that emanated from him.

'It is time to consider what you owe me.' He held out his hand to her. 'Come.'

Felicity eyed him warily. 'I do not understand you.'

He took her wrist. 'I am taking you back to Rosthorne House with me.'

'No! It is far too late at night.' She tugged against his iron grip.

He pulled her towards him and lifted her easily into his arms. Felicity gasped, then began to kick and struggle, but it was useless. His hold tightened, pinning her against his chest.

'Be still, woman. You did not fight me thus last night.'

Author Note

The Retreat to Corunna is one of the less well-known episodes of the Napoleonic Wars. The Spanish allied armies had been overwhelmed, and Sir John Moore found himself and his British troops alone in northern Spain, facing Emperor Napoleon's victorious French army. Moore retreated to the port of Corunna and managed to keep his exhausted men together as they struggled across the mountains during the depths of winter. He fought off the French at Corunna long enough to allow the British transport ships to come into the harbour and carry the remains of the army safely back to England. Travelling that same route in January 2009, I realised just how awful that journey across the mountains must have been. Many soldiers perished from cold and hunger, stragglers were cut down by the French, and the ragged, starving wretches marching back into Corunna aroused the sympathy of their Spanish hosts.

The story of THE EARL'S RUNAWAY BRIDE begins amongst the mayhem and confusion of that winter in Corunna. Felicity Bourne is alone and penniless in the city, and when she is rescued by a dashing British soldier she thinks him the hero of her dreams. Unfortunately, those dreams turn into a nightmare, and she is separated from Nathan Carraway for five long years, until the premature Peace Celebrations of 1814 bring them together again in London. Nathan and Felicity are both scarred by their wartime experiences. They must learn to forgive the past and work together for their future happiness.

I do hope you enjoy THE EARL'S RUNAWAY BRIDE. As an author I set scenes and drop my hapless characters into predicaments that I would certainly not wish to experience, but they battle through, survive and succeed, often in ways that surprise even me!

THE EARL'S RUNAWAY BRIDE

Sarah Mallory

First published in Great Britain 2010
Large Print edition 2010
Harlequin Mills & Boon Limited,
Eton House, 18-24 Paradise Road, Richmond, Surrey TW9 1SR

© Sarah Mallory 2010

ISBN: 978 0 263 21166 5

Harlequin Mills & Boon policy is to use papers that are natural, renewable and recyclable products and made from wood grown in sustainable forests. The logging and manufacturing process conform to the legal environmental regulations of the country of origin.

Printed and bound in Great Britain
by CPI Antony Rowe, Chippenham, Wiltshire

Sarah Mallory was born in Bristol, and now lives in an old farmhouse on the edge of the Pennines with her husband and family. She left grammar school at sixteen, to work in companies as varied as stockbrokers, marine engineers, insurance brokers, biscuit manufacturers and even a quarrying company. Her first book was published shortly after the birth of her daughter. She has published more than a dozen books under the pen-name of Melinda Hammond, winning the Reviewers' Choice Award in 2005 from Singletitles.com for *Dance for a Diamond* and the Historical Novel Society's Editors' Choice in November 2006 for *Gentlemen in Question*.

Recent novels by the same author:

WICKED CAPTAIN, WAYWARD WIFE
MORE THAN A GOVERNESS
  (part of *On Mothering Sunday*)
THE WICKED BARON

For my editor, Lucy,
with thanks for all your help and support.

Chapter One

Felicity was angry, blazingly angry. All her terror and anxiety at being alone and penniless in a strange country was forgotten, superseded by rage that the portmanteau packed with her last remaining possessions had been snatched away from her. Without a second thought she gave chase, following the ragged Spaniard in his leather waistcoat away from the Plaza and into a maze of narrow alleys that crowded about the harbour at Corunna. She did not stop; even when a sudden gust of wind caught her bonnet and tore it off her head she ran on, determined to regain her property. Only when they neared the harbour and she found herself in an unfamiliar square bounded by warehouses did she realise the danger.

She saw her bag handed to a young boy who ran off with it while the thief turned to face her, an evil grin splitting his face. Felicity stopped. A quick glance over her shoulder revealed two more menacing figures blocking her escape. Felicity summoned up every ounce of authority to say haughtily, 'That is my bag. Give it back to me now and we shall say no more about this.'

The response was a rough hand on her back, pushing her forward. She stumbled and fell to her knees. Quickly she scrambled up, twisting away as one of the men reached out to grab her. There was only the one man in front of her, if she could get past him—with a guttural laugh he caught her by her hair and yanked her back, throwing her into the arms of his two accomplices. Felicity fought wildly, but it was impossible to shake off their iron grip. They held her fast as the little man with his yellow teeth and stinking breath came close, leering at her as he ripped open her pelisse.

She closed her eyes, trying to blot out their cruel laughter and ugly jests. Then she heard another voice—slow, deep and distinctly British.

'Move away from the lady, my good fellows.'

Felicity's eyes flew open. Beyond the thief stood a tall British officer, resplendent in his scarlet tunic. He looked completely at his ease, regarding the scene with a slightly detached air, but when her tormentor pulled a wicked-looking knife from his belt the officer grinned.

'I asked you politely,' he said, drawing his sword. 'But now I really must insist.'

With a roar the two men holding Felicity released her and rushed forward to join their comrade. She backed against the wall and watched the red-coated officer swiftly despatch her attackers. He moved with surprising speed and agility. A flick of his sword cut across the first man's wrist and the knife fell from his useless fingers. A second man screamed as that wicked blade slashed his arm and when the officer turned his attention to the third, the man took to his heels and fled, swiftly followed by his companions.

The officer wiped his blade and put it away. Sunlight sliced through a narrow gap between the houses and caught the soldier in a sudden shaft of light. His hair gleamed like polished mahogany in the sunshine and he was grinning down at her, amusement shining in his deep brown eyes as if the last few minutes had been some entertaining sport rather than a desperate fight. He was, she realised in a flash, the embodiment of the hero she had always dreamed of.

'Are you hurt, madam?'

His voice was deep and warm, wrapping around her like velvet. She shook her head.

'I—do not think so. Who are you?'

'Major Nathan Carraway, at your service.'

'Then I thank you for your timely assistance, Major.'

'Come along.' He held out his arm to her. 'We should get out of here in case they decide to come back with their friends.'

'But my portmanteau—'

'I think you should resign yourself to its loss, madam. Was it very valuable?'

'Priceless.' She swallowed. 'It contains everything I own in the whole world.' Suddenly she felt quite sick as she realised the enormity of her situation. 'What am I going to do now? I have nothing, no one…'

Instinctively she turned to the man at her side. Looking into his eyes she was conscious of a tug of attraction, a sudden conviction that in this man she had found a friend. Her fear and anger faded away. He gave her a slow smile.

'You have me,' he said.

'Good morning, miss. I've brought your hot chocolate.'

Felicity stirred, reluctant to leave her dream, but when the maid threw back the shutters her room was flooded with sunlight, banishing any hope of going back to sleep.

'What time is it, Betsy?'

'Eight o'clock, miss. With Master John and

Master Simon gone off to school you said not to wake you too early this morning.'

Felicity sat up. She hadn't bargained for the extra hour's sleep being haunted by her dreams!

She did not linger in her bed but dressed quickly and made her way down to the schoolroom. It was eerily quiet: after four years of looking after two energetic youngsters and watching them grow into schoolboys it was not surprising that she now missed their presence. As their governess she had grown very fond of them, and they had provided her with an excellent distraction from her constant, aching sadness.

'Fee, Fee, where are you?'

Felicity heard Lady Souden's soft calls and hurried across the room to open the door.

'Do you need me? I was just tidying up.'

Lady Souden entered the sunny schoolroom and looked around, sighing.

'It does seem so *quiet* with the boys away at school, does it not? But you are no longer the governess here, Felicity.' She rested her hands upon her stomach. 'At least not until this little one is of an age to need you.'

'And that will not be for some years yet,' observed Felicity, smiling.

'I know, but oh, Fee, is it not exciting? The boys are darlings, and I adore being their stepmama, but I cannot *wait* to have a baby of my own.' Lydia shook her head, setting her guinea-gold curls dancing. 'After five years I thought it would never happen! But that is not what I wanted to say to you. Come away now; you do not need to be toiling up here.'

Felicity scooped up another handful of books from the table.

'This isn't toiling, Lydia, I enjoy being useful. Besides, the boys will still use this room when they come home, so it is only fitting that it should be as they left it.'

'If it is to be as they left it you had best spread their toys over the floor and pull *all* the books from the shelves! Oh, Fee, do leave that now and come into the garden with me. It is such a lovely morning and I want to talk to you.'

'Oh, but another five minutes—'

'No, now. It is a command!'

As Felicity accompanied Lady Souden down the stairs she reflected that few people could have such an undemanding mistress. They had been firm friends at school, and when Felicity had come to her, penniless and desperate to find work, Lydia had cajoled her doting new husband into employing her as a governess to his two young sons— Lydia's stepchildren. Felicity knew she was very fortunate. Sir James was a considerate employer and she was thankful that her excellent education allowed her to fulfil her duties as governess to his satisfaction. So pleased had he been with her performance that when the boys finally went away to school he raised no objections to Lydia's suggestion that Felicity should stay on at Souden Hall as her companion. The arrangement worked extremely well, for Sir James was often away from home and said it was a comfort to him to know that his wife was not alone. Felicity's only complaint was that she had so little to do, but when she taxed Lydia with this, Lady Souden merely laughed and told her to enjoy herself.

Now, walking in the shrubbery arm in arm with Lydia, Felicity gave a little sigh of contentment.

'Happy?' asked Lydia.

Felicity hesitated. She was content: there was a world of difference between that and true happiness, but very few people could aspire to such a luxury. She said, 'Who could not be in such lovely surroundings? The gardens here at Souden are so beautiful in the spring. Are you still planning to lay out a knot-garden? I have been studying the pattern books in the library and would dearly like to help you draw it up.'

'Oh, yes, if you please, but I am afraid that will have to wait. James has written to say he wants me to join him in London next month. For the Peace Celebrations.'

'Oh. Oh, well, while you are away I could—'

'You are to come with me, Fee.'

Felicity stopped.

'Oh no, surely that is not necessary.'

'*Very* necessary,' said Lydia, taking her hands. 'With the boys at school there is no reason for you to hide yourself away here. Besides, you have read the news sheets, you know as well as I that any number of important personages will be in London for these celebrations: the Emperor of Russia and his sister the Grand Duchess of Oldenburg, the young Prussian princes and—oh, too many to name them all now! And James has already been informed that he will be expected to entertain them all. Just think of it, Fee, dinners, soirées and parties—dear James has also said he wants us to hold a ball! So I shall need you to help me with all the arrangements. I could not possibly cope with it all.'

'Should you be coping with any of it when you are with child?'

'Oh, Fee, I am not *ill*! I am more likely to die of boredom if I stay here with nothing to do. Besides, the baby is not due until the autumn and the celebrations will be over by then. Do not look so horrified, Fee, look upon this as a rare treat.'

'A treat! Lydia, you know I am...not good in company. I fear I should let you down.'

'Nonsense. You have very good manners, it is merely that you are out of practice—and that is because your horrid uncle dragged you away from the Academy to make you his drudge!'

'Lydia! Uncle Philip was not horrid, he was... devout.'

'He was a tyrant,' returned Lydia with uncharacteristic severity. 'He tried to beat all the joy out of you.'

Felicity hesitated.

'It is true my uncle considered all forms of pleasure a sin,' she conceded, 'but that was only because he was deeply religious.'

'Then he should have hired a *deeply religious* servant to take with him rather than dragging you off to deepest Africa!'

Felicity laughed at that.

'But he didn't! We only got as far as northern Spain! Poor Uncle Philip, he convinced himself that the Spanish Catholics were as much in need of saving as any African tribe, but I have always suspected the truth was he could not face another sea journey.'

'Well, it was very wrong of him to take you away instead of giving you the opportunity to marry and have children—'

Felicity put up her hand in a little gesture of defence; she did not want to contemplate what might have been.

'What's done is done,' she said quietly. 'I am very happy here at Souden, and I would much rather stay here while you go to London.'

'But I shall need you!'

Lydia's plaintive tone carried Felicity back to their schooldays, when her friend had often begged her for company. Poor Lydia could never bear to be alone. Now, as then, Felicity found it impossible to resist her. Sensing her weakening, Lydia pressed her hand.

'Do say you will come, Fee—you are so *good* at organising parties.'

'But you will not expect me to *attend* any of these parties.'

'Not unless you want to, my dear.'

'You know there is nothing I would want less!'

'Then you may remain behind the scenes, invisible.'

Felicity laughed at her.

'But I cannot possibly be your paid companion if I never leave my room. Sir James will not countenance such a thing!'

'I shall tell him that you have a morbid fear of strangers,' said Lydia. 'He will understand that, for he has a cousin who is very much the same, only because he is a man, and rich, it is *quite* acceptable for him to be a recluse. And James knows how much I rely upon you, especially now that I am increasing.'

'Perhaps you should not go at all,' said Felicity, clutching at straws.

Lydia gave a little gurgle of laughter.

'But of course I should! I have never felt better, and the doctor says I must not pamper myself but carry on very much as normal. Oh, *do* say you will come with me, Felicity: you are very necessary to my comfort, you know.'

Felicity could not resist Lydia's beseeching look.

'You have been so kind to me that I cannot refuse you.'

'So you promise you will come to town with me?'

'Yes, I give you my word.'

Lydia gave a huge sigh.

'I am so relieved!' She linked arms with Felicity again and gave a little tug. 'Come along, now: we must keep moving or we shall grow too chilled. It is only April, after all.'

They walked on in amicable silence for a few more minutes.

'Is that what you wished to say to me,' asked Felicity, 'that we are to go to town?'

'Well, yes, but there is a little more than that, my dear.'

'Now, Lydia, what mischief are you planning?'

'None, I promise you, but there is something you should know.' Lady Souden gave her arm a little shake. 'Remember, Fee, you have given me your word!'

'Very well. Tell me.'

'The Earl of Rosthorne will be in town.'

Felicity's heart lurched. The Earl of Rosthorne—Nathan Carraway, her handsome hero. The man who still haunted her dreams, but had proved to be a master of seduction. She swallowed nervously, trying to remain calm.

'How do you know that?'

'James wrote to me—'

'Lydia, you haven't told him—!'

'Of course not, I promised I would not give you away. No, his letter was full of the plans for the celebrations. He said that Carraway had been ordered to London, not only because he is now Earl of Rosthorne, but because he is—or was—a military man and Prinny is quite *desperate* to impress. The royal parks are to be opened, there will be displays, and fireworks, and—oh, Felicity, it will be so exciting—are you not the *teeniest* bit curious to see it all?'

'Not if there is the teeniest risk of meeting Lord Rosthorne!'

Lydia turned her wide, blue-eyed gaze upon her.

'I know he treated you badly, my dear, but are you not curious to see him again?'

Felicity hesitated. Nathan had rescued her, given up his lodging for her, bought her new clothes. He had taught her to love him and then broken her heart.

'No. I have no desire to see him again.'

'Felicity, you are blushing. You still care for him.'

'I do not! It was five years ago, Lydia. I am over him.'

'Well, perhaps you no longer cry yourself to sleep every night, as you did when we first took you in, but at times, when you are sitting quietly, there is that faraway look in your eye—'

Felicity laughed.

'Lydia, you are too romantic! That faraway look was most likely exhaustion, having had the care of two energetic boys for the day!'

'Well, it does not matter what you say, I have the liveliest curiosity to see the man who—'

'Lydia!' Felicity stopped abruptly. 'Lydia, you promised me when I came to you that you would respect my secret.'

'And so I shall, my love, but—'

'Pray let us say no more about the odious Lord Rosthorne! If you insist upon my coming to town with you then I will do so, but pray understand that upon no account must he know I am there. It would be embarrassing to everyone.' She swallowed hard. 'I am dead to him now.'

Lydia threw her arms around her, enveloping Felicity in a warm, scented embrace. 'Oh, my dear friend, you know I would do nothing that would make you miserable!'

'No, of course you would not. Not intentionally, that is.' Felicity glanced up. 'The rain clouds are gathering. The sun will soon disappear; I think we should go indoors now.'

They did not speak of London again, or of the Earl of Rosthorne, but when Felicity retired to her room that night he was there, in her head, as close and as real as ever.

'The Earl of Rosthorne, sir.'

The butler's sonorous tones filled the small, book-lined study, investing the announcement with considerable gravitas. Nathan squared his shoulders. After twelve months he was still not comfortable with the title. The gentleman sitting behind the large mahogany desk jumped up immediately and came forward to meet him. Nathan regarded him with interest. He knew Sir James Souden only by reputation but even if he had not heard that the man was an active supporter of Lord Wellesley, he would have been disposed to like him, for there was a look of intelligence and humour in his face and an energy in that lean body. Here was a man who was used to getting things done. He was smiling now at Nathan and waving him towards a chair.

'Welcome, my lord, and thank you for coming so promptly.'

Nathan bowed.

'Your message was waiting for me when I arrived in town this morning, Sir James.'

'Ah, but knowing the object of this meeting I would not have been surprised if you had put it off.'

The twinkle in the older man's eyes drew a wry grin from Nathan.

'Always best to attack the unpalatable without delay, I find.'

'Spoken like a true military man.' Sir James gestured towards the decanters lined up on a side table. 'You'll take a glass with me, my lord? I've a very fine cognac—stolen from the French, of course, so you might appreciate it.'

'I would, thank you.'

'So,' said Sir James, when the glasses had been

filled and his guest was sitting in one of the comfortable padded arm-chairs that faced the desk. 'So, my lord, how much have you been told?'

'Only that his Highness wants me to help with the entertaining of his royal visitors.'

'Aye. He's turning the town into a damned beargarden for the summer,' said Sir James, shaking his head. 'But there, it's all in a good cause. Peace, don't you know, so I suppose we shouldn't complain.'

Nathan sipped at his brandy. It was smooth and aromatic and definitely not to be hurried.

'I am at a loss to know why he has summoned me here,' he said at last. 'I would have thought there were hostesses enough in London to entertain all the crowned heads of Europe. Mine is a bachelor establishment; my mother does not come to town. You may know she is an invalid and spends all her time at Rosthorne Hall—'

'Oh, his Highness ain't looking for you to give parties and all that sort of nonsense. The ladies will be falling over themselves to do that—and in fact I have asked Lady Souden to come to town for that very purpose—not that she needs any persuading to hold a party! But the Regent wants military men around him, especially to accompany Marshal Blücher: the old Prussian is so highly esteemed that even Prinny is in awe of him. There will be so many of 'em, you see: Blücher, the King of Prussia and all those princes, not to mention Tsar Alexander. And his sister, of course, the Grand Duchess... So we are all recruited to help: an army of attendants to ensure that his royal guests are not left to themselves for a moment. Your first task is to head up the Tsar's escort from Dover. I know, I know, my boy; I can see from your face that you don't like the idea.'

'You are right,' replied Nathan. 'I begin to wish I had never left the army!'

Sir James laughed and got up to refill their glasses.

'Do you miss it, my lord, the military life?'

'It was the only life I had ever known, until last year. I obtained my commission in the Guards when I was sixteen.'

'The title came as a surprise?'

Nathan nodded. 'Quite. The old Earl, my uncle, had three healthy sons, so I never expected to inherit. But the two youngest boys perished in Spain.' Nathan paused for a moment, recalling the icy winters and scorching summers: the torrential rain, cloying mud, flies and disease that took their toll of the troops. It was said more men were killed by disease and the weather than by Bonaparte's army. The scar across his left eye began to ache. Too many memories. He shook them off. 'Their loss may well have hastened the old man's end. He died at the beginning of the year '12 and his heir took a fall on the hunting field less than six months later. When the news came I thought it my duty to come home. Boney was on the run, after all.' He allowed himself a little smile. 'Since then I have been so tied up with my new duties I've had no time to miss the army.'

'And do your new duties include looking for a wife? You will need an heir.'

Nathan's reply was short. 'My cousin is my heir.'

'The ladies won't see it that way.' Sir James winked. 'You are now the biggest catch on the Marriage Mart.'

An iron claw twisted itself around Nathan's guts. 'I do not think so.'

'Oh? From all I've heard of you, my boy, you have never had trouble attracting women. Your reputation precedes you,' said Sir James, when Nathan raised his brows. 'It is said that Europe is littered with the hearts you have broken. Although to your credit, I have never heard that you seduced innocent young virgins.'

No, thought Nathan bitterly. *Only once did I break that rule, to my cost!*

His lip curled. 'With such a reputation I would

expect the doting mothers to keep their chicks away from me.'

'But they won't, believe me. They will be planning their own campaigns once they know you are in town.' Nathan's hand briefly touched his temple and Sir James smiled. 'And don't think that scar will frighten them away—'tis more likely to fascinate 'em; it will add to your attractions!'

Hurriedly Nathan rose. 'If there is nothing else to discuss I must be away.' He saw his host's brows rise and tried to moderate his tone. 'I do not think there is much that can be done until the allied leaders arrive next month.'

'You are right, of course. We will meet again before then to discuss our roles.' Sir James chuckled. 'Thank God his Highness is too busy designing new uniforms for his troops and working on his plans for a grand spectacle in Hyde Park to worry about us. Goodbye, then, for the moment, my lord. If you have no other engagements, you might like to join me for dinner on Wednesday night. I am expecting Lady Souden to be here by then, but we shall not be entertaining: just a snug little dinner, if you care for it.'

Nathan bowed. 'My presence in town is not generally known yet, so I have no fixed engagements.' He bowed. 'Thank you, sir. I should be delighted to join you.'

* * *

London, thought Felicity gloomily as she gazed out of the carriage window, was crowded and noisy and so very dirty. The roads were thick with rubbish and droppings from the hundreds of horses and oxen that plodded up and down, the cobbles only visible in the wheel tracks or where a crossing sweeper cleared a temporary path for a pedestrian and earned a penny for his pains. The cries of the flower-seller mingled with those of the knife-grinder and the hot-pie man as they hawked their wares from street to street. Rows of tall houses lined the road, mile upon mile of brick and stone with barely a patch of grass to be seen.

In one corner of the carriage, Lady Souden's severe-looking dresser was snoring gently while Lydia herself was sitting bolt upright, staring out of the window, her eyes shining and a little smile of anticipation lifting her mouth. She was born to be a society hostess, thought Felicity. She delighted in parties and balls and could not understand Felicity's reluctance to come to town. After all, she reasoned, if Felicity refused to go into society, what did it matter if she was in London or at Souden?

But it did matter. Felicity knew that there was danger in London.

Nathan Carraway was in London.

Chapter Two

The carriage drew up outside Sir James's house in Berkeley Square and Felicity followed Lydia through the gleaming front door and into the study on the ground floor, where Sir James was waiting for them. Lydia ran in, cast aside her swansdown muff and threw herself into her husband's arms. He kissed her soundly before holding her away from him.

'Well, well now, puss, have you missed me?' he said, laughing. 'What will Miss Brown think of this very unfashionable display of affection?'

'Miss Brown is delighted with this display of domestic harmony,' murmured Felicity, her grey eyes twinkling.

Sir James grinned at her, keeping one arm about his wife's still tiny waist.

'I'm glad to hear it. And I am glad to see *you*,

Miss Brown. I hope Lady Souden has warned you, we are to be very busy for the next two months.'

'She told me you would be entertaining a great deal, Sir James.'

'Aye, dukes, duchesses, crown princes—and never a moment to call our own. What do you say to that, Miss Brown?'

'I say Lady Souden is equal to the challenge, sir.'

'Aye, so do I,' declared Sir James, giving his wife another kiss. 'But I rely upon you to look after her when I am not here, Miss Brown. Lydia is far too careless of her health, especially now.'

Felicity met his eyes and said resolutely, 'You may depend upon me, Sir James. I would not wish any harm to come to Lady Souden or the unborn child.'

Sir James bestowed a grateful smile upon her.

'Thank you, I am sure I may. Lydia has told me of your fear of going out, Miss Brown, and I will do everything I can to lessen your own discomfiture. A carriage shall be at your disposal at all times, you have only to say the word. Now upstairs and unpack, the pair of you, for we have a guest for dinner.'

'Oh?' Lydia clapped her hands delightedly. 'Is it someone I know?'

'No, a young man I met only t'other day, but he

is very agreeable, I assure you. He will set all the young ladies' hearts a-flutter this summer, I have not a doubt.'

'Oh, who?' cried Lydia. 'Do tell me, my love!'

Sir James kissed her nose.

'He is a young nobleman. Rich, handsome and most clearly in want of a wife.' He looked from Felicity to Lady Souden, his smile growing. 'It is the new Earl of Rosthorne.'

Felicity's hands tightened on her reticule. What cruel trick was fate playing upon her, to force the earl upon her notice so soon? She cast an anguished look at Lydia, who attempted a little laugh as she turned to her husband.

'R-Rosthorne? Well, bless me! How is this, my dear?'

'He is newly arrived in town,' explained Sir James. 'We met to discuss the arrangements for looking after his Highness's guests at the forthcoming Peace Celebrations and he struck me as a very pleasant young man. I thought it would please you to meet him, my love.'

'It—it does,' stammered Lydia. 'It is a little sudden, that is all. Having just arrived…'

'Well, he is not expecting any formal ceremony. Just a snug little dinner, I told him, so off you go and put on one of those pretty gowns of yours, my love. You are required to look charming tonight, nothing more.'

'Then perhaps Lady Souden should come up-stairs and rest for a little while,' suggested Felicity, edging towards the door.

With another slightly hysterical laugh Lydia allowed Felicity to lead her away, leaving Sir James still chuckling to himself.

'I am sorry, Fee,' she whispered as they went up the stairs. 'I had no idea James would invite Rosthorne to the house!'

Felicity sighed. 'It was inevitable, I suppose, but I did not expect it to be *today*.'

Lydia squeezed her hand. 'You must not worry, my love, you need not see him. This house has so many rooms the earl could be *living* here and not know of your existence!'

Despite Lady Souden's assurances Felicity found herself growing ever more anxious as the hour approached for Lord Rosthorne's arrival. For five years she had done everything in her power to remain hidden from Nathan Carraway and the thought that he would shortly be in the same house terrified her. Not least because she had an overwhelming desire to see him again.

It was dangerous, but she could not resist. A few minutes after Lydia had gone down to the drawing room, Felicity slipped out of the little chamber that Lady Souden had decreed should be set aside as her own private sitting room. The entrance hall of Souden House extended up to the roof and a glazed dome provided natural light for the ornate staircase that rose from a central point to the half-landing before splitting into two flights that curved around the side walls to the first floor and the main reception rooms. From there a narrower stair curled up to the second floor where a small balcony overlooked the hall below. During past seasons Felicity had often brought her young charges on to this balcony when Sir James was entertaining and they had spent many a happy hour watching the arrival of the guests. Now she decided to use it for her own purposes.

Feeling very much like an errant schoolchild, she crept towards the edge of the balcony and sank down. Felicity knew from experience that visitors rarely raised their eyes beyond the ornately decorated first floor. Her dark-grey gown blended well with the shadows and through the balusters she had an excellent view of the front door and entrance hall as well as the first rise of the staircase. The long-case clock on the landing below chimed the hour. It was followed almost immediately by the sounds of an arrival. Felicity knew a sudden, irrational desire to laugh—trust Nathan to be so punctual, it was the soldier in him.

Then he was there. They were in the same house, the same space. She leaned forward, straining to see him. Her heart turned over as he walked into the hall, but his curly-brimmed beaver hat obscured her view of his face. She had never seen him in anything but his scarlet regimentals and thought him handsome in uniform but now, seeing his tall, athletic figure in the plain black swallow-tailed coat, she almost fainted with a wild yearning to run down the stairs and throw herself into his arms. She stifled it, reminding herself of how he had betrayed her. She hated him, did she not? She had vowed she was done with him for ever. Yet here she was, hiding in the shadows, desperate to see the man who had broken her heart.

He spoke to the footman as he handed over his hat; she could not make out the words but his warm, deep voice awoke a memory and sent a tingle down her spine. She noticed that his brown hair was no longer tied back but cut short so that it just curled over his collar. He turned to ascend the stair and she was momentarily dazzled by his snowy white neckcloth and waistcoat. As he lifted his head she put her hand to her mouth, stifling a cry. A disfiguring scar cut through his left eyebrow and down across his cheek. His face was leaner and his mouth, which she remembered as almost constantly smiling, was turned down, the lines at each side more pronounced. She had expected him to look a little older, but the severity of his countenance shocked her.

Felicity had followed his career as closely as she could. She knew Nathan's regiment had been involved in several bloody battles so she should not have been surprised to see he had been wounded, but the scar made it suddenly very real.

Do not be so foolish, she told herself. *You should rejoice that he has been punished for the way he treated you!* She closed her eyes and shook her head slightly. It had been her uncle's way to call down fury and retribution upon the heads of those that had offended him. But she was not like her uncle and the thought of Nathan's suffering sliced into her heart. She stared again at the tall figure ascending the stairs.

Look up, she pleaded silently. *Look at me.*

As Nathan reached the top of the first flight of stairs he paused. Felicity's heart was thudding against her ribs: if he raised his head now he would see her! For one joyous, frightening, panic-filled moment she thought he would do just that, but then he was turning to greet his host and Sir James's bluff good-humoured voice was heard welcoming him.

'Come along up, my lord, do not hesitate out there! Here is my lady wife waiting to make your acquaintance...'

The drawing room door was closed, the voices became nothing more than a low drone. Felicity slumped down, her head bowed. She had seen him. He was alive and apart from that scar on his face he looked well. A burst of laughter reached her: he even sounded happy.

And he was not aware of her existence.

Hot tears pricked her eyelids and she berated herself for her stupidity. It had been foolish to come to London, knowing he would be here. She should have known it would only bring pain. She dragged herself back to her room. It was senseless to think of him, laughing and talking with Lydia and Sir James in the gilded splendour of the dining room below. She would be best to put him out of her mind and go to sleep. That was the sensible thing to do.

But when the Earl of Rosthorne left the house several hours later, the silent grey figure was again watching from the upper balcony.

Having lost his first wife in childbirth, Sir James was morbidly anxious for Lydia. Felicity was aware of this and resolutely stifled her own misgivings as she offered to accompany Lady Souden about the town. Lydia's delighted acceptance of her company was at least some comfort.

'Oh, I am so pleased! I knew how it would be, once you saw how exciting it is going to be in town this summer. I only wish we could have been here for the procession in honour of King Louis last month, but there is so much to look forward to; it will be *so* entertaining.'

'I am sure it will,' said Felicity bravely.

Lydia gave her a long look. 'And Lord Rosthorne?'

Felicity hesitated. 'I must do my best to avoid him. If I dress very plainly I shall not attract attention. It is possible that he would not even recognise me now. Perhaps, when we go out during the day, I might be veiled.'

Lydia clapped her hands. 'How exciting! But people will be so curious! We could say you are a grieving widow…'

'No, no, Lydia, that will not do at all.'

But Lady Souden was not listening.

'Smallpox,' she declared. 'You have been hideously scarred—or mayhap your head was misshapen at birth.'

In spite of her anxieties, Felicity laughed.

'Shall I pad my shoulder and give myself a hunchback as well? That is quite enough, Lydia. We will say nothing.'

'But people will think it very odd!'

'I would rather they think me eccentric than deformed!'

Glancing at her reflection in the mirror the following day, Felicity could see nothing in her appearance to cause the least comment. Lydia had informed her that they were going to drive out in Hyde Park at the fashionable hour. Felicity's russet-brown walking dress was not quite as fashionable as Lady Souden's dashing blue velvet with its military-style jacket but it looked well enough, and the double veil that covered her face was perfectly acceptable for any lady wishing to protect her complexion from the dust kicked up by the carriage horses.

The drive started well, but there was such a number of carriages in the park and so many people claiming acquaintance with the fashionable Lady Souden that it was impossible to make much progress. Lydia was enjoying herself hugely. She introduced 'my companion, Miss Brown' with just the right amount of indifference that very few bothered to spare more than a glance for the plainly dressed female with her modest bonnet and heavy veil. Felicity was beginning to relax and enjoy the sunshine when she spotted yet another carriage approaching, but this one was flanked by two riders, one of them the unmistakably upright figure of Lord Rosthorne.

She gripped Lydia's arm and directed her attention to the coach.

'Heaven and earth, Lady Charlotte Appleby! I had no idea she was in town.'

'But Rosthorne is with her,' exclaimed Felicity. 'Can we not drive past?'

'Too late,' muttered Lydia, pinning on her smile. 'They have seen us.'

She was obliged to order her driver to stop. Felicity held her breath and sat very still, praying she would not be noticed.

With the two carriages side by side, Nathan brought his horse to a stand and raised his hat to Lady Souden.

'Good day to you, ma'am. You know my aunt, of course.'

'Yes indeed.' Lydia Souden turned her wide, friendly smile towards Lady Charlotte and was rewarded with no more than a regal nod. Nathan's lips tightened. His aunt made sure no one ever forgot she was the daughter of an earl. Lady Charlotte raised her hand to indicate the second rider.

'Let me present my son to you, ma'am. Mr Gerald Appleby.'

Nathan grinned inwardly as his cousin took off his hat and greeted Lady Souden with all the charm and courtesy that his mother lacked. Young scapegrace!

'Delighted, ma'am! But we are remiss here, I think—will you not introduce your friend?'

Nathan blinked and berated himself. It was unusual for Gerald to show him the way, but he had not even noticed the rather dowdy little figure sitting beside Lady Souden, still as a statue.

'Oh, this is my companion, Miss Brown. Lady Charlotte, you are in town for the Peace Celebrations?'

'Yes. We were obliged to hire, since Rosthorne House is no longer available.'

'You know that if you had given me sufficient notice I would have had rooms prepared for you, Aunt,' replied Nathan.

'In my brother's day there were always rooms prepared and ready for me.'

'Heavens, Mama, the house has been shut up for the past year or more,' replied Gerald Appleby. 'Nathan wasn't expecting to come to town this summer, were you, Cos?'

'No. Consequently I have only opened up such rooms as I require.'

'Fortunately my man was able to secure a house in Cavendish Square,' Lady Charlotte addressed Lydia. 'With so many visitors in town this summer there was very little to suit. So different in Bath, of course, where I have my own house…'

'My dear ma'am, there was any number of apartments that would have been ideal if you had not insisted upon having so many servants with you.' Gerald glanced at his audience, a merry twinkle in his eye. 'Only imagine the task: not only had her poor clerk to find somewhere with sufficient rooms for Mama's household, but *then* he was obliged to find stables and accommodation for her coachman and groom, too!'

'Really, Gerard, do you expect me to do without my carriage?'

'No, but you might well do without your groom. You no longer ride, ma'am.'

'Harris has been with me since I was a child. He comes with me everywhere.'

'I wonder if perhaps he might have enjoyed a holiday,' observed Gerald, but his mother was no longer listening.

'My man had instructions to find me the very best,' she announced. 'And I do not think he has managed so ill.'

Nathan's attention began to wander as the ladies discussed the forthcoming arrival of the foreign dignitaries. Gerald, he noticed, was passing the time by trying to flirt with the veiled companion. While his mother's attention was given to speculation about the Grand Duchess of Oldenburg's latest conquest, Gerald was leaning over the side of the carriage and murmuring outrageous remarks. The poor little dab looked quite uncomfortable. Nathan tried to catch Gerald's eye. Damnation, why couldn't the lad behave himself? Nathan's hand clenched on the reins. He must get out of the ridiculous habit of regarding Gerald as a boy. He was eight-and-twenty, the same age as himself, but his cousin had not served a decade in the army, an experience that Gerald declared had left Nathan hardened and cynical. It might well be the case, but it was quite clear that the little figure in the carriage was not enjoying Gerald's attentions. He was leaning closer now, his hand reaching out towards the edge of the veil.

'Cousin, you go too far!' Nathan's voice cracked across the space between them. It was the tone he had used on new recruits and it had its effect. Gerald's hand dropped.

'I beg your pardon,' Nathan addressed the rigid little figure. 'My cousin sometimes allows his humour to go beyond what is pleasing.'

She did not reply and merely waved one small hand. He threw an admonishing glance at his cousin, who immediately looked contrite.

'Indeed, Miss Brown, Rosthorne is right; I went too far and I beg your pardon.' Gerald directed his most winning smile towards her. 'Well, will you not speak? Pray, madam, take pity on me: I vow I shall not rest until you say that you forgive me. Miss Brown, I *beg* you.'

Nathan could not but admire Gerald's tenacity. He was—

'I do forgive you, sir. Let us forget this now.'

His head jerked up. That voice, the melodic inflection—it struck a chord, a fleeting memory: surely he had heard it before. He stared at the lady, trying to pierce the thick curtain of lace that concealed her face.

'Forgive me,' he said, frowning. 'Have we—?'

'Forgive *me*, my lord,' interposed Lady Souden with her sunny smile. 'We are causing far too much congestion on this path. That will never do; we must drive on. If you will excuse us…'

There was nothing to do but to pull away and allow the carriage to pass.

'Well, well, one must admit Lady Souden to be most charming,' declared Lady Charlotte graciously. 'She intends to hold a ball later this year. I have told her I shall attend. And you must come too, Gerald.'

Mr Appleby grinned across at his cousin. 'Not really my line, Mama, but if you insist. What of you, Cos?'

Nathan shrugged. 'If I receive an invitation I

must go, I suppose.' His thoughts returned to the veiled figure in the carriage. Something nagged at the back of his mind, a thought that he could not quite grasp. He said, 'Who was the female with Lady Souden? Miss Brown. Have you met her before, Aunt?'

'Lady Souden said she was her companion,' replied Lady Charlotte. 'No doubt she is some penniless relation.' She turned to address her son. 'And as such she can have no attraction for *you*, Gerald.'

'Devil a bit!' responded Gerald, grinning. 'Just trying to be friendly, Mama.'

'Better that you should remain aloof, like your cousin,' retorted Lady Charlotte.

'What, be as grim as Rosthorne?' Gerald laughed. 'Impossible! I swear his dark frown could turn the milk sour!'

Nathan allowed himself a smile at that. 'Try for something in between, then, Cousin.'

'Precisely.' Lady Charlotte nodded. 'You must remember your breeding, my son.'

As the carriage pulled away Gerald threw a rueful glance across at Nathan. 'When am I ever allowed to forget it?'

'So. It is done. I have met him.'

Felicity closed the door of her little bedchamber and leaned against it. Her legs felt very unsteady, so much so that she dare not even attempt to walk across the room to her bed. She closed her eyes. Nathan's image rose before her, so familiar, so dear. She had studied him closely while the two carriages were stopped. In profile she thought him even more handsome than when they had first met, his face leaner, his look more serious. Even when she saw again the scar across the left side of his face she was no longer horrified by it. She was thankful the dreadful disfigurement did not seem to have affected his sight; his eyes were as keen as ever and for a moment she had quailed beneath her thick veil, convinced that he would recognise her. Even worse than the fear of detection was the fierce disappointment she had known when he had addressed her; he was clearly unaware of her identity and his indifference hit her like a physical blow.

'But it is done,' she said again. 'Now I have seen him I know what to expect, I am prepared.'

However, being prepared did not prevent her from feeling slightly sick when Sir James announced cheerfully that she would be required to accompany his wife to Lady Somerton's later that night.

'I know I promised to attend, but I have fallen

behind with drawing up my plans for Tsar Alexander's arrival in London—I gave my word that I would report to Carlton House tomorrow morning.'

'Then you must remain here and finish them,' replied Lydia calmly. 'But there is not the slightest need for Felicity to come with me: Lady Somerton is such an old friend…'

Felicity felt Sir James's eyes upon her and she said immediately, 'There is nothing I should like more than to go with you, Lady Souden.'

Lydia blinked. 'You would?'

'Of course,' Felicity lied valiantly. 'You will recall you showed me Lady Somerton's invitation and said she hoped that Lord Byron would be there and would read for her.'

'But I thought you disliked Byron,' objected Lydia.

'His style of living, perhaps,' Felicity persisted. 'His poetry is quite—quite impressive.'

Her friend looked at her in surprise. Felicity maintained her calm, aware that Sir James was also regarding her, but with approval, and she drew some comfort from this as she ran upstairs after dinner to change her gown. And what if Nathan should be there? Felicity knew this question would be on Lydia's lips as soon as they were alone together. She had no answer, and could only pray that the earl was not a lover of poetry.

Lady Somerton's tall, narrow town house was crowded and noisy. Felicity followed Lydia as she swept up the stairs to the main reception rooms, ostrich feathers dancing, and was immediately surrounded by her friends and acquaintances. Felicity stayed very close. In her plain grey gown she elicited barely a glance from the gentlemen vying for the beautiful Lady Souden's attention and no glance at all from the matrons who came up to claim acquaintance with one of the most fashionable personages of the *ton*.

Lady Somerton laughingly chided Lydia for arriving so late and ushered them into a large salon where the poetry reading was about to begin. Felicity followed on, but such was the crush that she was unable to secure a seat beside her friend and was obliged to find a space for herself towards the back of the room. This suited her very well, for she was able to observe the crowds from the shadowy recesses.

Any hopes that Nathan might not attend were soon dashed when she saw him stroll into the room. At first she thought it was her imagination that there was a change in the atmosphere as he entered, but there was a definite murmur of excitement rippling around the salon. A young lady to her right fluttered her fan and muttered, 'Mama! The Earl of Rosthorne is come.'

'Then stand up straight, Maria,' retorted her turbaned parent. 'You will not catch his attention if you slouch. Shoulders back, my love; he is surveying the company.'

The young lady plied her fan even faster. 'Oh, Mama, he looks so severe, I vow he frightens me!'

'Nonsense, child, it is merely the effect of that dreadful scar. Smile now... Oh, how vexing, Lady Somerton is carrying him off. Never mind, Maria, while he is in the room there is still hope. Keep your head up. And do not squint, girl! You will need all your wits about you if you wish to become a countess.'

A cold chill settled around Felicity's heart. Was that the reason Nathan was in town, to find a wife? Why should he not? she asked herself miserably. She had done her best to disappear, doubtless he had forgotten her in the inevitable confusion of removing the army and its followers from Corunna.

The evening dragged on. Felicity heard very little of the poetry—her attention was fixed on Nathan. At one point he looked around, as if conscious of her gaze, and she was obliged to draw back into the shadows. When there was a break in the recital Felicity noticed that he was immediately surrounded by ladies, all eager for his attention. The turbaned matron lost no time in joining the throng and was soon presenting him to her daughter. Felicity longed for it to be *her* hand he was carrying to his lips, *her* words that made him smile. She forced herself to look away. It would do her no good to dwell on what could never be.

She spotted Lydia at the centre of a laughing, chattering group of ladies and seeing that she was as far from Nathan as the room would allow, Felicity made her way across to her. Lady Souden looked up as she approached, excused herself with her charming smile and stepped away from the group to take Felicity's arm.

'Well, my dear, what do you think to it?' Lydia giggled. 'I have rarely heard such execrable verse, I think.'

'Was it so very bad? I was not really listening...'

'Dreadful, my dear,' Lydia murmured, smiling across the room at their hostess. 'Rosthorne is here, have you seen him?'

Felicity almost laughed at that. She had eyes for no one else!

'Yes. By staying in the shadows he has not noticed me.'

'But you are uneasy.' Lydia patted her hands. 'Shall we make our excuses and leave? If Lord Byron had been here I might have made a push to stay and be sociable but as it is, I think I would prefer to be at home with darling James.'

Felicity nodded. She looked across the room at Nathan. She would have liked to stay and prolong the torture of watching him, but she knew that was senseless, so with a word of acquiescence she turned and followed Lydia out of the room.

They were in the entrance hall, waiting for their carriage when Lydia reached over and deftly flicked up the hood of Felicity's cloak.

'Cover yourself,' she murmured. 'Rosthorne is coming.' She gave Felicity's shoulder a reassuring pat before turning. 'My lord.'

Felicity stepped behind Lydia and out of Nathan's direct gaze.

'Going so soon, madam?'

'Why, yes, my lord.' Lydia gave him her charming smile. 'I find a little poetry goes a long way.'

The corners of his mouth lifted. 'Well said, ma'am! I expected to see Sir James with you.'

'Unfortunately his work on plans for the Tsar's entertainment would not allow him time to come with me this evening. I have no doubt that when we get back we shall find him still poring over his notes.'

'Well, ma'am, if you have no escort, you must let me accompany you to Berkeley Square—'

Lydia gave a little laugh. 'I would not dream of taking you away from Lady Somerton, my lord.'

'If your opinion of the readings this evening is the same as mine, you will know that I welcome the distraction.'

The boyish grin that accompanied the words was like a physical blow to Felicity. Nathan suddenly looked so much younger, so much more like the handsome hero of her dreams.

'But I will not hear of it,' Lydia was saying to him. 'We have our footmen and link boys, so I need not trouble you, my lord.'

'It will be no trouble at all,' replied Lord Rosthorne, walking to the door beside her. 'In fact, it suits me very well, for I need to see Sir James and it is so early that I am sure he will not object to my disturbing him. Therefore I will come with you—I beg your pardon, Miss Brown, did you say something?'

'She coughed,' said Lydia quickly. 'But really, my lord, there is no need—'

'Madam, I insist.' Nathan held out his arm and after a brief hesitation Lydia placed her fingers upon his arm and allowed him to escort her to the waiting carriage. Felicity followed closely. She was aware of an unnerving and quite illogical temptation to reach out and cling to the skirts of Nathan's black evening coat.

Nathan had been quite sincere in his assurances. He was glad of an excuse to quit Lady Somerton's soirée. He had never intended to remain there for long, and if by escorting Lady Souden to her home he could have five minutes' conversation with Sir James it would save him time in the morning.

He handed Lady Souden into the carriage then turned to her companion. The little hand in its kid glove trembled beneath his fingers but that did not surprise him; Miss Brown seemed to be a very nervous person. She did not even lift her head to thank him as he helped her into the coach.

The journey to Berkeley Square was short and Lady Souden kept up a flow of conversation to which Nathan willingly responded, although he found his attention straying to her companion, sitting quietly in the corner. Even enveloped in her cloak there was something familiar about the way she held herself. Who was she? Why did he feel that he should know her?

He thought of the women he had met during his days with Wellington's army and a silent laugh shook him. Perhaps one of the lightskirts he had known had come to England and decided to turn respectable. They would be very likely to take an innocuous name such as Brown! He glanced again at the little figure sitting bolt upright by the window. No, that was not the answer. His instinct told him the chit was no straw damsel. From what he had seen of her, she behaved more like a nun.

Nathan realised Lady Souden was still talking to him, and he broke into her nervous chatter to say with a touch of impatience, 'I fear my presence makes you uncomfortable, ma'am.'

'No—no, not at all,' stammered Lady Souden.

'Be assured that I have no intention of stepping beyond the bounds of propriety. Besides, you have Miss Brown here to act as your chaperon.'

'Oh—no, no, you misunderstand me, my lord,' Lady Souden stammered. 'If—if I seem a little anxious, it is because—because I have a headache!'

Nathan was thankful for the dark interior of the carriage, for he was sure his scepticism was evident in his face. Something was upsetting Lady Souden, but if she wished to lie to him rather than explain, then so be it. He had long ago given up trying to understand women.

'I am sorry to hear it,' he replied quietly. 'But if that is the case, perhaps we should not talk for the remainder of the journey.'

The uncomfortable silence that ensued was mercifully short. When they arrived in Berkeley Square, Nathan lost no time in handing down Lady

Souden and escorting her to the door, where she thanked him prettily enough for his trouble. As soon as she had directed a footman to take him to Sir James, she grabbed her companion's hand and hurried away.

Felicity said nothing as Lydia almost pulled her up the stairs and into her luxurious apartments. As soon as she was sure they were alone, Lydia leaned against the closed door and let out a long sigh.

'Of all the unfortunate circumstances! When Rosthorne insisted upon coming with us I did not know where to look.'

'That was quite apparent,' replied Felicity, a reluctant smile tugging at the corners of her mouth. 'I have never seen you so flustered.'

Lydia shook her head wearily. 'Oh, Fee, I cannot like this! Rosthorne is not a man I like to deceive. Will you not call an end to this charade?'

Felicity put back her hood. 'I cannot, Lydia. You know I cannot.' She turned away, her head bowed as she struggled with the strings of her cloak. Too much had happened that neither of them could forgive. She sighed. 'I am dead to him. It is better that way.'

Lydia swung her around, saying fiercely, 'No, it is not! You have not given him a chance to explain himself.'

'There is nothing to explain. He was desperately in love with another woman.' Felicity shook off her hands. 'He has forgotten me. Let it be, Lydia, it is over.'

'If you do not wish to tell him then there is an end to it. But I do not see how you can maintain this subterfuge. The earl is not a fool, he will recognise you eventually.'

Felicity sighed. 'If I am very careful he need never know I am here.' A sad little smile pulled at her mouth. 'After all, there are plenty of pretty young ladies to distract him.'

'Then you must go back to Souden. You would be safer there.'

'But then who would look after you? A poor companion I would be if I deserted you now! No, I shall do my duty, Lydia, and accompany you whenever Sir James is not available. After all, I am not likely to see Lord Rosthorne so very often: Sir James will be at your side for most of the balls and concerts you will attend this summer and I may remain safely indoors.'

Lydia did not look completely satisfied with this answer but Felicity was adamant, and at length her friend shrugged.

'Very well, if you are sure it is what you want,' she said. 'Ring the bell, Fee. We will take hot chocolate here in my room. I would like to change out of this gown and go and find Sir James, but Rosthorne may still be with him, and it would look very odd if my headache had disappeared so very quickly!'

An hour later Felicity made her way back to her own apartment. It was not yet midnight, but she felt very tired. The strain of being so close to Nathan had exhausted her, and yet as she lay in her bed thinking over the evening she realised she would not have missed seeing him for the world. It was not without pain, to be sure. He knew her only as Lady Souden's companion, Miss Brown, and his indifference cut her deeply, but there was some comfort in watching him, in being near him. More comfort than she had felt for the past five years.

As the first grey light of dawn seeped into the master bedroom of Rosthorne House, Nathan threw back the bedcovers and sat up, rubbing his temples. Why, after all this time, should he dream of little Felicity Bourne?

He went to the window and pressed his forehead against the cool glass. The view from his bedroom was a pleasant one, for it overlooked the Green Park but this morning Nathan saw nothing; he was thinking of those hectic days in Corunna five years ago. He had been sent ashore by Sir

David Baird to help with the delicate negotiations with the local Spanish *junta*, trying to persuade them to allow the British troops to disembark. It was slow, frustrating work and it took all his attention—until one day he had turned a corner and seen three men attacking a young woman. Felicity.

She had looked magnificent with her dark gold hair in disarray about her shoulders and her eyes flashing with anger. He summed up the situation in one glance and when they dared to lay hands on her, he intervened. It was a brief tussle and they soon retreated, leaving Nathan to receive his reward, a grateful look from those huge grey eyes.

'So, madam, where may I escort you?'

'I do not know. That is, I have no place to stay here in Corunna.' She paused. 'I—I need to go to Madrid. I have friends there.'

Nathan hesitated. With no effective government in Spain he would not advise anyone to set out for Madrid without an escort, especially such a fragile little thing as this.

'After what has just happened perhaps it would not be wise for me to travel alone.'

Her quiet words touched a nerve deep inside him, awaking every chivalrous instinct. It was all he could do not to tell her she need never be alone again. His reaction surprised him and he took a small step away.

'On no account must you travel out of the city,' he said decisively.

She turned to him. 'But what am I to do? I am homeless, penniless—' she indicated her muddied pelisse '—and now I am not even presentable.'

'Hookham Frere, the British Envoy, will be setting out for Madrid in the next few days,' said Nathan. 'I have no doubt that he would be happy for you to travel with his party. Will you allow me to escort you to him?'

The relief in her face was evident. 'Thank you, yes, that would be very kind of you.'

Nathan gave her what he hoped was a reassuring smile. He had little experience of dealing with delicately reared young ladies and this one unsettled him. The sooner he could pass her over to the relative safety of the diplomatic party the better. He held out his arm again and hesitantly she laid her gloved hand on his sleeve. He noted idly that her head barely reached his shoulder.

'How comes it that you are separated from your friends, Miss Bourne?'

'Oh, as to that I…' Her words trailed off. He felt the weight of her on his arm.

'Miss Bourne, are you ill?'

'I beg your pardon, I—that is, I have not eaten for a few days…'

She was near to collapse. Nathan quickly revised his plans.

'If you can walk a little further, I have lodgings near here in the Canton Grande. Allow me to take you there, and when you are fed and rested we will continue.'

A slight nod was the only answer he received. He put his arm around her and led her through the narrow streets to a neat house whose wide door and shuttered window sheltered beneath a mirador, an upper-floor balcony completely enclosed by glass panels. He saw his man sitting in the doorway, smoking his pipe.

'Sam, run and fetch Señora Benitez!'

'Now that I can't do, Major,' Sam replied slowly. 'She's gone to stay with 'er daughter for a couple o' days. She told you so herself, this morning, if you remember.'

'Damnation, so she did.'

Felicity gave a little moan and collapsed against him. Swiftly he lifted her into his arms. She was surprisingly light, and fitted snugly against his heart. Something stirred within him.

'And just what have we here, sir?' asked Sam, jabbing his pipe at Felicity.

Nathan allowed himself a swift, wry smile. 'A

damsel in distress, Sam. Go ahead of me and open the door, man.'

'You ain't never going to put her in your room!'

'Where the devil do you expect me to put her?'

'Well, there's always the nuns…'

'No.' Nathan's arms tightened around her. He remembered the look in her eyes when she had turned to him. It was a mixture of trust and dependence and something more, a connection that he could not explain, but neither could he ignore it. 'No,' he said again. 'I shall look after her.'

Chapter Three

'Well my love, you can be easy now,' said Lydia at breakfast a few days later. 'James and Rosthorne have gone off to Dover to meet the royal visitors and bring them back to London. The Prince is planning a royal procession through the town to St James's Palace and James has hired rooms for us overlooking the route, so we will be able to watch the procession in comfort.'

Felicity received the news with mixed feelings. She should be relieved that there was no possibility of meeting Nathan for a while, instead she was disappointed.

'Will Sir James and the earl be riding in the procession?' She tried to sound indifferent but she blushed when she looked up and found Lydia smiling at her.

'Yes they will. James tells me the Prince has insisted that Rosthorne should wear his dress uniform: he will look so dashing that I am sure all the ladies will be swooning over him.'

Felicity scowled into her coffee cup.

'Let them swoon,' she muttered. 'I am sure I do not care!'

But when the day arrived Felicity could not deny a frisson of excitement as she and Lydia sat in the window of the hired room.

'People have been gathering since dawn,' remarked Lydia. 'Everyone is eager to see the Emperor. They have even erected stands along the route, but I doubt that even they will have such a fine view as this.'

There was a sudden stir in the crowds below.

'They are coming,' declared Lydia, leaning towards the open window.

Felicity could hear the rattle of drums. A cheer went up as the cavalcade approached, a long column of bright colours and nodding plumes. Felicity watched, fascinated by the never-ending ranks of soldiers and dignitaries passing beneath her.

'There's Prinny!' cried Lydia, pointing. 'And that must be the Prussian King.'

Felicity looked down at the upright, soldierly figure in his topboots and white pantaloons. He looked very serious, but she could not help thinking that was much more regal than the portly Prince Regent. Lydia grabbed her arm.

'Look, there's James!' She waved her handkerchief wildly at a group of riders following the royal party and was rewarded when Sir James looked up and raised his hat to her. 'Oh, he is so handsome. And he looks so well on horseback, does he not?'

Felicity murmured a reply. She was searching the colourful columns, eager to catch a glimpse of Nathan. What had Sir James said about their escort duties? Nathan was to accompany the Emperor of Russia.

'I have not yet seen the Tsar,' she murmured, her eyes raking the crowds.

'Perhaps he is gone another way.' Lydia laughed. 'I would not be surprised if his sister has told him to come direct to her at the Pulteney Hotel. James says she has taken a dislike to the Prince Regent!'

Felicity was aware of a searing disappointment and berated herself fiercely. For five long years she had resolutely tried to forget Nathan Carraway— now he was out of her sight for just a few days and she was pining for him! She stared out at the colourful cavalcade passing beneath the window and made a decision. She would speak to him. At the very next opportunity she would reveal herself to Nathan. She would watch his reaction carefully; if he wanted nothing to do with her then she would ask Lydia to send her back to Souden and she would do her best to make a life for herself without Nathan Carraway. But perhaps, just perhaps... She hugged herself, trying not to fan the tiny spark of hope that refused to be extinguished. Whatever was decided, surely it would be better than this half-life she was living at present? Beside her, Lydia gave a little tut of exasperation.

'It does not look as if the Tsar is going to appear. How tiresome! But we shall discover the truth tonight.' Lydia sighed. 'Such a lot of new faces, and James will expect me to know them all, for he will be inviting them to our ball! Well, Fee, my dependence is upon you to remember them, so that you can prompt me if I forget their names!'

'So, James, what happened? Where was the Tsar?' Lydia drew her husband into her private sitting room. 'It is no good telling me you have been ordered to dine at Carlton House; you are not leaving until you tell us everything. Is that not so, Felicity?'

'If you could spare us five minutes, Sir James, we would be grateful.'

Her calm tone belied her impatience to know why Nathan had not been in the procession. Sir

James allowed himself to be pulled down on to a sofa beside his wife.

'Oh, very well. So you and Miss Brown watched the proceedings, did you?'

Lydia shook his arm. 'You know very well we did, sir, for you saw us there when you rode past. But what happened to the Tsar?'

'Aye, well…' Sir James shook his head. 'We made good progress coming up from Dover. There were people lining the streets and hanging out of upstairs windows, all cheering, but the crowds were so thick as we came into London that the royals grew nervous.' He tried and failed to hide his grin. 'They ain't used to the mob, you see. All the people wanted to do was to cheer their heroes, unbuckle the horses and draw the carriages through the streets themselves, but the sovereigns didn't want it. Then someone took a pot-shot at the Tsar.'

'No!'

'Yes, my love. Only the shot went wide and hit Rosthorne instead.'

'Was—was he badly hurt?' Felicity asked, her hands straying to her cheeks.

Sir James laughed. 'Not at all, but the bullet took his hat clean off! I didn't have a chance to talk to him, for he was obliged to set off after the Emperor, who was determined to join his sister.'

'At the Pulteney.' Lydia nodded sagely. 'You said he might do that.'

'Did I, by heaven?' exclaimed Sir James. He lifted her hand to his lips. 'What a clever little puss you are to remember that! Well, I hope he's comfortable there. The Lord Chamberlain, two bands and I don't know how many others had been waiting since dawn to receive him, then Rosthorne sends a message to say Tsar Alexander came into town by way of the turnpike at Hyde Park Corner and would be staying at the Pulteney. Prinny is as mad as fire, of course, but forced to put on a brave face. That is why I must go now, my love. His Highness is not in the best of moods, so it will not do for me to be late!'

'Poor James,' said Lydia, kissing his cheek. 'I think these celebrations are going to be anything but peaceful! But I must confess a desire to see this Emperor of Russia. Will he be at Lady Stinchcombe's ball tomorrow night, do you think?'

'He has certainly been invited; we must see if Rosthorne can bring him up to scratch!'

Felicity looked up to find Lydia giving her a rueful glance.

'Then I regret I must ask you to come out with me again tomorrow, Fee—I cannot wait for James to finish his interminable meetings before going to the ball.'

Felicity nodded. Inside, she was aching to see for herself that Nathan was unhurt. Tomorrow night could not come soon enough.

The carriage turned into a cobbled street off Piccadilly and pulled up outside a pretty red-brick house set back in its own grounds. Lady Stinchcombe greeted them warmly.

'There is no ceremony here tonight,' she said gaily. 'The Emperor sent Lord Rosthorne to make his apologies, but we shall do our best to enjoy ourselves without him. Wander where you will, although the garden illuminations will not be at their best until it is properly dark.'

'I suppose we should wait until the last of the daylight has gone before we look at the gardens,' said Lydia. She led the way towards the card room. 'Have a care, Fee,' she murmured, pausing in the doorway. 'Rosthorne is here.'

Grateful for the warning, Felicity stayed in Lydia's shadow as she followed her into the room. She spotted the earl almost immediately. He was playing picquet with another gentleman while a crowd of admiring ladies stood at his shoulder, vying for his attention.

'Poor man, how very distracting for him.'

Hearing Felicity's comment, a gentleman standing near them gave a laugh.

'There's no distracting Rosthorne! Even being
shot at don't make him turn a hair. Some dashed
fool nearly blew his head off yesterday.'

'Aye, I heard about that.' A bewigged man in
a faded frockcoat nodded. 'Pretty wild shot if it
missed the Tsar and hit Rosthorne. Who did it,
some drunken lunatic?'

'They didn't catch him,' replied the first man.
'He got away in the crowd. Made no odds to
Rosthorne, he merely followed on after the
Tsar.'

'He is very brave,' murmured Lydia.

The bewigged man shrugged. 'Rosthorne's a
soldier. He thought nothing of it. Ruined a perfectly good hat, though.'

Pride flickered through Felicity. Of course
Nathan would think nothing of the danger. He
did not know the meaning of fear. Lydia took her
arm.

'Even so, we shall not add to the distraction,' she
murmured. 'Let us move on to the music room.'
She patted Felicity's hand. 'My dear, what is this?
You are shaking.'

'I am a little shocked to hear of such violence,'
whispered Felicity. 'Pray do not mind me, Lydia;
let us go on.'

She was being irrational, she told herself. Nathan had been in danger any number of times when he was a soldier, so why should the news of this incident affect her so? She chewed her lip. Because it was here, in London, where one did not expect such things. She glanced back at Nathan, sitting at the card table.

And because she still cared for him.

They wandered into the next room where Miss Stinchcombe was performing upon the harp. As the final notes died away and they applauded her performance, Felicity saw Gerald Appleby approaching them.

'Lady Souden, how do you do! And Miss Brown. A delightful evening, is it not? Mama is sitting over there by the window, may I take you over? I know she will want to talk to you…'

He led them across the room, chatting all the time until they came up to Lady Charlotte, who greeted Lydia with a regal smile. Felicity she acknowledged with no more than a flicker of her cold eyes before engaging Lady Souden in conversation. Felicity gave an inward shrug and would have moved away, but Mr Appleby stopped her.

'How are you enjoying the music, Miss Brown?'

'Very well, sir, thank you.'

'I think the harp very over-rated and much prefer the pianoforte,' he continued, smiling at her. 'Do you play at all, Miss Brown?'

'The pianoforte, a little.'

'Ah, all young ladies say they only play a little and then they perform the most complicated pieces for us. Shall we have the pleasure of hearing you this evening, ma'am?'

'No, Mr Appleby, I do not play in public.'

'What, never? But why? This must be remedied immediately,' he cried gaily.

Felicity tried to step away but found the wall at her back. 'No, I assure you, sir—'

He took her hand and leaned toward her, smiling. 'This is no time for bashful modesty, madam. Let me take you to the piano—'

'Gerald!' Lady Charlotte's strident tones interrupted him. 'Gerald, leave the gel alone. It is beneath you to flirt with the hirelings.'

'I beg your pardon, Lady Charlotte, but Miss Brown's birth is equal to my own,' said Lydia, bristling in defence of her friend.

'So I should hope,' returned Lady Charlotte, unperturbed. 'I would expect nothing less in any companion of yours.'

Felicity observed the angry flush on Lydia's cheek and slipped away from Gerald to take her arm.

'You wished to look at the lamps in the garden, my lady...'

'Insufferable woman,' muttered Lydia as they walked away. 'She is so set up in her own importance!'

'I was quite thankful for her intervention,' returned Felicity. 'Mr Appleby is far too mischievous.'

'Perhaps he is trying to fix his interest with you.'

'Oh, Lydia, surely not!'

'You may look surprised, Fee, but he is quite taken with you.'

'But I have done nothing—'

'No, nothing more than look adorably shy.' Lydia gave a soft laugh. 'There is no need to colour up, my love; you have an air of fragility that makes men want to protect you.'

Felicity put up her chin. 'But I do not want to be protected! Oh dear. I had hoped, by dressing plainly and not putting myself forward, that I would not be noticed.'

'And in general that is the case,' Lydia reassured her. 'Mr Appleby is perhaps trying to make amends for his mother's ignoring you.'

'Yes, that is very possible,' mused Felicity. She looked up, a smile lurking in her eyes. 'And it is a very lowering thought!'

Her companion laughed. 'Yes, it is! But it is quite your own fault, Fee. If you were to put on a fashionable gown and stop dressing your hair in that dowdy style I have no doubt that we would have dozens of gentlemen clamouring to make your acquaintance!'

Still chuckling, they wandered out on to the terrace where a familiar voice cut through the darkness.

'So there you are! Now what in heaven's name are you two laughing at?'

Sir James's bemused enquiry brought his lady flying to his arms.

'Oh, my dear, you are here already! How wonderful! No, no, you must not ask about our silly jokes. I did not expect to see you here for another hour yet!'

'Well, having delivered his Highness to our hostess I have left him being toad-eaten by any number of the guests! What a crush. Scarcely room to move in the ballroom!'

'I know, that is why we came out here to look at the lamps. They are very pretty, are they not?' Lydia took her husband's arm. 'Shall we take a stroll through the gardens? Come with us, Fee.'

'If you do not object, I think I might stay here for a little while.' Felicity had spotted the earl slipping out of the house on the far side of the terrace.

She nodded at Lydia. 'Please, go on without me. I shall be perfectly safe here.'

As soon as Lydia and Sir James had disappeared into the gardens, Felicity ran across the terrace and down the steps in the direction that Nathan had gone. This was her opportunity to reveal herself to him. It was much darker on this side of the house, for the path led away from the main gardens, where myriad coloured lights were strung between the trees. As she hurried through the gloom her step faltered. Nathan might have an assignation—how would she feel if she came upon him with his arms around another woman? She put up her chin. If that was the case then she would rather know of it. Then she could put him out of her mind and end this growing obsession.

Away from the house there was just sufficient light for her to see the grassy path. It ran between tall bushes with the ghostly outlines of marble statues at intervals along its length. Nathan's tall figure was ahead of her, no more than a black shadow in the darkness. At the end of the avenue he hesitated before disappearing to the right. Felicity followed and found herself stepping into a rather unkempt shrubbery.

'Why are you following me?' Felicity turned to flee, but Nathan's hand shot out and grasped her wrist. 'Oh, no. You will not leave until I have an explanation!'

Felicity swallowed. It was far too dark to see clearly and she only recognised Nathan by his voice. She lowered her own to a whisper in an attempt to disguise it.

'I—I came out here to...' Felicity hesitated. Should she reveal herself, tell him she had followed him? Her courage failed her. 'I do not like the noise and chatter.'

That much at least was true. She heard him sigh.

'Nor I.' He released her. 'In fact, I can't think why I came tonight.'

Felicity knew that she should pick up her skirts and run away, but her wayward body would not move. To be here, alone with Nathan, talking to him—it was very dangerous, but she could not resist.

'Why remain in town, sir, if you do not enjoy society?'

'I have duties to perform.' He turned his head suddenly, peering at her. 'Do I know you?'

Felicity shrank back. 'No,' she said gruffly. 'No. I do not move in your circle.'

Nathan shrugged. He had come out into the gardens to enjoy a cigarillo in peace but it was not his house, he could hardly tell this young person to go away. The strains of a minuet floated out on the night air.

'The dancing has begun. Do you not wish to join in?'

'No.'

Her laconic reply surprised him into a laugh.

'I thought all young ladies love to dance.'

'I do not dance. I have not danced since I was at school.'

He heard the wistful note in her voice and held out his hand to her. 'Would you like to try now? Here?'

The stillness settled over them. Nathan had the impression the little figure before him was holding her breath. He saw her hand come up, then it dropped again to her side.

'Thank you, but no. Companions do not dance.'

So that was her role. He felt a stir of pity.

'But out here we do not need to abide by society's rules.' He reached out and took her hand, pulling her towards him. 'Here we are no more than a man and a woman. We may dance if we wish to, or…'

His words trailed away as he drew her closer. He had not intended to take her in his arms, but as she stepped forward it seemed natural to embrace her. She leaned against him, her head just below his chin. He breathed in the subtle fragrance of flowers and sunshine and—

'Oh, dear heaven, let me go!'

She was struggling like a frightened bird against this hold. Immediately he released her.

'Oh, I do beg your pardon,' she gasped. 'That was not meant to… I must go!'

'As you wish.' She stood before him in the darkness. He could not see her face, but he knew that she was troubled. He said gently, 'Did I frighten you?'

'No…' Her voice caught on a sob. 'No, never.'

She turned and disappeared into the night. Nathan watched her go, then with a faint shrug he reached into his pocket for his cigarillos.

Felicity flew out of the shrubbery and stopped, panting once she reached the grass path. What had she been thinking of? To talk to Nathan had been foolish enough, to allow him to take her in his arms was sheer madness. Why had she not told him who she was? She bowed her head. She could imagine his reaction. Anger and revulsion. How had she ever dared to hope that he might want her back? Yet even now she could not bring herself to walk away.

Give him the chance to decide.

Felicity crept back to the edge of the path and

peeped around the corner. She could just make out Nathan's dark figure a short distance away, only his white neckcloth and waistcoat showing against the black shadows. He was moving quite slowly and as she watched he tilted his head back and exhaled a little cloud into the night air. A tangy, unusual fragrance wafted towards her. He was smoking a cigar. She had seen the officers in Corunna smoking these little cylinders of rolled tobacco and guessed that Nathan had picked up the habit during his years as a soldier. A movement in the shadows caught her eye. There was someone else in the shrubbery. Immediately she was on the alert, sensing danger. Nathan had turned away from that corner of the garden and Felicity saw a sudden flash, a glint of metal in the moonlight.

'Behind you, sir!' Felicity's shout cut through the silence.

Nathan wheeled about, fists raised. 'Who's there?'

A dark shape broke away and fled, all attempts at stealth gone as it crashed through the bushes.

Felicity stepped back into the shadows. She had succeeded in putting Nathan on his guard. Now she must remove herself. Picking up her skirts, she raced back towards the terrace, veering off along the path leading to the main gardens.

'Sir James, Sir James!'

Lydia and her husband were strolling arm in arm beneath the coloured lamps. They looked up at her call. She ran up to them.

'Sir James, there is—an—intruder,' she gasped out the words, impatient to make him understand. She pointed. 'Over there in the shrubbery.'

Sir James immediately ran to the terrace and pulled one of the torches from its holder, calling to a footman to follow him. He turned to Felicity.

'Very well, show me.'

'James, be careful!' cried Lydia, running along behind them.

They were halfway along the path when they met Nathan coming the other way. Felicity dropped back immediately into the darkness.

'Rosthorne,' Sir James called to him. 'There's a report of an intruder. Have you seen him?'

'Aye, there was someone. He took off through the garden door when I challenged him. I followed him outside, but the alley was deserted.'

Sir James turned to the footman. 'Could he have got in that way?'

The servant shook his head. 'No, sir. Her ladyship insists we keep the door locked.'

'Well, it was used tonight,' said Nathan. 'There are bolts top and bottom. I was close behind the man as he opened the door. He did not have time to draw them back. Either he had prepared his escape, or someone let him in.'

'Good heavens!' gasped Lydia, clinging to her husband's arm.

'I will talk to Stinchcombe,' said Nathan. 'He can have the servants search the house, to check if anything is missing.'

'Make sure you do not alarm the rest of the guests,' Sir James called after him. He patted Lydia's hand. 'There is nothing more to be done here, so I suggest we go back indoors. Come, Miss Brown. You may rest easy now; there is no one here.'

Sir James took the ladies back to Berkeley Square soon after, and the incident in the Stinchcombes' garden was not mentioned again, but it remained in Felicity's mind when she went to bed that night. Sir James had spoken to his hostess before they had left and she had assured him that nothing had been taken from the house, and no uninvited guests had been seen in the building. For all that Felicity was still uneasy. It would be a very bold thief who would risk entering a house full of guests. There had been something menacing about the way the figure had moved in the shadows, the way it had approached Nathan and the glint of metal she had seen. Could it have been a knife blade? She shuddered. There were so many strangers in London for the Peace Celebrations: perhaps not all of them were friendly.

'Now you are being fanciful,' she muttered, pummelling her pillow. 'It was probably some poor starving creature looking for a little food, nothing more. You were overwrought. Most likely you are making a mountain out of nothing more than a worm-cast!'

Nevertheless, the feeling persisted that by being there she had saved Nathan's life.

However, there was no talk of intruders the next morning; Lydia's thoughts were all on a forthcoming treat.

'In general James does not like masked balls and I feared that he would cry off from Lady Preston's masquerade next week,' she said, with a twinkling look at her husband. He grinned back at her.

'His Highness insists we all attend, and that we wear a costume of his own designing.'

Lydia laughed. 'How galling that I must be grateful to the Prince Regent for my husband's company!'

Felicity turned to Sir James. 'His Highness wishes you *all* to attend?'

'Aye, Miss Brown. Neither Rosthorne nor I will

be escorting the royal party that night, but we are still obliged to wear the Regent's costume.'

Felicity digested this while Sir James took his leave of them and went off to his study.

'I am glad for your sake that James will escort me to Lady Preston's,' said Lydia, when they were alone again. 'It means that you are not obliged to come with me, Fee, so it works out very neatly.'

'Actually, I would like to go to the masquerade, if I may.'

Lydia turned an astonished gaze upon her. 'Fee, my dear, you cannot wish to go!'

Felicity looked down at her hands. 'It is not so long ago we thought I should be attending as your companion,' she reminded Lydia. 'You expressly requested Lady Preston to send me an invitation, did you not?'

'Yes, yes, I know that, but…oh, Fee, are you sure you want to attend? Have you considered?'

'Yes, I have. It is to be a masked ball, so I may be quite disguised. And I shall leave before the unmasking at midnight.'

'But Rosthorne will be there!'

'I know. That is why I want to go.'

With a tiny squeal Lydia sat up. 'Have you run mad?' she demanded. 'Do you know the risk you will be running to attend a masquerade?'

Felicity nodded. 'I have considered that. But I

want to see him again, Lydia.' She clasped her hands tightly in her lap. 'It is the perfect opportunity for me to talk to him.'

'But as soon as you speak to him he will recognise you.'

Felicity shook her head. 'He will not be expecting to see me there.' She thought back to their time together in the shrubbery. 'I doubt he even remembers my voice.'

'This is madness,' Lydia said again. 'Think of the danger, Fee. These events can be very…wild.'

'It is no matter,' said Felicity calmly. 'All I want is to dance with Nathan. We have never danced together, you see. And I would so like to know how it feels. Just once.'

Lydia looked at her, tears starting in her blue eyes. 'Oh, my dear—'

Felicity quickly put up her hands. 'No, please, Lydia, do not pity me or I shall start to cry, too. Instead I would like to ask you to help me in another way.' She fixed her eyes upon her friend. 'I will need some dancing lessons. Apart from a few country dances at Souden I have not danced, not *properly* danced, since we were at the Academy together…'

'And you were always such a graceful dancer. I shall ask my old dancing teacher, Signor Bellini, to come here and I shall play for you,' declared

Lydia. 'Oh, Fee, this is so exciting. And when Rosthorne discovers who you are...'

'You go too fast, Lydia!' Felicity frowned. 'I am not at all sure I am ready to reveal myself to him.'

Lady Souden looked as if she would say more, but after a brief hesitation she merely smiled, and nodded. 'Very well, my love. Now, let us think of a disguise for you.'

'I thought you might have a domino that I may borrow. And a mask.'

Lydia sat back and regarded her friend. After a few moments a mischievous little smile tugged at the corner of her mouth. 'I think I can do much better than that for you, my love.' She shook her head. 'No, I will tell you nothing more now, except that you must leave everything to me!'

Lady Souden refused to say any more.

Felicity was obliged to curb her curiosity until the very day of Lady Preston's masquerade, when she accompanied Lydia on another of her shopping sprees. This included the purchase of a pair of scarlet stockings, which Lydia presented to her friend.

'What on earth would I want with these?' asked Felicity, laughing.

'They will add the finishing touch to your costume this evening.'

'What are you planning for me, Lydia? Do tell!'

But Lady Souden merely looked mysterious and bade her to wait until the evening.

'How fortunate that dear James could not dine with us tonight,' remarked Lydia as she took Felicity upstairs to her apartment. 'I can help you to dress without fear that he will want to know what we are doing.'

'I am becoming mighty anxious about this myself,' said Felicity as she followed her hostess into the white-and-rose dressing room. 'The thought of those scarlet stockings is quite alarming.'

Lydia giggled. 'Nonsense, they are just right!' She smiled at her maid, who was standing beside an open trunk. 'Well, Janet, have you put everything ready, as I instructed?'

'Aye, m'lady.' She reached into the trunk and with a rustle of tissue paper she pulled forth a gown. Felicity stared.

'Lydia,' she breathed, 'I couldn't...can you not find me a plain domino? That is all I require...'

'Nonsense, you will look wonderful in this. We are very much of a height, so it will fit you very well. I would wear it myself but...' Lydia smiled and placed her hands on her waist '…I would not look my best in it this year.'

Felicity looked again at the gown the maid was holding up for her inspection. It was a heavy brocade gown with full skirts and a narrow, boned bodice, but it was not the old style that made Felicity's eyes widen. It was the colour. The gown was a vividly patterned scarlet-and-black, trimmed with black lace.

'Begging your pardon, my lady, but I am not sure this is a suitable gown for Miss Brown,' offered Janet, eyeing the gown doubtfully.

'Pho, it is for a wager,' Lydia responded in an airy tone. 'Come now, we must help Miss Brown to dress. Quickly, Janet, for there is much to do.'

Felicity submitted meekly to their ministrations. Soon her light, flowing muslin gown had been replaced by pads and hoops and petticoats. She gasped as Janet tugged on the laces of her bodice, fitting it tightly into the curve of her waist. When Lydia sent the maid off to pack away her discarded clothes, Felicity gave a little whimper.

'I can scarce breathe.' She regarded herself in the mirror. The tight bodice emphasised her tiny waist and the creamy swell of her breasts above the low neckline. As she raised one hand to her throat the black lace ruffles fell back softly from her white arm. 'Oh dear, Janet is right: I should not be wearing this.'

'You want to dance with Rosthorne, do you not?' said Lydia, eminently practical. 'Trust me, he will not be able to resist you in this gown.' She sighed, a faraway look creeping into her eyes. 'The modiste named this gown "Temptation". I remember when I wore it: James could not take his eyes off me.' Lydia gave another sigh, but as her handmaid came back into the room she recollected herself and said in a very businesslike tone, 'Now for the headdress. Sit down here, my love, while Janet helps me.'

A heavy black wig was fitted over Felicity's soft gold-brown hair and she watched in some consternation as Janet pulled up a side table and began to set out a frightening array of powders and paints.

'Is this really necessary?' protested Felicity. 'I am sure—'

'Hush,' Lydia told her. 'You must look the part.'

'Why, 'tis no more than a little powder, miss,' said Janet. 'Thirty years ago no lady would ever leave her room without painting her face as white as snow.'

'And what is that you are putting on my eyes?'

'Nothing more than a little burnt cork, miss.'

And so it went on. Felicity stared ahead of her as Lydia and her maid worked their transformation.

The daylight faded and was replaced by the soft glow of candles before the maid began to pack away the little pots and brushes.

'Can I look in the mirror now?'

'Just a few more touches,' said Lydia.

She handed Felicity a length of black ribbon embroidered with gold thread.

'To tie up your stockings, of course,' she said in answer to Felicity's questioning look. 'And finally, these.'

She produced a square leather jewel case and lifted from it a heavy ruby necklace. 'This belonged to my grandmother, but no one wears such things now. There...and the ear-drops...well—' she caught Felicity's hands and pulled her up to stand before the long glass '—what do you think of yourself?'

For a long, silent moment Felicity gazed at her reflection. A strange, exotic creature stared back at her. A dark-haired stranger with white skin and light grey eyes framed by long dark lashes.

'Well?' said Lydia again.

'Even *I* do not recognise myself.' Even as she spoke her eyes were fixed upon her mouth: plump, sensuously curving lips painted a vivid red contrasted with the whiteness of her skin.

Lydia gave a little crow of laughter. 'That is precisely what we want!' She handed Felicity a mask, a black-and-gold creation with long black ribbons to fasten around her headdress. 'Now, you are to sit down and keep still while Janet helps me into my dress. Tonight I shall be Aphrodite, the goddess of love.' She gave her friend a mischievous smile. 'Quite appropriate, do you not agree? Goodness, look at the hour! We must be quick, Janet, Sir James will be here any minute and we cannot risk him coming upstairs and finding Miss Brown dressed like this!'

The maid's head shot up. 'Sir James doesn't know that Miss Brown is attending—?'

Lydia shushed her maid and waved an impatient hand. 'I told you it is for a wager. Now not another word from you, Janet, and make haste to help me into my costume!'

Lydia was giving her golden curls a final pat when word arrived that Sir James was waiting below.

'I must go,' she said. 'I have given instructions for your coach to be at the door for you in half an hour. Janet has looked out a domino for you, so your costume will be completely concealed when you leave here.' She gave her friend a final hug. 'Do take care, Fee. I will be sure to keep James away from you tonight.'

'Are you afraid he might recognise me?'

Lydia picked up her mask. 'No,' she said, going to the door. 'I am afraid he might find you too, too attractive.'

Chapter Four

Nathan prowled restlessly around Lady Preston's magnificent ballroom. The walls were covered with swathes of midnight-blue silk that seemed to absorb the light from the huge chandeliers. The colourful costumes lost something of their brilliance as the movement of the dance took the dancers away from the centre of the room and they were eager to push back into the middle of the swirling, swaying mass. Not so Nathan, who took advantage of the shadows to hide himself away against the dark walls or in the shadowy corners of the room. He tugged at his collar: it was very warm, despite the tall windows being thrown wide. Impatiently he fiddled with the strings of his mask and heard a quiet laugh at his shoulder.

'No, no, my lord, it's not time for the unmasking yet.'

He turned to find Sir James and Lady Souden beside him.

'Fie upon you, sir, that is no way to address someone at a masquerade.' The lady was smiling at him through the scrap of lace that served as her mask.

'Well, I'm dashed if I'm going to ask Rosthorne if I know him,' retorted Sir James. 'It's perfectly plain to see who he is. But you don't look as if you're enjoying yourself, my boy.'

Nathan shrugged. 'I have been here for most of the day, sir. His Highness got wind of the fiasco in the Stinchcombes' garden and I was despatched to check that the grounds here are secure.'

'Ah, yes. We cannot risk another assassination attempt,' replied Sir James. 'That would really put a damper on the celebrations. But having done your duty you are free to enjoy yourself now, Rosthorne.'

'To tell the truth I wish this whole evening was over,' replied Nathan, grimacing.

'Is it really so bad?' Lady Souden gave him a sympathetic smile.

'I would be more comfortable in a plain domino, but this—' Nathan indicated his costume, an over-elaborate variation of a hussar's uniform in royal blue, red, white and gold.

Sir James nodded. 'Garish, ain't it? And even

the mask don't conceal one's identity. But his Highness insists. A display of solidarity for his guests, I think.'

'And they haven't even put in an appearance,' declared Nathan bitterly.

'But they will.' Sir James patted him on one heavily gilded shoulder. 'Bear up, Rosthorne. Prinny and his royals will turn up shortly and depart again even sooner, no doubt. When they have gone you can take your leave.'

'Aye, I'll go home and change.' Nathan grinned. 'I pity those poor fellows in the Prince's Own if their uniform is anything like this.'

'Well, I think you both look very dashing,' laughed Lydia as Sir James led her away to join the dancing. 'Every woman will want to dance with you.'

And that's the problem, thought Nathan as he drew back once more into the shadows. It seemed to him that all the matchmaking mothers in London had begged, borrowed or stolen an invitation to this masquerade for no better purpose than to fling their marriageable daughters at his head. Lord, what a conceited fool everyone would think him if he expressed such a view aloud, but it was true Sir James himself had called him—what were his words? The biggest catch on the Marriage Mart. Nathan's mouth twisted in distaste. When he had been a mere Major Carraway no one had cared about his marital status, but the wealthy Lord Rosthorne was the subject of constant speculation.

Nathan had not expected to become Earl of Rosthorne, but when he had inherited the title he had thought it his duty to sell out and interest himself in his estates. Now, as he dodged behind a pillar to avoid the gaze of another predatory matron, he began to wish he had remained in the army.

'Do I know you?' A soft voice at his side uttered the familiar words.

He looked down to find an exotic, black-haired creature standing beside him. Her silvery eyes glittered through the slits in her black velvet mask and as he met her gaze she looked away, bringing up a black feather fan to hide her face.

'Do I know *you*?' he countered.

Running his eyes over the delightful figure enshrined in the rich scarlet-and-black gown, he could not bring to mind any woman of his acquaintance. As if aware of his appreciative glance at her full, rounded breasts she lowered the fan a little to cover them.

'I am Temptation,' she murmured. 'Have you never known me?'

'Not recently,' he responded, entering into the

spirit of the game. A footman walked by with a tray full of glasses and Nathan reached out to seize two of them. 'Will you take wine with me, madam?'

Her scarlet lips curved upwards. 'With pleasure, my lord.'

'Ah, you *do* know me!'

She looked at him over the rim of her wineglass. 'Everyone knows the rich Lord Rosthorne.'

'Then you have the advantage of me, madam, for I cannot put a name to you.'

'I am Temptation,' she repeated. 'I exist only for tonight.'

Her voice was low and slightly breathless. He found the combination very alluring. Nathan leaned closer.

'And are you Temptation for all men, or only for me?'

The eyes behind the black mask widened slightly. 'For you alone, sir, if you wish it so.'

He stared at her, intrigued. There was something vaguely familiar about the woman, in the tilt of her head, the soft cadences of her voice. Those carmined lips belonged to the mouth of a wanton, but her low, musical voice was cultured and there was no suggestion of a bold swagger in her movements, nothing to suggest she was anything but a lady. And yet…

'Tell me—' He broke off as a female dressed as a milkmaid dashed by, screeching. She was closely followed by two gentlemen in Turkish costume. For a moment he watched their progress. They were heading towards Sir James. He was standing nearby with his wife upon his arm and was obliged to pull Lady Souden out of the way of an imminent collision. Catching Nathan's eye, he shook his head at him.

'What is it that makes these affairs so dashed boisterous?' he demanded, coming up. 'Damme, but my poor Aphrodite already has wine stains upon her skirts!'

'I told you we would be safer dancing,' remarked Lady Souden, dismissing her spoiled robes with an airy wave of her hand. She pulled Sir James back into the crowd and they were soon lost to sight. Smiling faintly, Nathan looked around for the lady in the scarlet-and-black gown, but she had gone.

Lady Preston presented a dancing partner to Nathan, a young woman in a pink domino who appeared to have no conversation and even less sense. Nathan led her on to the dance floor, but soon grew tired of trying to talk when the only response to his efforts was a giggle. The music ended and he escorted his partner back to her party, where her effusive mother made every effort to keep him at her side. A flash of scarlet and black caught Nathan's eye. The dark-haired beauty was moving across the floor almost within arm's reach. His curt 'Excuse me' cut off the matron in mid-sentence but he hardly noticed her indignant gasp for he was already pushing through the crowd.

He was closing on his quarry when a large be-whiskered cavalier stepped in front of her. She tried to move around the fellow but he blocked her escape, pushing himself against her and laughing at her attempts to evade him. Nathan did not hesitate. In two strides he was beside her.

'My dance, I think.' His tone was pleasant, but the savage look he bestowed on the cavalier made the man step back, muttering something that could have been an apology. Triumphant, Nathan put his arm around the lady's tiny waist to lead her away.

'You are trembling,' he said.

'Because you are holding me.'

Her words were quiet, almost lost in the noise and chatter of the room. Almost, but not quite: a bolt of pleasure shot through him. He was unaccountably pleased by her reply. With some reluctance he released her to take her place in the set.

'I thought you were going to tempt only me this evening.'

She smiled, displaying white even teeth between

those luscious scarlet lips. 'For that I need your company, my lord.' She reached out for his hand as the music began.

Nathan had never danced such a measure before. Perhaps it was the wine and the warm, heady atmosphere of the crowded room that had confused his senses. His partner fascinated him; he had to force himself to turn away from those glittering eyes when the movement of the dance demanded that he should do so. The laughter and chatter around him died away, he heard nothing, saw nothing, only her. They danced down the line and separated and he found himself impatient to have her beside him again, resenting the other men who enjoyed her smiles, however brief. The dance brought them back together and as he reached for her hand he felt her fingers tremble in his grasp. His heart leapt; so she felt it too, this attraction. The music was ending, the couples were bowing to each other, walking off the floor. Only Nathan and his partner remained, standing breast to breast, staring at one another. As if in a dream he reached out his hand to her. Slowly, the fingers in their black satin glove came up, slid into his. Pulling her hand on to his arm, he led her through the crowd. He saw Sir James ahead of him, his mask failing to conceal his curiosity as he observed Nathan's partner. Even as Nathan was wondering how he would introduce his mysterious companion, Lady Souden glanced in his direction, gave a faint smile and with a word to her husband she led him away. Nathan could not be sorry; he wanted nothing to break the spell that surrounded him.

The orchestra was striking up again as they moved to the side of the room and he took his partner to a less crowded spot near the wall. A nod at a hovering footman provided two glasses of wine; in the dim light it appeared as black as the panels of her gown.

There was a sensuous pleasure in watching her take a sip from her glass. A ripple of excitement pulsed through him when the tip of her tongue slid across her lip. She was temptation indeed. He moved closer until the skirts of her gown brushed his legs.

'So, madam, will you stay with me for the rest of the evening?'

A warm sense of satisfaction spread through Felicity. She looked up at Nathan, noting the way his dark eyes glittered through the slits of his mask. He wanted her! Or, rather, he wanted the beautiful, entrancing creature she had become. Felicity had no illusions; people behaved differently as soon as they put on a mask. She had experienced it herself. As soon as she walked into the ballroom she had been aware of the admiring glances, and safely disguised beneath the mask and the beautiful scarlet-and-black gown, her nerves had disappeared. She was not herself, but an enchantress, powerful and alluring, capable of seducing any man in the room. It was a role she was happy to play, if it kept Nathan by her side. She smiled up at him.

'If you so wish, my lord.'

'I do wish,' he said softly. 'I wish it very much indeed.'

Slowly he lowered his head and touched his lips against hers. Felicity trembled but did not recoil. She tasted the wine on his lips, breathed in the subtle spicy fragrance that hung around him and knew a momentary desolation when he raised his head. He gave her a reassuring smile and turned to watch the dancers. She stood beside him, observing the little smile hovering around his mouth, wondering if she dare reach up and plant a kiss on his lean cheek. She desperately wanted to be close to him, to feel his arms around her. She realised with a shock that she wanted him to make love to her.

It is the wine, she told herself fiercely. *It is making you reckless. You must be careful.* A little devil in her head mocked at her caution. *This may be your only chance*, it taunted her. *Take it!*

As if aware of her scrutiny Nathan turned and looked down at her. He put down his glass and held out his hand. 'We should dance again, I think.'

Nathan was entranced: the woman had intoxicated him. He was aware of the envious glances of the other men and the glares of the ladies, but only for a moment, for he found he wanted nothing more than to look at his partner, to watch her eyes glint with laughter when he said something to amuse her, to admire the slender column of her throat, the white, smooth skin of her shoulders and the soft, rounded breasts that nestled in the lace of her bodice. A flurry of activity near the door indicated the arrival of the Prince Regent's party, but Nathan took no notice. He only had eyes for the temptress beside him.

They danced and danced again and when she declared herself too warm he led her to one of the open windows and out on to a narrow terrace.

'Here.' He took the feather fan from her hands and began to wave it gently.

'Thank you, that is much better.' She leaned back against the wall and closed her eyes, smiling slightly.

Nathan looked at her. The ruby necklace glinted in the moonlight, inviting him closer. He reached up one hand to cup her face and slowly brought his mouth down upon the side of her neck. She trembled and slipped her hands over his shoulders, her fingers driving through his hair, holding him close. A tiny, whispering breath escaped her and he lifted his head.

'What did you say?'

'I sighed, merely.'

'You called me Nathan.'

'No. You are mistaken.'

He looked at her closely. 'We *have* met before, I know it.'

She gave the tiniest shake of her head. 'In our dreams, perhaps.'

'Now I have it! You were the mysterious lady in the Stinchcombes' shrubbery. My guardian angel.'

Her grey eyes glittered and a small dimple appeared at one side of that delicious mouth.

'That is a compliment indeed, my lord.'

'I must know who you are.'

He reached out towards her mask but she caught his hand, her eyes darkening, suddenly serious.

'No. If you unmask me I shall be obliged to leave. Let us enjoy this one brief moment.'

'But—'

She put her fingers to his lips saying softly, 'I am Temptation, nothing more.'

Her hands cupped his face. Gently she drew him to her until their lips were touching. The first, gentle contact deepened almost immediately into something much more passionate and Nathan gave himself up to the desire that had been building all evening. He gripped her shoulders, his mouth coming down hard upon hers, forcing her lips apart. She responded eagerly, tangling her tongue with his. Again, he revised his opinion of her: this was no shy lady out of her depth. The passion of her response fired him. She was eager for his touch and offered herself with a fierce abandon. He slid one hand around her back while his right hand caressed her neck, his thumb moving lightly along the line of her jaw. She clung to him, her body leaning into his. The blood pounded in his veins. He felt more alive than he had for years. He tore himself away from the delights of her mouth and began to kiss her breasts, desire slamming through him when he heard her moan softly.

Cry off, before it is too late.

The warning flashed through Felicity's head. She had never intended to let it get this far to-night—one dance was all she had hoped for, but the wine and Nathan's attentions had swept her up into a dream world where nothing else mattered, except being in his arms. The warning cried again in her mind but she ignored it; her body was yearning for Nathan to make love to her as he had done during those brief heady days in Corunna. She was overwhelmed by the white-hot passion cascading through her. She clung to him, giving him back kiss for kiss. She revelled in his touch, gasping as his hand slipped beneath the black lace of her bodice and caressed her breast. A fierce elation filled Felicity—she felt alive, irresistible. Dangerous.

Nathan raised his head, gazing deep into her eyes. 'Shall we finish this?'

She rested her cheek against his coat and heard the rapid beat of his heart beneath his jacket. 'We should go back into the house,' she whispered.

He sighed. 'I am not ready for this to end.' His hands tightened around her. 'Come with me,' he whispered urgently. 'Come away with me, now. Tonight.'

It was tempting. They could run away and continue this idyll—until he discovered her identity, then the questions would begin. There would be accusations, bitterness. Sadly, Felicity shook her head. 'I cannot.'

'Why? Is there a jealous husband ready to call me out?'

'No, but I cannot leave here with you.'

Silence stretched between them. Finally, with

a little nod Nathan stood back and held out his arm.

'Then shall we go back inside?'

For a moment he thought he saw a shadow of unhappiness in her eyes and she stared at him as if trying to memorise every detail of his face.

'One last kiss,' she whispered.

Nathan obeyed. The heady fragrance of flowers filled his senses. He looked down at the woman in his arms. 'This cannot end here.'

'It must, my lord. It is the nature of the masquerade.'

'But you must tell me your name.'

A smile trembled on her lips. 'I have done so, sir. You need know nothing else of me.'

He gave a little growl of frustration. 'I need to know everything about you. I shall not let you go until I know everything about you!' A nearby church clock struck the hour. Nathan raised his head, counting. 'Twelve.' He laughed. 'Midnight! It is time for the unmasking.'

She put her hands against his chest. 'You go in—I need a moment to compose myself.'

He hesitated, covering her fingers with his own as his eyes searched her face. He said at last, 'Very well, but only one moment.'

She nodded. 'I will follow you. Now go.'

Nathan could not resist stealing one final kiss

before he tore himself away and slipped back into the ballroom.

The orchestra played a fanfare as the last strokes of midnight died away and amid much laughter, cries and shouts the guests abandoned their disguises. Through the crowds Nathan could see Sir James and Lady Souden embracing, their masks discarded. Now was the moment. He tore off his own mask, glad to be free of it at last. He looked around for his lady. She had not yet come in and impatiently he stepped out on to the terrace.

It was empty. He walked the length of it and back again, but there was no sign that she had ever been there, save for a black feather fan lying discarded on the floor.

Swiftly Nathan ran down the steps into the garden. He tore around the side of the house to the front drive. Just in time to see a carriage driving out through the gates.

'Damnation!'

He watched the coach vanish into the darkness. It was too late; even if he called for his own chaise his quarry would have disappeared by now, effectively hidden amongst the other carriages filling the London streets.

Exhaling slowly, Nathan sat down on a low wall and stared into the darkness, aware of an overwhelming sense of loss. Temptation. She had named herself well. She had moved him more in a few short hours than any other woman he had ever known. His head went up. All except one.

Chapter Five

Only when she was safely inside the carriage and on her way back to Berkeley Square did Felicity allow herself to consider what she had done. She had spoken to Nathan, danced with him—and so much more. For a few brief hours he had been hers alone. In vain did she tell herself it meant nothing to him, that he would view it as a mere flirtation with a stranger. She had been in his arms, experienced his passion and nothing could crush the little seed of hope growing within her. She crossed her arms, hugging herself. Her body still burned from his touch. She closed her eyes and relived the evening, going over every word he had spoken to her, every little action. When she thought of their time together her insides melted again, just as they had done when he had taken her in his arms. She had spent so long trying to forget him and it had all been for nothing. She loved him now quite as desperately as she had done five years ago.

The pain and anger she had felt at his betrayal were diminished. Perhaps she had expected too much of him. Seeing Nathan again, being in his arms, had convinced her that she would rather be a small part of his life than to be out of it completely. If he would take her back. Slowly she removed her mask. Perhaps she should have revealed herself to him; she had heard that men would promise anything when they were in the grip of passion. She had been very tempted, but something had held her back, a fear that when his passion cooled he would regret his actions, and she could not bear to think of that.

She nibbled pensively at the tip of one finger as she considered what she should do next. It was a problem that occupied her thoughts for most of the night.

With the morning light came a solution. Determined to waste no time, she dressed quickly and made her way to Lydia's bedchamber. As Felicity followed the maid into the room, Lady Souden gave a little shriek.

'Heavens, Fee, what are you doing here so early? Go away, do, until Janet has had time to make me presentable!'

Felicity regarded her friend's frothy lace bedgown and the very fetching cap tied over her golden curls.

'You look very presentable, Lydia, and you are well aware of it. Now do, pray, let me talk to you. It is important.'

'Oh, very well.' Lady Souden waved her maid away. 'I confess I am desperate to learn how you went on last night—I saw you dancing with Rosthorne and could scarce contain my curiosity. If James had not been with me I vow I should have had to come to your room last night to find out what happened! He did not recognise you?'

Felicity perched herself on the edge of the bed. 'No. I left before the unmasking.' That at least was true.

'But he danced with you, several times, and I saw him taking you outside.'

Felicity's cheeks grew warm under her friend's scrutiny. 'Yes. He…kissed me.'

'Yes?' Lydia put down her cup. 'Is that all?'

Felicity hung her head, feeling the heat spreading from her cheeks—even the tips of her ears felt warm. 'It was a very—a very *passionate* kiss,' she mumbled.

'Oh, I knew it!' Lydia clapped her hands. 'I knew he would not be able to resist you! And he looked so preoccupied when we saw him later in the evening.'

'He did?'

'Quite distracted, my love! He left soon after midnight. Ring the bell, Fee! I must get dressed and we must think what to do—'

'I have decided what I must do,' Felicity interrupted her. 'I must write to him. I shall not give him my direction; I would not have him blame you or Sir James for my deception.' She clasped her hands together tightly in her lap. 'I shall explain everything, and throw myself upon his mercy. If… if he wishes to see me again it shall be arranged. If not…' she tried to smile '…I hope you will let me go back to Souden.'

'Of course you may, but I do not think that will happen. Once Rosthorne sees you again he cannot fail to want you.'

Felicity could not share her friend's optimism—there was so much Lydia did not know. She said in a low voice, 'There is no guarantee he will want to acknowledge me. In Spain he looked after me out of pity.'

'It was not pity that kept him at your side last night,' observed Lydia drily. She reached out and clasped Felicity's hands between her own. 'Have faith in yourself, Fee. I am confident the earl will want you back.'

'We shall see. Whatever the outcome, I am truly sorry to leave you without a companion—'

'That is of little consequence compared to your happiness. Besides, there is always my widowed cousin Agnes; she would dearly love to come and bear me company. But we have talked enough. I have arranged for us to go to the silk mercers in Covent Garden this morning, but after that I shall not need you, and you will be free to write your letter!'

However, when Lydia peeped into her room just before the dinner hour, Felicity was still at her writing desk.

'But how is this? Have you not finished yet?'

Felicity indicated the scrunched-up balls of paper littering the floor. 'All my attempts so far have come to nought. It is proving far more difficult than I thought to explain everything.'

'Perhaps you should just ask him to meet you.'

Felicity grew cold at the thought. 'But I behaved like a wanton last night—what will he think of me?'

'You have hidden yourself from him for five years,' retorted Lydia. 'Do you think Rosthorne will forgive that more easily?'

'No, I suppose not.'

'I do wish I could stay and help you with your

letter,' said Lydia, 'but James and I are prom-ised to attend the Prince Regent at the theatre to-night. You must wait up for me and I will tell you all about it. James has heard that the Princess of Wales will put in an appearance!'

'Poor woman,' murmured Felicity. 'I am sure she regrets her marriage. I know she does not behave very well—both she and the Regent are shockingly indiscreet—but one cannot help but feel sorry for her.'

'Feel sorry instead for James,' Lydia urged her. 'He will have the unhappy task of soothing the Prince's ruffled sensibilities if the Princess makes an appearance, as well as explaining away any awkwardness to the Tsar and his sister!'

After a solitary dinner Felicity returned to her desk, but soon discovered that her wasted efforts had exhausted her supply of paper and ink. Rather than disturb the servants she decided to go down to the morning room and make use of Lady Souden's elegant writing cabinet.

One of the best things about living in Berkeley Square, thought Felicity, was that Sir James or-dered candles to be kept burning throughout the house during the evening, in readiness for his return from the nightly round of balls and parties that he and Lady Souden were obliged to attend.

There was therefore no need for Felicity to use her bedroom candle to light her way down the stairs, nor did she have to send for more lights in the morning room: she had only to move a branched candlestick to the top of the writing cabinet to provide her with ample illumination. She spent some time searching for plain paper and mending her pen, then, unable to put it off any longer, she began to write.

She had scarcely finished the first line when she heard the door open and the footman's echoing utterance.

'The Earl of Rosthorne!'

The pen dropped from her nerveless fingers. She turned in her chair and stared as Nathan strode into the room.

The candlelight, which Felicity had thought so beneficial moments ago, now seemed far too glaring. There were no concealing shadows that she could step into, even if she could have made her limbs obey her, which she couldn't—they seemed to have turned to stone.

'So. It *is* you.'

Felicity could not speak. The footman withdrew, closing the door behind him. Fear tingled down her spine as she saw the glitter in Nathan's eyes. The thought flitted through her mind that she would be safer shut in with a wild animal.

'I thought you were dead.'

'No, I—' Her mouth felt very dry. 'How did you discover me?'

He put his hat and gloves upon a side table. The candlelight glinted on the heavy signet ring he wore on his left hand.

'Your disguise last night was very clever, but there was something…familiar about you. I couldn't put my finger on it, until you had gone.'

'How…who told you I was here?'

'You did.'

She shook her head. 'But I never—'

'The Stinchcombes' garden,' he cut in. 'You told me you were a companion. It did not take any blazing intelligence to think of the self-effacing Miss Brown, Lady Souden's drab little attendant.'

She flinched, hurt by his scathing tone as much as his words. He crossed the room and stood over her.

'What was your plan?' he demanded. 'Did you think to ensnare me? To entangle me in a web of desire before revealing yourself?'

'No! I am even now writing a letter to you—'

'More lies!'

'No, I swear—' She forced herself to stand up. It was not quite so intimidating, even though her eyes were only level with the snowy folds of his cravat. 'Nathan, listen to me, please. I had no intention of *ensnaring* you. When I left Corunna I had no thought of ever seeing you again.'

'Until I became an earl!' he bit out. 'You had no wish to be the wife of a poor army officer, but a countess—no doubt you find the title irresistible.'

'That is not true!' She stepped away, trying to ignore the sheer animal power that emanated from him. She said slowly, 'Last night should not have happened. I meant only to dance with you.' She winced at his bark of disbelief. 'I thought, later, that there might still be some…hope for us. I have been trying to compose a letter to you.'

'Do you think you can explain everything?'

She was silent. The idea of baring her soul to this hard, angry creature was unthinkable.

'I tried to find you,' he said at last, rubbing at the scar above his eye. 'I put notices in the newspapers. Did you not see them?'

'Yes,' she said unhappily, 'but—'

'I told myself there could only be two reasons why you would not respond. The first was because you were dead, the second that you did not want to be found. I had hoped it was the first.'

She closed her eyes. How many times in those first months back in England had she indeed wished to die?

'What did you do with the money?'

'I beg your pardon?'

'My prize money. Every penny I had saved. I left it with you before I marched out of Corunna.'

'I...spent it.'

'Oh? How long did it last you?'

'Six, seven months.'

She shrank from the blaze of anger in his eyes.

'By God, madam, you must have lived high to spend it all in so short a time! Well, I hope you enjoyed it, because you won't get another groat out of me!'

'I do not want your money!' she shot back at him. 'I want nothing more from you. Ever!'

'Then why did you seek me out last night?'

Felicity glared at him, her bottom lip caught between her teeth. Her hopes and dreams seemed foolish now, but even so she could not bear to have him sneer at them.

'Think what you like of me,' she said coldly, turning away. 'I do not need to explain myself to you!'

He caught her shoulders and swung her round to face him. 'By God, I think you do, madam! Last night you seduced me—'

'I did not seduce you!'

'Hah! Then what would you call it? No mere maid would know such tricks.'

'If I used any *tricks*, sir, then I learned them from you!'

'Do you expect me to believe there has been no man in your life since you left me?'

She wrenched herself from his grasp. 'I do not *expect* you to believe anything I say!'

He folded his arms. 'Then you wrong me. I am very ready to be convinced.' He waited, and when she did not reply he said, 'Perhaps you can explain what brought you to this household?'

'Lydia—Lady Souden and I were at school together. When—when I came back to England I had nowhere else to go, so I contacted her and—and she took me in.'

'And you have been her pensioner for the past five years.'

'Not at all.' Felicity's chin went up. 'Until very recently I was governess to Sir James's two sons.'

'And you call yourself Miss Brown.'

She looked away. 'I wanted to forget the past.'

'You thought that could best be done by starting a new life, with a new name?'

She shrugged. 'I did not wish to be any trouble…'

'Trouble!' With a grunt of exasperation he turned and strode about the room. At last he stopped by the fireplace. 'Did you think you would cause no trouble if you disappeared? Heaven and earth, do you have any idea how it was in Spain that winter?' He stared down into the empty, blackened hearth.

'We marched through hell to get back to Corunna, and all the time the French were snapping at our heels! My men were starving, we had scarcely one good pair of boots between us and we knew we would have to make a stand against the French with the sea at our backs. I expected you to be there, in Corunna, waiting for me—and then to find you gone! The town was in chaos, I did not know what to think, where to look. There were more than twenty thousand soldiers to be ferried out to the waiting ships and brought home. Do you think anyone had time to help me find one woman at such a moment? I prayed you had found safe passage back to England, but I could not discover it. Five years. *Five years* and not one word from you. Then I find you living here, right under my nose!'

'I did not plan this!' she cried.

'Then why did you come to London?'

'Lady Souden is in a—a delicate condition and asked me to accompany her, to be with her when Sir James cannot be at her side.'

'No doubt you both thought it a good jest to bamboozle me.'

'Not at all! I—I did not want to come to town. I knew it might be difficult but Lydia begged me—and I owe her so much.'

'Well, consider that debt paid. It is time to

consider what you owe me.' He held out his hand to her. 'Come.'

She eyed him warily. 'I do not understand you.'

He grabbed her wrist. 'I am taking you back to Rosthorne House with me.'

'No! It is far too late at night. What will everyone think?'

'I neither know nor care.'

She tugged against his iron grip. 'No, I will not go with you!'

'And I say you will.'

He pulled her towards him and lifted her easily into his arms. Felicity gasped, then began to kick and struggle, but it was useless. His hold tightened, pinning her against his chest.

'Be still, woman. You did not fight me thus last night.'

She gave a sob. 'Let me go, you monster!'

He laughed harshly. 'Monster, madam? I am your—'

'What the devil's going on here?'

Sir James Souden stood in the open doorway, Lydia behind him, her eyes wide with amazement. Felicity's cheeks flamed. She stopped struggling and glanced up at Nathan. He seemed quite unperturbed.

'I am sorry to tell you, Sir James,' he said, 'that you have been harbouring an impostor.'

'Have you been drinking, Rosthorne? Put Miss Brown down immediately.'

Nathan merely tightened his hold. 'Ah, now there we have it. This is *not* Miss Brown.' His angry gaze scorched Felicity. 'This is my wife, the Countess of Rosthorne.'

Chapter Six

Sir James's brows snapped together. 'Good God, man, now I *know* you are foxed!'

A sardonic smile stretched Nathan's mouth. Felicity wished she could free her arm, for her hand itched to slap his face.

'Not at all,' said Nathan smoothly. 'Ask Lady Souden. I believe she knows the truth.'

Lydia pulled her husband into the morning room and shut the door upon the interested gaze of the footmen standing in the hall.

'I was aware of a connection, but not...' She stared at Felicity. 'It is a little complicated...'

Sir James had been a diplomat for too long to be shocked by anything. With a sigh he gently disengaged himself from his wife's grasp and turned again towards Nathan.

'Very well, then I demand an explanation of just what is going on in my house. Rosthorne, kindly unhand the lady and tell me what this is all about.'

Sir James's calm tones had their effect. Nathan set Felicity on her feet. She stepped away from him, smoothing down her crushed skirts and glowering fiercely.

Sir James smiled. 'Well now,' he said, at his most urbane. 'Shall we send for some wine?'

Nathan waited silently while Sir James rang the bell. The speed at which its summons was answered suggested that the footman had been standing very close to the door. Probably with his ear to the panel. Lady Souden had coaxed Felicity to the sofa where she sat very stiffly, her eyes downcast. With her disordered curls tumbling about her shoulders and a delicate flush on her cheeks he thought she had never looked more tantalising. Damn her.

Nathan had been perfectly ready to carry the wench off to Rosthorne House, but as his white-hot anger cooled he realised the situation would have to be handled much more delicately if they were to avoid a scandal. His only thought in calling at Souden House had been to prove that his guess was correct, but the shock of finding Felicity had been overwhelming. She was even more beautiful than he remembered, her face a little thinner, the cheekbones more defined, but those huge grey eyes still had the power to send his thoughts crashing into disarray. And remembering her passion last night on the terrace he had become prey to such a bewildering array of emotion that he had quite lost his usual iron control. Relief, joy, pain and anger had all fought for supremacy. Anger had won the first victory.

They waited in silence until refreshments were served. As he sipped at his brandy Nathan noted that Felicity's hands were not quite steady when she took a glass of burgundy. It was some consolation to know that she was suffering too.

'Now,' said Sir James, sitting back at his ease and smiling at the company. 'Who is going to explain? Lady Rosthorne, perhaps you would like to begin.'

Lady Souden sat up, her eyes shining. 'Rosthorne rescued Felicity from a group of desperate *bandidos* in Corunna!'

'Perhaps, my dear, you would allow the lady to tell her own story.' Sir James turned to the Felicity. 'I think I should like to know what you were doing in Spain in the first place—succinctly, please. It has been a long evening and I would appreciate brevity.'

Felicity was very still for a moment, as if gathering her thoughts. 'My parents died when I was very young. I was left in the guardianship of my uncle, but he was a bachelor and could not be expected to take me in. However, my parents left sufficient funds for me to live at an excellent school.'

'The Academy,' nodded Lydia. 'Where we met. She was Felicity Bourne then, of course—'

'Thank you, my dear,' said Sir James. 'Please continue, my lady.'

'I travelled to Spain in June in the year '08 with my uncle, Philip Bourne. He is—was—a clergyman. He had planned to go to Africa, as a missionary, but our ship docked at Corunna and we came ashore. Uncle said we would remain there, that it was his calling. He hired rooms for us and talked of opening a church, to cater for English travellers, but somehow it never came about. He was never well enough. He caught a fever within weeks of arriving in Spain, you see, and never recovered fully. In October he fell ill again and this time—' Felicity bit into her lower lip but Nathan observed how her little chin trembled. 'My uncle was not the best at keeping his accounts. I did not know how little money there was until—' She sighed. 'By the time I had paid the doctor and buried Uncle there was not enough left for my lodgings.'

Nathan watched as she collected herself and settled her hands once more in her lap. Pity stirred; this was difficult for her. There was a look of great determination in her face as she continued.

'I sold everything I could, hoping the money would last until I could find some kind of employment, but I was too young.' She raised her head. 'I was nineteen. If I had remained at the Academy I would have had charge of the younger girls by then, and in Corunna I saw women of my age with families of their own, but it seems that I was not to be taken seriously, except for...'

Nathan's hands clenched into fists. He had heard this. He knew what she was about to say.

'Except for?' Sir James prompted her gently.

Felicity shuddered. 'Our landlord said I could stay on in the rooms if—if I allowed him certain...favours. So I left. I was on my way to the town centre when I was accosted, and my bag was stolen.'

'Which is when the then-Major Carraway came to your aid.'

'Yes, Sir James. We...we were married a week later.'

Sir James sipped at his wine. 'Incomprehensible,' he murmured at last.

Nathan leaned back and shut his eyes.

Incomprehensible indeed, when stated so baldly. But not then. Then it had seemed the most logical thing in the world.

He had taken Felicity to Casa Benitez, fed her

and put her to bed, removing her muddied clothes, bathing the dirt from the cuts and bruises on her arms. He held her when she awoke, terrified, from a nightmare, and watched over her when she drifted back to sleep. Even now he remembered staring at her exquisite profile with its straight little nose and determined chin, and her hair fanned out over the pillow like a deep, golden storm.

He had planned to be the perfect gentleman, but when she woke up and gave him a sleepy smile, he leaned over to drop a kiss on her forehead. Her eyes widened and he recognised the spark of desire in their grey depths. Her mouth had formed a little O of surprise and Nathan could not resist. He brushed her lips with his own and when she did not recoil he slid his mouth over hers. A little tremor ran through her, then she was kissing him back. Her inexpert embrace ignited his soul. He sensed the passion within her, wild and untamed and he wanted to be the one to release it. Their first, long kiss was deep and satisfying, but her inexperience tugged at his conscience and he broke away. She lay back against the pillows, breathing heavily, her eyes the colour of a stormy sea. Reluctantly he pulled himself away from her.

'Felicity. Listen to me: I have work to do this morning, but later today I shall take you to the British Envoy and we will explain your situation.

Once he takes you under his protection you will be safe.' He turned, afraid that if he looked into her huge grey eyes again he would forget his honourable intentions. 'I must go out now. I have to talk to the local council about bringing our men ashore. You must remain indoors, do you understand? You must stay here where I know you are safe.' He heard her sigh and added more gently, 'I am sorry I have to leave you here, but I have a job to do.'

'Of course,' she said quietly. 'I understand that you must do your duty, Major.'

Three hours later Nathan had returned to the Casa Benitez, grinding his teeth in frustration and consigning all bureaucrats to the devil. He ran quickly up the stairs to his apartment to find Felicity waiting for him. As he entered the room she gave him her wide smile. It was like a burst of sunshine. Suddenly the day did not seem quite so bad. He felt his tension draining away.

'Is that your old dress? It has come up very well.'

She spread her skirts and dropped him a little curtsy.

'Thank you, Major. Sam managed to get nearly all the dirt out of it, and I have reworked the lace that was torn around the neck.'

'Very ingenious. Has that taken you all morning?'

'Most of it.' She pointed to the enclosed balcony. 'Since then I have been sitting in the mirador, looking out for you.'

He grinned. 'A tedious job!'

'Not at all. The Canton Grande is very busy, so there is always something interesting to be seen.' She indicated a little tray. 'Sam brought in your sherry. He thought we should fortify ourselves before we go off to see the British Envoy.' She poured out two glasses and handed one to Nathan. 'I admit I am a little nervous.'

'There is no need—Hookham Frere will find you charming,' said Nathan.

She sighed and put down her glass. 'I have had time to reflect upon my situation, Major, and I can quite see that you might not wish to be associated with me.'

His brows snapped together. 'What the devil—?'

She put up her hand. 'You have done more than enough for me already, sir, and I know you are very busy. I have no wish to importune you further, so if you would give me Mr Hookham Frere's direction I will make my way there alone and ask for his protection. If I can find someone to lend me the money for my passage home, I can contact the family lawyer; it may be that there is something left of Uncle Philip's estate to allow me to pay my debts. And if not I can return to the Academy and earn my living as a—'

'No!'

She turned her clear grey eyes upon him. 'I beg your pardon?'

'You should not do that.'

'You are being nonsensical, Major. I must do *something*.'

'Then you should marry me.'

'You said something, Lord Rosthorne?'

Nathan opened his eyes to find Sir James and Lady Souden watching him.

'The chaplain married us,' said Nathan crisply. 'It was a drumhead wedding, but perfectly legal. I marched out of Corunna with my regiment later that day, and that was the last I saw of my wife. I could find no trace of her and was forced to assume that she was dead. Until tonight.'

'And do we know why the lady ran away from you?' Sir James asked quietly.

Nathan glanced at Felicity. There was a hunted look in her eyes. No doubt she expected him to announce to all the world that she had stolen his prize money!

'A misunderstanding,' he replied curtly.

Her grey eyes flickered over his face. 'Yes,' she whispered miserably. 'A misunderstanding.'

Sir James bent an enquiring gaze upon his wife. 'And you knew all this, my dear?'

Lydia plucked nervously at her skirts. 'Not *everything*. Felicity came to me for help, and I could not refuse her.'

'Please, you must not blame Lady Souden,' Felicity put in. 'She knew nothing of my marriage.'

'Besides,' said Lydia. 'Lord Rosthorne—or Major Carraway as he was then—had returned to the Peninsula by the time Felicity wrote to me, so—so there really was nothing else to be done.'

Nathan could not but appreciate the imploring glance she cast at her husband. It was a nice mixture of regret, apology and entreaty. He found himself wishing that Felicity would direct such a look at *him*, but she merely sat with her head bowed. A sudden irritation came over him.

'Enough of this,' he declared, rising. 'It is very late. If you will excuse me, I will take my wife home now.'

From the tail of his eye he saw Felicity's head snap up.

Sir James set down his glass.

'I appreciate how eager you are to be—er—reunited with your wife, Rosthorne, but perhaps Miss…perhaps Lady Rosthorne should remain here for a little longer.' Before Nathan could object

Sir James continued in the same thoughtful tone. 'A couple of points for you to consider, my dear sir. One, Rosthorne House is a bachelor establishment, is it not? Surely you would wish to make a few changes before you install your bride there. Two—and possibly of more concern—if the *ton* wake up tomorrow morning and discover you have a wife it will make you the object of speculation for every gossip-monger in town.'

'After what has occurred here, your servants will already be speculating,' Nathan retorted.

Sir James dismissed this. 'I pay my people well for their silence, but once outside this house you will find the world is less discreet. You will not deny that you have allowed everyone to think you are unmarried.'

Nathan flushed at the gentle rebuke. 'It was unconsciously done,' he said stiffly. 'Those who knew of my marriage were fighting in the Peninsula with me. Most perished there. When I came back to England, there seemed no point in dragging up the past.'

'Quite, but now it will be—er—dragged up, discussed and pondered over in every salon and coffee house in London,' observed Sir James. 'It cannot be avoided.'

'Yes, it can.' Felicity spoke up. She was very pale

and was holding tightly to Lady Souden's hand. 'I could disappear again.'

'No!' Nathan's anger flared. In heaven's name, why did this woman hold him in such aversion? Even the French prisoners he had taken in battle had shown less desire to run away from him.

'I'm afraid that is impossible, my dear,' said Sir James, gently. 'You are Rosthorne's legal wife—we cannot ignore that fact. But perhaps we can take a little of the sting out of the gossip and speculation.'

Nathan sat down again. 'Go on, sir.'

'We could spread it about that you sent your wife back to England for safety,' suggested Sir James. 'After all, the war was going badly at that time, so no one would think anything amiss there. And what more natural that she should wish to stay with her lifelong friend?'

'For *five* years?' Nathan could not keep the sceptical note out of his voice.

'The war has only been over a few months, my lord.'

'And why did she not take my name?'

Sir James allowed himself a little smile. 'A foible. Women are prone to them, I believe.'

'Oh, well done, my love!' exclaimed Lydia, clapping her hands. 'An excellent notion!'

Sir James accepted his wife's praise with a faint

smile, but his eyes were fixed upon Nathan, awaiting his response.

Nathan shrugged. 'I have no objection, but will Lady Rosthorne agree to it?'

Silently Felicity nodded, so pale and unhappy one would have thought she was agreeing to her own execution. Pity gnawed at Nathan and made him uncomfortable. Impatiently he rose again to his feet.

'Good, then it is settled,' he said. 'I shall return in the morning to collect my wife—' He observed the look upon Sir James's face and said impatiently, 'Good God man, what is it now?'

'I said at the outset that your wife should remain here and I still think that. Not only would it give both of you time to come to terms with the new situation but...' Sir James gave the slightest of pauses '...one must consider his Highness.'

Nathan stared at him. 'What the d—! What in heaven's name has the Regent to do with this?'

Sir James spread his hands. 'We are in the middle of his Peace Celebrations,' he said apologetically. 'They are not going well. Only tonight the Princess of Wales appeared at the theatre and drew everyone's attention. The sensational news that the Earl of Rosthorne has a wife could have very much the same effect, and you know how Prinny hates anyone to steal his thunder.'

He paused. 'The Regent would make a powerful enemy, Rosthorne.'

Nathan was about to damn the Prince to perdition when his eyes fell upon Felicity. The abject misery in her face gave him pause. He could shrug off whatever the gossips said of him—it did not matter to him if the Prince turned him into a social outcast—but it would be different for his countess. He might disdain the Regent's good opinion, but there was no doubt that his Highness could make life very difficult for his wife. If the fashionable tabbies of the *ton* decided to unsheathe their claws they could destroy any chance she had of being accepted in town. They could make her unhappy, and much as he was tempted to wring her pretty little neck he was damned if he would let anyone else hurt his wife. He rubbed his chin.

'Your duties as escort to the Emperor of Russia will leave you very little free time for the next two weeks,' Sir James reminded him. 'I understand there are visits planned to the Royal Exchange, the Tower and the Abbey as well as various engagements in the City…'

'Very well, you need not go on. I will leave her in your care until the Tsar leaves London,' agreed Nathan. He directed a hard look towards Lady Souden. 'I make you responsible for my wife, madam; I shall hold you accountable if she slips away from me again!'

'P-perhaps I should leave town,' suggested Felicity.

Nathan shook his head. 'No. I want you here, where I can see you.'

Sir James agreed. 'If you remain here, my dear, it will give you and Lord Rosthorne an opportunity to get to know one other again.'

Lydia looked up, a speculative light in her eyes. 'My lord, will you allow Felicity to continue as my companion while she is here?'

'I do not see that that is his lordship's decision,' Felicity objected.

'Well, it would need both of you to agree, of course,' replied Lydia, unabashed, 'but it would mean that you could come about with me, at least until Cousin Agnes arrives.' She turned a hopeful face towards her husband. 'Would you agree to that, my dear?'

'Since my primary concern is your welfare, love, of course—but I think it is for Lord Rosthorne and his countess to decide.'

Nathan hesitated. He did not want Felicity to be anyone's companion save his own, but after making such a mull of this encounter he realised that it might be to his advantage.

At last he nodded. 'I will allow this charade to continue for a while longer.'

'Excellent.' Sir James rose. 'Now I think that is quite enough for one night. I think we would all benefit from a little sleep. Allow me to escort you to the door, my lord.'

Nathan turned towards the ladies, but observing the way Felicity shrank away he merely bowed to them before accompanying Sir James out of the room.

'A most interesting evening,' murmured Sir James, linking his arm through Nathan's.

'That, sir, is an understatement!'

'So you and Miss Bro—Miss *Bourne*—met and married within a week? Hardly time to get to know one another.'

Nathan thought back. He had known after one day that Felicity was different from any other woman he had ever met. That she was the only woman he wanted for his wife. Nothing had happened in the last five years to change that.

Sir James continued, 'It is to be hoped you can find some time amid your duties as royal escort to plan your campaign.'

Nathan lifted an eyebrow. 'Campaign, sir?'

The older man's smile widened and he patted him on the back. 'Why, man, to court your wife all over again!'

Chapter Seven

Felicity awoke to the usual morning sounds: birdsong, the clatter of wheels and hooves on the cobbles beneath her window, the creak of floorboards. Sounds she had heard every morning since her arrival in Berkeley Square, but this morning something was different, something that made her stir restlessly against her pillows. Then it all came back to her and she was sitting up in bed, clutching at the bedcovers. Last night had not been a nightmare, Nathan really had come to the house. He really had recognised her.

She slipped out of bed and went to the chest by the window. Reaching beneath the neatly folded chemises and petticoats in the top drawer, her fingers closed around a small leather pouch. She pulled it out and tipped it up over her hand. Two rings tumbled into her palm.

Felicity remembered with perfect clarity when

Nathan had given her the diamond ring. It was the eve of their wedding. Nathan came to collect her to take her to dinner, to meet his fellow officers. They had not gone many yards along the road when he stopped.

'Almost forgot. I bought you this today.'

He reached into his pocket and pulled out a small box. Felicity took it, a smile of anticipation hovering around her mouth, which turned into a gasp as she opened the lid to find an exquisite diamond ring winking up at her.

'Oh, it is beautiful.'

'We are to be married tomorrow, and I cannot introduce you as my fiancée if you have no ring. Take off your glove and put it on. I hope it is the right size.'

'It is perfect,' she breathed. 'Thank you, Major.'

'I have a name, you know; I think it is time we were a little less formal.'

She looked up at him, smiling shyly. 'Yes, of course. Thank you, *Nathan*.'

She smiled up at him, flushing as she observed the warm glow in his eyes. She thought that only the fact that they were on a busy thoroughfare prevented him from pulling her into his arms and kissing her. Instead he looked away and cleared his throat.

'You had best put your glove on again.'

'Must I?' She looked down at her fingers. 'I want everyone to see my ring.'

He laughed at that. 'Very well—' he tucked her hand in his arm '—but these sea winds will chap your skin.'

'It will do no harm, this once. But should I not give *you* a ring?'

'That is not necessary; I have this.' He pulled a heavy gold ring from his right hand. 'My mother gave me this when I came of age three years ago. I shall wear this on my left hand from now on.'

'And the other ring, the band on your little finger?'

'A present from my grandfather when I joined the army. He said it would buy a few nights' lodging, or a pair of boots if ever I was in need.'

'It is very unusual,' she remarked, leaning closer to study the ring by the light of the torchères burning outside one of the houses.

'Yes, it is a thorn bush, the Rosthorne family symbol—a rose thorn, you see.'

Felicity looked at the gold band with its engraving of thorns running around it. She had a fleeting thought that he might have given her the smaller ring, rather than buying her a new one, but a glance at the little diamond on her finger, flashing fire as it caught the light, quelled any dissatisfaction. The diamond ring fitted her slender finger perfectly and she would treasure it always.

'Tell me again where we are going, Major.'

'To the hotel Fontana d'Oro. I want to introduce you to Adam Elliston. He and I grew up together, we are almost like brothers.'

'Then I should be delighted to meet him,' she replied, smiling.

He hesitated. 'He will be accompanied by a...' he coughed '...by Mrs Serena Craike. She is the wife of Colonel Craike.'

'And will Colonel Craike be there, too?' Felicity asked innocently, but then she glanced up at him. 'Oh, you—you mean that she, that she and your friend are...are *lovers*?' she whispered the last word.

'Well, he is besotted with *her*, but as for *love*—' Nathan's mouth twisted in distaste.

'Perhaps she is unhappy in her marriage,' mused Felicity.

'Perhaps. Adam is not the first man to fall under her spell.'

'Oh. Is she very pretty?'

'A beauty, if your taste runs to ripe redheads.'

Felicity picked up the second ring, a plain gold band, and held it between her fingers. She could remember only disjointed images from her wedding day. Being surrounded by men in bright uniforms, a loud-voiced officer with bushy side-whiskers barking orders at the chaplain, telling him to get on with it since the Guards were already marching out of Corunna, the officer's wife pressing a small posy of wild flowers into her hands. One or two of the officers she recognised, but Nathan's best friend, Adam Elliston, could not be spared from his duties and she was sorry for it, for Nathan's sake. She had no friends there but she wanted none, for Nathan was constantly at her side, making his vows with clipped assurance, sliding the wedding ring on to her finger, brushing her lips with his own.

'Well, Mrs Carraway…' Nathan turned his head to look at her. 'How do you feel?'

'Very strange,' she said slowly. 'I feel—no different.'

'Forgive me—to be married in such haste, at the drum's head—'

She put her hand to his lips. 'It is the vows one makes that are important, Nathan, not where one makes them.'

He handed her a small purse. 'This is all I have now. There is more than enough to keep you until we are together again. I have paid for board and lodging here for the next three months, by which time I hope to be able to send for you.' He put his arm around her. 'I am sorry to be leaving you so alone…'

'No, no, you must not worry for me. You have your duties to attend to, and as for being alone, I lived very isolated with my uncle, so I am used to that. At least now I have Señora Benitez, who is very kind, and I shall soon become acquainted with the other English ladies of the town.'

Smiling, he caught her hand and pressed a kiss in the palm. Then he put his hand under her chin and tilted her face up to kiss her, very gently, on the lips.

The shock set the nerves tingling throughout her body. She closed her eyes, relishing the sensation of his mouth on hers, the scent of his skin. She wanted it to go on for ever.

He took her back to the apartment on the Canton Grande and carried her into the bedroom.

'But, Nathan, your men.' Her protest was half-hearted. 'The colonel said you have to catch up with them…'

'Let them wait,' he muttered, setting her gently on her feet. 'I will ride all night if I have to.'

He put his hands on her shoulders and she trembled at his touch. She said shyly, 'How much time do we have?'

Nathan smiled at her. It sent a warm thrill down her spine and on, right to her toes.

'As long as we need, sweetheart.'

* * *

Felicity gave herself a shake. She dropped the rings back into the pouch and buried them deep in the drawer again. It was over. She had loved him, trusted him, and it had cost her dear. She would not allow that to happen again.

'Oh, what a fool I have been!' she exclaimed.

'What was that, my love?' Lady Souden came in, closely followed by Betsy with her morning tray.

'I wish I had stayed at Souden,' said Felicity morosely.

She allowed Betsy to place the tray on the bed, but she did not drink her hot chocolate, merely stared into its muddy depths. When the maid had left the room she looked up.

'Oh, Lydia, what am I to do?' she wailed.

'Do?' Lydia helped herself to one of the dainty strips of buttered toast lying on the tray. 'Why, my love, you must learn to be a countess.'

'But Rosthorne hates me!'

'No, no, Fee. He was a little put out last night, to be sure, but that is understandable. It was quite a shock for him to find you in London.' She giggled. 'It was quite a shock for *me*, when I followed James to the morning room and found you in Rosthorne's arms. I had not considered him to be such a passionate being.'

'It was not funny,' retorted Felicity, offended. 'It was quite frightening. I have never seen Nathan so angry. Heaven knows what would have happened if you had not arrived when you did.'

Lydia gazed at her, a knowing twinkle in her eyes. 'Do you not, love?' Felicity's cheeks flamed and with a soft laugh Lydia reached out and patted her hand. 'I beg your pardon; I will not tease you any further. I thought James handled the whole thing very well, did not you? He is always so calm and sensible. And how delightful that Rosthorne has agreed to your remaining here with me.'

'But for how long?' replied Felicity. 'I am very tempted to keep to my bed, knowing that he might call at any time.'

As if to prove her words, there was a light scratching on the door and a flustered maid peeped in to announce that Lord Rosthorne was below and wishful to see Miss Brown. Felicity grew pale and turned her frightened eyes towards her friend. Lydia merely patted her hands.

'Tell Lord Rosthorne that if he would care to wait, Miss Brown will be with him in thirty minutes,' she said to the maid. She turned back to Felicity. 'Betsy shall help you into your gown and I will send Janet to dress your hair for you. Now that the earl knows who you are there is no need for you to look quite so Quakerish!'

'My uncle would have said it was a very appropriate look.'

'Your uncle tried to beat your self-esteem out of you,' retorted Lydia. 'The Academy trained us to be fitting partners for our husbands, not meek little servants. Remember that.'

Slightly more than half an hour later, Felicity was ready to descend. 'I wish you would come with me.' She gave Lady Souden a beseeching look.

'I am not yet dressed,' exclaimed Lydia, fingering the folds of her frothy negligee. 'Besides, Rosthorne would only request that I leave the two of you alone, I am sure.' She gave Felicity a reassuring pat on her shoulder. 'Go on now, and stand up to him; he is a gentleman, after all.'

Felicity cast her a darkling look. 'I hope Lord Rosthorne remembers that!'

She found the earl waiting for her in the library. He was standing by the window, his buckskins, topboots and the tight-fitting jacket he wore combined to accentuate his athletic form. He was idly spinning the terrestrial globe on its stand and did not look up immediately.

Felicity waited. With the light behind him she could not read his expression.

He said abruptly, 'I came—that is, I wanted to apologise for my boorish behaviour last night.'

She inclined her head. 'We were all a little on edge, my lord.'

'You have dressed your hair differently.'

Flushing, she put a hand up to her head. It felt strange after so long to have curls falling about her shoulders.

'Lady Souden suggested…'

'Ah, I should have guessed. She knows how to please a man.'

Felicity's cheeks burned at the inference. She pulled herself up a little taller. 'What can I do for you, my lord?' Her tone was as frosty as she could make it, but it had no visible effect upon the earl.

'May we not sit down?'

She sank into a chair, tensing herself as he chose to sit opposite her. She tried to ignore his searching gaze.

'You do not look to have slept well,' he said at last. 'If it is any consolation, neither have I. Your appearance in town was quite a shock for me.'

'I had hoped to break the news a little more gently.'

'It should not have been necessary to break it to me at all,' he ground out. 'You entered into a legal contract when we married, madam. It seems those vows that you professed were so important meant very little to you, since you ran away from me at the first opportunity!'

'No, no…' She must try to make him understand. 'You had a…' She fought to speak calmly. 'Someone said you had a mistress.'

'A mis—!' He raised his brows. 'And you believed that? Without even asking me?'

'It is unlikely that you would have told me the truth!' she retorted. 'Besides, you had already left Corunna.'

'Then you could have written to me—but that is not the point. What did it matter if I had a whole *string* of mistresses, you were no less my wife! You had no right to leave without a word. What in heaven's name was I to think?' He paused and drew a breath. 'When I returned to England I tried everything. I set the lawyers to work, I even sought out your late uncle's man of business. You might have applied to him for funds, you know, your uncle did not die a pauper.'

'I was afraid if I went to him he would tell you of it.'

Felicity kept her head bowed, but she could feel his eyes boring into her.

'Did I frighten you so much,' he asked quietly, 'that you cut yourself off from everyone who could help you?'

'Not quite everyone…'

'No.' The sneer in his voice was unmistakable. 'You went to Lady Souden. No doubt she thought it very romantic to take you in, to hide you away—'

'She wanted me to contact you! I made her promise to tell no one, not even Sir James!'

'So not only did you disregard your own marriage vows, but you persuaded your friend to deceive her husband.'

Felicity jumped up. 'When I left Spain I was hurt and angry. I wanted only to get away from you. I was…ill for a while and by the time I had recovered your regiment had sailed again for the Peninsula. Lady Souden offered me a home, and an occupation. It seemed best to take another name, to forget that we had ever married. I never thought to see you again.'

Nathan watched her, his arms folded across his chest and a cynical curl to his lips. 'Do you take me for a fool, madam?'

It was Felicity's turn to sneer. 'Is it so hard to believe that I wanted nothing more to do with you?'

'Oh, no, I am quite ready to believe that you were happy to abandon a penniless officer. Quite a different matter when you realised your husband was the Earl of Rosthorne.'

She gave him a scorching look and turned away from him.

'Yes, that would make sense,' he said, getting up and coming to stand behind her. 'To be married to a rich lord would be much more comfortable than to be the wife of a poor soldier, would it not? A handsome jointure might even reconcile you to my—ah—diversions.'

She swung round to find him so close that she was obliged to look up to meet his hard, angry eyes.

'I have never wanted your money! If I had done so I should have declared myself as soon as you became the Earl of Rosthorne.'

'Why did you not? Why leave me to think myself a widower? Good God, I might have taken another wife. Would you make a bigamist of me?'

'Of course not!'

She went to step away, but he grabbed her arms.

'So what *would* you have done if I had chosen another bride? Come to the church, perhaps, and declared yourself on my wedding day!'

'No! I never thought of that—I merely planned to hide myself away, to live quietly, under another name...'

'And now? What are we to do now?' His fingers dug into the flesh of her arms. 'Well, madam?'

She struggled angrily against his grip. 'I could go away, live abroad.' Her head went up. 'Or there is always divorce—heaven knows your name has been linked with any number of women!'

She met his gaze squarely. There was a flash of something in his eyes. Rage, surprise, she could not tell. He released her and she quickly moved out of reach, rubbing her arms. Scowling, he walked away from her and stood for a moment, staring out of the window.

'Is that what you want?' he said at last. He waited, then said harshly, 'I presume your silence means you do.' Slowly he turned to face her. 'Well, I'm *damned* if I'm going to make it that easy for you, madam. You married me, for better or worse. I give you fair warning that I intend to claim my wife!'

'That smacks of vengeance, my lord,' she challenged him. 'Hardly the sentiments of a civilised man.'

'Very likely,' he retorted. 'But I do not feel very civilised at the moment.'

'Well, let me remind you, sir, that this is a gentleman's house, and until you can act in a civilised manner I suggest you stay away!'

With that she swept out of the room, closing the door behind her with a decided snap.

Felicity flew the stairs. Her spine tingled. She was afraid that Nathan might follow her and drag her back, but it was only when she reached the second floor that she heard his booted tread on the marble floor below. Running to the balcony, she was in time to see him leave the house.

'Felicity, my dear, what happened?' Lydia appeared on to the landing. 'I heard raised voices.'

'As well you might,' replied Felicity, her voice shaking with anger. 'The man is a boor and a bully. I cannot think how I ever thought I could like him!'

Lydia drew her into her room and closed the door. 'What did he say?'

Felicity hunted for her handkerchief and defiantly blew her nose. 'I told him I knew of his mistress and he—he did not even care! He said he might have dozens of them, but it did not give me the right to leave him!'

'Well, legally, he is correct…'

'I do not *care* about the law,' declared Felicity. Her eyes narrowed. 'He says he will not let me go.'

'Well, that is a good sign, isn't it?'

'I am not sure. I think it is just that he does not like to be thwarted.' She sighed. 'He is so hard, Lydia, so angry; nothing like the kind, gentle man I knew in Corunna. Perhaps I was naïve to expect him to be the same; perhaps I never really knew him at all.'

Lydia patted her hands. 'You have startled him, that is all. I have always found Rosthorne a most charming man, and James thinks very highly of him. I think he will make you a very considerate husband.'

'And what of his mistresses? You have heard the gossip, Lydia—Europe is littered with them. It is not to be expected that he will change.'

'But it *is* possible,' said Lydia. She added gently, 'We must face facts, my dear. Many men take a mistress, although I do not think that James has ever…but he is the exception, I fear. To have a kind, generous, considerate husband is more than most women dare hope for and I think Lord Rosthorne is all of those things. When you have had a little time to grow accustomed I feel sure you will deal very well together. But, there is nothing else to be done about it at the moment, so go and change into your walking dress. A little exercise will do you good. I shall expect you downstairs in half an hour.'

'Why, where are we going?' called Felicity as Lydia went to the door.

'To New Bond Street,' came the airy reply. 'We are going shopping!'

It was three days before Nathan managed to catch up with his wife again. In between riding out to Richmond to escort Tsar Alexander back to town and accompanying Marshal Blücher when he attended a military review, he had called at Berkeley Square, only to be told that Lady Souden and Miss Brown had gone out and were not expected back until the evening. He had called again while the Tsar and his sister were at one of the innumerable parties being held in their honour and was informed that the ladies of the house were dining out.

The following day he had dashed off a terse note, requesting an appointment and received a very civil response from Lady Rosthorne explaining that the ongoing Peace Celebrations were causing such a clash of engagements that she could not possibly say with any certainty when she would be at home. Nathan was not taken in by the apologetic tone of the note, which he ground savagely between his fingers. It was plain that Felicity was avoiding him.

When he had worked off his anger with a strenuous bout of fencing practice Nathan was able to look back upon his last meeting with Felicity, and to acknowledge that he had given her little reason to seek out his company. It seemed they could not meet without ripping up at each other. But surely he had reason to be angry. Her erroneous belief that he had been keeping a mistress in Corunna was a feeble excuse for running away from him. It was much more likely that she wanted his money—he would not be the first soldier to fall victim to a heartless adventurer. But Felicity was not heartless, he would stake his life on it, and it was quite possible that she had needed his money when she returned to England—had she not told him that she had been ill? He needed to talk to her.

With this in mind he presented himself at Lady Templeton's rout the next night. He was in no very cheerful mood as he entered the crowded ballroom. When he was given leave from his escort duties the last thing he wanted to do was to attend another party, but this promised to be one of the most glittering occasions of the season and he was confident he would run his quarry to ground there. It appeared that all London was crammed within its elegant walls. He stepped quickly into the crowd to avoid Lady Charlotte, looking magnificent in diamonds and lace, and he soon spotted his cousin Gerald flirting outrageously with the Tsar's sister, the Grand Duchess of Oldenburg.

He turned away, thankful that for tonight at least the royal party was not his concern. His height gave him the advantage as he swiftly surveyed the room and he soon spotted Lady Souden talking to their hostess and—yes, standing behind her was Felicity. He noticed immediately the subtle difference in her appearance. She wore no concealing fichu around her neck and her gown of rose-coloured muslin accentuated the creamy whiteness of her flawless skin. Her honey-coloured hair was no longer combed flat and constrained in a knot but now hung in soft curls about her head, with one glowing ringlet coaxed to hang down beside the slender column of her neck and rest upon the gentle swell of her breast. Little changes, but the effect took his breath away.

Felicity saw Nathan as soon as he entered the room and it was with some unease that she watched him pushing his way through the crowd, a determined look on his face. She touched Lydia's sleeve and was gratified when her friend reached out to give her hand a reassuring squeeze. As Nathan came up Lydia smoothly ended her conversation with Lady Templeton and turned to greet him.

'My Lord Rosthorne, how delightful.' She held out her hand and he could do nothing but take it, although his impatience was ill-concealed.

'Your servant, my lady. Miss Brown.'

Remembering their last meeting, Felicity gave him only a cool nod of recognition.

'I wonder, Miss Brown, if you would do me the honour—'

'Oh, you would like Miss Brown to dance with

you!' Lydia broke in. 'Yes, yes, do go along, my dear, I do not need you for the moment.' She put her arm across Felicity's shoulders and pushed her forward. 'There you are, my lord, a charming partner for you. But be sure to bring her back to me directly the dance is ended!'

'You were not going to ask me to dance, were you?' Felicity challenged him as he led her away.

'No. I want to arrange a time to see you. Alone.'

Her spirits dipped. There was nothing of the lover in his tone. 'That may not be possible, we are very busy...'

'So I understand.' He took his place opposite her in the line, his frowning gaze never leaving her face. 'But it must be done.'

The music began. Felicity gave him her hands, stepped close, then back, all the time gazing up at her partner. He looked so stern that it was difficult to believe he was the same man she had danced with at the masquerade. Then there had been a smile on his lips and a glint in his brown eyes. But *then* he had not known who she really was.

'You sigh, Miss Brown. Do you find me so tedious as a partner?'

They were so close it was safe to reply without anyone overhearing.

'I was thinking of the last time we danced, my lord.'

'At the masquerade?' He brought his head closer. 'I have told you, madam—that was not so much a dance as a seduction.'

She flushed. 'I beg your pardon. I behaved then like a wanton.'

His grip on her hand tightened painfully, but before he could respond the dance drew them apart. Her spirits dipped even further. He had not contradicted her; perhaps such behaviour was acceptable in a mistress but not in a wife.

'So will you tell me when I may see you?' he asked, when at length they came back together. 'I could call tomorrow morning.'

'Lady Souden and I are going out—'

'Tell her you cannot go.'

'No.' Felicity recalled the scandalised faces of the servants the last time they had been alone together in Berkeley Square. She did not think her reputation would withstand another such meeting. 'I cannot meet you alone at the house.' A muscle flickered in his cheek, as if he was keeping his temper with difficulty and she added quickly, 'I—I will think of somewhere… Pray give me a little time.'

Again that iron grip squeezed her fingers. 'You have until the end of the evening, madam!'

They finished the dance in stony silence and Nathan escorted her off the floor with almost indecent haste, his countenance shuttered and cold. It seemed to Felicity that he could not wait to part company. She moved towards Lady Souden, only to find Gerald Appleby blocking her way.

'Well, well, Miss Brown I must take you to task! I was led to believe you never danced, yet I have been watching you on the dance floor with my cousin here. If you can dance with Rosthorne, then you cannot say nay to me! Come along, Miss Brown.' As he reached for her hand Nathan stepped up and grabbed his arm.

'You are too impatient, Appleby. The lady has not consented.'

Felicity blinked, startled by the icy menace in his tone.

Gerald regarded him with a mixture of laughter and surprise in his face. 'What have you done to my cousin, Miss Brown? He looks ready to call me out.'

Nathan released his grip. 'I would not have you importune the lady, that is all,' he said coolly. 'If she wishes to dance with such a fribble that is her choice.'

'A fribble, am I?' Gerald grinned and cocked an eyebrow at Felicity. 'Well, ma'am, will you dance with me?'

She hesitated. Beyond Gerald, Lady Souden was smiling at her and nodding, but Nathan bent on her a furious glare. Perhaps he was not quite so indifferent after all. Her shoulders straightened. She lifted her head. 'Why, yes, Mr Appleby, I will dance with you.'

Nathan's lips thinned and he bowed, unsmiling, to Felicity. 'Until later, Miss Brown.'

Chapter Eight

Dancing with Gerald did much to restore Felicity's spirits. She was amused by his cheerful banter but more than this, she was aware of Nathan's eyes upon her throughout the dance.

'I vow I am much encouraged by Lord Rosthorne's behaviour,' murmured Lydia as they made their way to the supper room soon after. 'To accost Mr Appleby in such a manner is most unlike him. There can be only one explanation, Fee. He is jealous!'

'Do you really think so?'

'Why, yes, I do! The whole time you were dancing he stood by and watched you, his arms across his chest and such a dark and brooding look upon his face I declare no one dared approach him.' She gave a little giggle. 'Very romantic—just like Lord Byron's *Corsair*.'

'I have not yet read that so I have no idea what

you mean.' Felicity tried not to think of Nathan as dark and brooding, it made her knees grow weak. Instead she tried to think of somewhere safe to meet him on the morrow.

In the supper room a deferential footman approached and murmured quietly to Lady Souden. Following his oustretched hand Felicity observed Lady Charlotte Appleby on the far side of the room, nodding and smiling towards them. Lydia allowed herself one swift, rueful glance at Felicity.

'We are summoned,' she murmured.

Lydia led the way across the room, greeting Lady Charlotte in her soft, well-modulated voice and sinking gracefully on to a chair.

'My dear Lady Souden, such a crush, is it not? I thought it best to bring you here—heaven knows whom you might have found at your table with you.' Lady Charlotte's strident tones carried around the room and Felicity found several pairs of eyes turning towards them. Lydia turned off her comment with a soft, laughing rejoinder, but Lady Charlotte's attention had already moved on. She called for wine, then sat back and ran an appraising eye over Lydia.

'Sir James is not with you tonight?'

'No, ma'am, he is accompanying Marshall Blücher to a dinner in the city.' Lydia glanced briefly at Felicity and gave her a smile. 'But I am not unaccompanied.'

'No, I noticed.' Lady Charlotte sat up very straight. 'I saw your companion earlier. She was dancing.'

'Why, yes. Miss Brown is a very elegant dancer.'

'That is not the point,' declared Lady Charlotte. 'I saw her dancing with *Gerald*. It will not do.' She beckoned Lydia towards her. 'You should drop a hint to her, my dear Lady Souden. My son is a very engaging young man, but she must not set her sights in that direction. Gerald is not for her.'

Her carrying whisper reached Felicity's ears and continued on to the surrounding tables.

'No,' continued Lady Charlotte with a regal disregard for the smiles and smirks around her. 'He is Rosthorne's heir, you know. Gerald is destined for Great Things.'

Lydia's eyes darkened with anger, but she returned a non-committal answer and neatly turned the subject. Felicity kept her head down and picked at the choice morsels provided by Lady Templeton for the delectation of her guests. It was depressing to realise that if Lady Charlotte thought her too lowly for her son, she would certainly not consider her a fitting consort for Lord Rosthorne.

She was relieved when at last Lady Souden rose

from the table and carried her back into the ball-room, murmuring as she went, 'Poor Fee, what an evening we are having. Shall we go home?'

'When you are ready, my lady.'

'Then pray go downstairs and bespeak our wraps. I will take my leave of our hostess.'

Felicity hurried out of the room, but just as she reached the top of the stairs a drawling voice stopped her.

'Are you planning to run away without seeing me?' Nathan stepped towards her. Instinctively she put out her hand as if to ward him off. He took it in his own.

'L-Lady Souden wishes to leave.'

'But you would have sought me out, to say good-night.'

'I—' All she could think of was his thumb gently massaging the inside of her wrist. It robbed her of any power of speech.

'So have you decided upon a meeting place for us tomorrow?'

'It—it is so difficult,' she stammered. 'I am very busy.'

'So too am I,' he growled, pulling her closer. 'Let it be early then. Shall we say six o'clock? I do not think even Lady Souden will require your services at that time in the morning.'

She swallowed. 'N-no, of course not. A-and where shall we meet?'

'Green Park—the Queen's Walk. I shall be there at six.' He lifted her hand to his lips. 'Do not fail me!'

Felicity nodded. As Nathan turned and walked away, a movement to one side caught her eye— Lady Charlotte was standing at the supper room door, her cold eyes snapping.

'Quite the little belle of the ball tonight, are you not, Miss Brown?'

Without a word Felicity hurried off down the stairs.

London was surprisingly busy at six o'clock on a summer's morning. The *haut ton* were still in their beds, but an army of servants was already hard at work scrubbing and cleaning and polishing the grand houses while in the streets a steady stream of carts and wagons rumbled by, carrying everything from fresh vegetables for the markets to paper and board for the bookbinders. Felicity slipped out of the quiet house in Berkeley Square and into this busy, bustling world. No one took any notice of a little figure in a serviceable cloak and bonnet and she moved without incident through the early morning streets until she came to the gated entrance to Green Park. The path Nathan had mentioned was easily found. It was lined by trees and to her left the tall houses of Arlington Street rose up, their rear windows overlooking the path. One of those houses, she knew, belonged to Lord Rosthorne. She would be living there now, if Nathan had his way. She pushed the thought aside.

She moved deeper into the park, where the buildings were screened by high walls or bushes and the noise of the streets was replaced by birdsong. An early morning mist clung to the trees and she pulled her cloak about her, unnerved by the stillness around her after the bustle of Piccadilly.

Felicity began to wish that she had brought a footman with her. The path was deserted, but she glanced left and right, half-expecting a menacing figure to jump out. She had reached a slight bend in the path when her straining ears heard sounds that set her heard pounding: a grunt, succeeded by several dull thuds. She should turn and run, but instead her feet carried her on past the bush that obscured her view.

Nathan arrived at the rendezvous early, admitting to himself his eagerness to see Felicity again. He was still angry with her for hiding from him for all these years, but she was his wife and he was anxious now to bring this matter to a close.

He swiped at one of the bushes with his cane; Sir James had told him to court Felicity, but he was damned if he would do any such thing. Confound it—a man should not have to woo his own wife! A still, small voice in his head whispered that if he had courted her properly five years ago she might never have run away from him, but he swiftly quelled the thought.

A sudden sense of danger intruded into his thoughts. He was instantly on the alert. A slight sound behind him made him turn, just in time to see a heavy cudgel swinging towards his skull. Nathan ducked, but not quick enough and the club caught him a glancing blow to the head, sending his hat flying off. He dropped his cane and closed with his assailant, seizing his wrist in an iron grip and twisting until the club fell from his nerve-less fingers. His vision clearing, Nathan drew back and delivered a well-aimed fist to the man's body. He grunted and as he bent forward, winded, Nathan sent a second blow slicing upwards to his chin. The man collapsed and Nathan stood back, pausing to drag one arm across his eyes to wipe away the blood. In that brief moment his oppo-nent scrambled to his feet and dashed off into the bushes. Nathan was about to give chase when he heard a noise behind him and he looked round to see Felicity staring at him, white-faced.

'I beg your pardon,' he said. 'I would not have had you witness that.'

'You are bleeding.'

'It's nothing.'

'No, do not use your arm, you are wiping the blood over your face.' She came forward, pulling a handkerchief from her reticule.

Nathan reached into his pocket, saying, 'I have my own—'

'Then use it as a pad over the cut, while I clean your face.' She guided his hand to his head. 'There, you have covered it.'

Nathan held his breath; she was standing very close to him, her whole attention on the wound, but her face was only inches from his mouth. He was greatly tempted to lean forward and kiss her. As if suddenly aware of his thoughts she dropped her hand and stepped away.

'I am sorry,' he said. 'So much blood on my face—and with my scar, too, I must look monstrous.'

She smiled at that. 'Hideous,' she agreed. She moistened her own small handkerchief with her lips. 'Allow me to clean you up a little.'

He stood passively while she wiped the blood from his cheek and brow. Her hand faltered as she touched his scar.

'When did this happen?' she asked.

'Spain. We were withdrawing from a little village called Pozo Bello. I got in the way of a French cavalry sword.'

'I am so sorry.'

Nathan shrugged, uncomfortable with her sympathy. 'I was one of the fortunate ones. Elliston died there.'

Felicity's large grey eyes filled with tears. 'Adam Elliston? Oh, I did not know.'

'No, you had disappeared and I had no way of informing you.'

She recoiled at his tone and Nathan cursed himself for his clumsiness. He tried to think of something conciliatory but she forestalled him, saying in a matter-of-fact tone, 'You look a little more presentable now, sir. Has your head stopped bleeding? We should move back towards Piccadilly, I would prefer to be able to call for help should your attacker return.'

He picked up his hat and placed it gingerly upon his head, wincing a little as the brim pressed upon the fresh wound.

'He will not come back.'

'You cannot be sure of that.' She handed him his cane. 'I wish you will take care, my lord.'

'I do take care, but footpads are a hazard in London. I do not heed them, I have broad shoulders.'

'And a broad back for an assassin's blade!'

'Now what nonsense is this?' demanded Nathan.

'Three attempts upon your life, sir—'

He laughed. 'Are you thinking of the supposed intruder at the Stinchcombes' garden?'

'There *was* someone there, my lord, I know it, I saw them. And I saw something glint, like the blade of a knife. And the shot that took off your hat—'

'That was merely an accident.'

'But what if that was meant for you and not the Tsar?' she persisted.

With a smile he caught her hand and pulled it on to his arm. 'I am touched by your concern, but you must not let these events worry you. Why should anyone want to kill me?'

'I do not know, but—'

He put up his hand. 'Enough, now. I will give the matter some thought, I promise you.'

They began to walk back towards Piccadilly. Felicity tried not to cling too tightly to Nathan's arm, but her spine tingled uncomfortably as they made their way to the park entrance and she breathed a sigh of relief once they were in sight of the busy road.

'You are shaking,' observed Nathan. 'I shall escort you back to Berkeley Square.'

'There is no need, my lord.'

'There is every need.'

Felicity inclined her head. Secretly she was relieved that she did not have to make her way back to the house alone. She had been shaken to come upon Nathan fighting off an attacker and her knees were still inclined to be a little wobbly.

'You have not yet told me why you wanted to meet, sir.'

'Because I only ever see you in company. I confess I did not intend to put you in any danger; I thought the park would be safe enough at this time of day. Which puts me in mind of something,' he said suddenly. 'What in heaven's name are you doing abroad unattended? Why did you not bring a footman with you, or at the very least a maid?'

'I was trying to avoid gossip,' she retorted. 'Like you I thought it would be safe enough at this early hour.'

'Thank God that you did not arrive first in the park and fall victim to that ruffian. He was probably loitering near the gate, waiting for someone to turn into the park.'

Felicity bit her lip. She was still convinced that it was no random attack and was about to say so again when Nathan forestalled her.

'You are too careless of your own safety, Felicity. I begin to think it might be better for you to leave London after all.'

'But why should I do that?'

'Until it is known that you are my wife I cannot protect you.'

'I do not need your protection,' she retorted, nettled.

'No? Appleby is already paying you far too much attention.'

She raised her brows. 'Are you jealous of him, my lord?'

'Good God, no! I am merely concerned for you. Discretion is not one of Gerald's strong points.' He glanced down at her. 'So will you go out of town?'

Felicity hesitated. 'I am sorry, I cannot,' she said at last. 'Lady Souden needs a companion and her cousin cannot be here until the end of the month.'

'Two weeks! Surely Lady Souden can manage without a companion until then.'

Felicity shook her head. 'You know, of course, that Lady Souden is expecting a happy event in the autumn and Sir James wants someone to be with her at all times.' She paused and added with some difficulty, 'I know you cannot like the fact that she helped me to deceive you, but she has been a very good friend to me. Besides, carrying a child is an anxious time for any woman. I want to be with Lydia, to support her.'

Nathan did not reply immediately, but at last he

put up his hand and briefly covered her fingers where they rested on his sleeve.

'Very well, we will keep to the original plan.' He exhaled and Felicity heard a wealth of frustration in the sound. 'But you must take care—remain in the house as much as you can.'

Her lips twitched. 'That would hardly make me a good companion, sir.'

'Lady Souden cannot be out all the time!'

'Well, during the day there are carriage drives and morning calls to be made and at night of course there are parties, routs, balls—'

Nathan swore under his breath.

'My lord?' She glanced up innocently.

'And you have to be present at all these events?'

'Oh, no, not all of them. Only those that Sir James cannot attend.'

His jaw was clenched. 'Then when you are out make sure you do not attract attention.'

'Yes, my lord,' she answered meekly.

'And at the balls you are not to dance.'

'No?'

'No,' he said forcibly. 'At least, you are to dance with no one but me!'

Chapter Nine

Felicity's return to Berkeley Square did not go unnoticed and it was not to be expected that Lady Souden would let her rest until she had given her all the details of her morning adventure. Felicity was disappointed when Lydia made light of the attack upon Nathan.

'My dear, it happens all the time. No one is safe on the streets—and that reminds me: you should not have gone out without a footman—Sir James's staff are most discreet, especially if you slip them a few extra shillings! But what is this about Rosthorne wanting you to go out of town?'

'He is anxious for my safety.'

Lydia gave her a sideways look. 'He is very possessive of you, Fee.'

'He is not jealous, if that is what you mean.'

'No? Yet you say he gave you orders to dance only with him.'

'Yes.'

With a little cry of delight Lydia clapped her hands. 'It is a Case, I know it! Oh, if only we can persuade a few more gentlemen to flirt with you under Rosthorne's nose...'

'No! I will not tease him, Lydia. When he is in a passion he is...ungovernable.'

'That is because he is desperate for you, my love,' replied Lydia sagely.

Felicity shook her head. 'It is merely that he does not like to be crossed.'

'We shall see—oh, I know what I shall do!' declared Lydia, jumping up. 'I shall dash off a note to the earl now, asking him to join us for dinner before we go to the reception at Carlton House tonight.'

'Lydia, no!'

'Felicity, *yes*!' retorted Lady Souden, adding with spurious sympathy, 'Poor man. It pains me to think of him dining alone in that enormous town house of his.'

'Lydia, *please* do not write to him,' Felicity begged as she followed her down to the morning room. 'I would as lief not see him again so soon.'

'My dear, if it would upset you so very much then I shall not invite him, but why, my dear?'

'I am in turmoil, in here.' Felicity pressed her

fist against her chest. 'I need a little time to think everything over.'

'What is there to think of? He had a mistress so you packed your bags and left him. That was five years ago, my love. He was very angry that you ran away, but now you have explained it all to him, have you not?'

Felicity said nothing. There was a secret that she could never bring herself to share with anyone, especially Nathan Carraway.

When Sir James declared that he would be escorting his wife to the ridotto the next night, Felicity declined an invitation to accompany them.

'Pray do not think that I shall be bored here alone,' she explained, smiling. 'I have my books, and I think perhaps I should write to my uncle's lawyer, to advise him of my direction. If there is anything due to me from Uncle Philip's estate, it would be a comfort to know I do not go to Rosthorne penniless.'

As soon as Sir James and Lydia had left the house, Felicity made her way to the morning room. After several false starts she managed to compose a satisfactory letter and was fixing the seal when she heard the low rumble of voices in the hall. Some premonition of danger made her jump up, but before she had reached the door it opened and Lord Rosthorne entered.

'Miss Brown—please—do not run away.' Without taking his eyes from her he raised one hand and dismissed the footman. The door closed and he stood for a moment, watching her. His lips twitched. 'Poor Fee, you look as if you have been locked in a cage with a tiger.'

'S-Sir James and Lady Souden are out, my lord.'

'I know, I met them at the ridotto. That is why I am come here, to see you. Will you not sit down? I promise I mean to behave myself.' He guided her to the sofa and gently pushed her down, seating himself at the other end and turning a little so that he could look at her.

'How is your head now, sir?'

'Sore, but mending.'

Felicity bit her lip and twisted her fingers together nervously.

'You were not wont to be afraid of me, Fee.'

'You were not wont to be so severe.'

'No. Those years fighting in the Peninsula have taken their toll. I am not the same man I was five years ago.'

'I followed your progress as closely as I could,' she told him. 'Sir James has the London newspapers sent to Souden; I read all the reports.' She glanced at him. 'Such a long campaign. It must have been very difficult for you.'

'I found it more difficult when I sold out and took control of the Rosthorne estates.'

'But war is so terrible, so much violence and death—the loss of your friends, like Mr Elliston.'

He frowned and she thought for a moment he would not reply.

'Yes, that was bad,' he said at last. 'His parents live near Rosthorne Hall. I brought back what possessions he had when I came home, but at the time, writing to tell them Adam was dead was the hardest thing I ever had to do, I think.'

He stared down at his hands, his thoughts far away. Felicity let the silence settle around them for a few minutes, then she spoke again, trying to keep her voice light and indifferent.

'Do...do you ever see any of the people who were at Corunna? Colonel and Mrs McTernon, perhaps, or Mrs Craike...'

He looked up. 'The colonel and his wife are in France now. As for Mrs Craike, her husband died on the retreat to Corunna and she came back to England. Within a year she had married Sir Alfred Ansell.'

'Married! But I thought—' Felicity broke off, flushing.

'Did you think she would marry Adam?' His lip

curled. 'Adam was a diversion for her, but he was never rich enough to keep her interest. It amused her to beguile naïve young men.'

And you, Nathan, did she beguile you? The question hovered on Felicity's tongue, but she could not bring herself to voice it.

'Elliston was devastated when he heard,' Nathan continued. 'I think he could have borne it better if he thought she had married for love, but Ansell was old enough to be her grandfather—it was plain she took him for his money.' His next words answered her unspoken thought. 'I don't doubt you would have seen her in town, but Sir Alfred died last winter and she is still in mourning.'

Felicity looked down at her hands, clasped tightly in her lap. 'You seem to have followed her career quite closely,' she observed.

'One cannot avoid hearing the gossip.' He waved an impatient hand. 'Enough of this. I came here to talk about you.'

'A—about me?'

'Yes. I meant to ask you yesterday, but we were—er—distracted. I want to know all that happened to you after you left Corunna.'

'I—I bought my passage home.'

'And lived like a duchess until the money ran out.'

Felicity did not reply.

'I would not have left you with a penny if I had known how you would spend it!' growled Nathan.

Felicity's head went up.

'We had known each other but a se'ennight,' she challenged him. 'Would you have me believe you were heartbroken when you discovered I was gone?'

'Of course not. Inconvenienced, merely.'

She jumped to her feet and walked over to the window, staring out into the near-darkness. 'If I was such an…an *inconvenience*, I am surprised you want me back.'

Nathan had wondered about that himself. He believed it was because he could not resist a challenge, but there was something else. When he had danced with Felicity at the masquerade she had gazed at him as if he had been the only man in the room. It was an image that disturbed his dreams, but it would not do to own it. For now he needed to provide a logical answer. He said roughly, 'You are my *wife*, madam. We may have been married by an army chaplain but it is the vows that are important. *Your* words, Felicity, remember?'

'Yes, I remember—and I remember you promising to forsake all others.'

His brows snapped together. 'What the devil do you mean by that?'

'I too have heard gossip, my lord! You have not been monk-like these past few years.'

With a smothered oath he crossed the room in two strides and caught her by the shoulders, roughly turning her towards him. 'Dear heaven, you try my patience! By running away you gave me no *opportunity* to be faithful to you!'

'You blame me, then, for leaving you?'

'Yes, I do! I blame you very much for not waiting for me, for not giving our marriage a chance!'

Felicity stared at him, shaken by the violence of his outburst. Was it possible that she had been mistaken? Had she been wrong to leave him? If she had stayed, if she had not been weakened by that rough sea crossing...

Abruptly Nathan released her and turned away, running a hand through his hair. He did not mean to hurt her, but every time they met she roused such a passion in him!

'Perhaps,' she said haltingly, 'perhaps I should not have left Corunna. Perhaps it would have been better to wait, to talk to you.'

'Much better,' he said grimly.

She was hunting for her handkerchief. He held out his own and she took it, silently. His arms ached to hold her, but even as he reached out she stepped away from him. He said quietly, 'Let us leave the past. We can deal together better than this, Felicity. We need to get to know one another all over again.'

She blew her nose defiantly. 'I do not think we ever really knew each other.'

He risked stepping a little closer. 'Then we have that pleasure to come.'

One of her curls had worked itself loose. He reached out a hand to tuck it gently behind her ear, his fingers trailing lightly down her neck. She did not bat his hand away: that must be a good sign. He moved nearer.

'Do not be afraid of me, Fee.'

She finished wiping her eyes. 'I'm not,' she muttered, her restless fingers tugging at the handkerchief.

Another step brought him within kissing distance. He put his fingers under her chin. 'Then will you cry friends with me?'

His fingers, gentle but insistent, tilted her face up.

Felicity raised her eyes to his face and found him gazing down at her with such a tender look that it made her feel very weak. She was obliged to put her hands against his chest to steady herself.

'F-friends?'

Felicity could hardly hear his words over the pounding of her heart; it seemed suddenly to be trying to leap out of her breast.

'Yes. Very—good—friends.'

He smiled, sealing her fate. He bent his head, gently touching her lips with his own. It was the lightest kiss, as soft as a feather, and Felicity found herself stretching up on tiptoe to respond and prolong the pleasurable sensations he was arousing within her. Nathan took her in his arms, cradling not crushing, while his thorough, unhurried kiss went on and on, dispelling all the anger and the tension until there was nothing left but the warm, heady sensation of floating away—flying or drowning, she was not sure which.

After some time—but all too soon for Felicity—the kiss ended. Nathan kept his arms around her, and she still clung to his jacket, afraid that if she let go she would collapse.

'Oh, how can I *think* when you kiss me like that?'

He gave a low laugh. 'What is there to think about?'

She rested her head against his chest, listening to the steady thud of his heart.

'I need to think about what to do—how to behave properly.'

He kissed the top of her head. 'I consider you are behaving very properly.'

'No, no. I should not be alone with you,' she

murmured, but she knew her words lacked conviction.

'Sir James is a diplomat; his servants are well known for their discretion, although I have no doubt it will cost me at least a half-crown when I leave here.'

He led her again to the sofa, but this time they sat together, Nathan keeping a protective arm about her. He reached for her left hand, looking down at her bare fingers.

'I do have the rings you gave me,' she told him shyly. 'They are safely hidden in my room.'

'And will you wear them again for me?'

'Of course. I will look them out tonight, my lord.' She looked at his hands. 'You were wont to wear two rings, my lord.'

'What? Oh, yes.' He lifted his right hand and stared for a moment at the little finger where he had worn the small gold band with its pattern of rose thorns. He said curtly, 'That one was lost, a long time ago.'

The faraway look in his eye and the faint sigh that accompanied his words pricked at the bubble of happiness inside Felicity, but she stifled her doubts. It was time to forget the past.

She went to rise, but he pulled her back.

'No, stay and talk to me.'

'Talk of what, sir?'

'Anything. The weather, the theatre—I do not have to be back at the ridotto for another hour.'

With a laugh she settled back against him. 'I am afraid I cannot converse to order, my lord.'

Nevertheless, she found that, once they began, the conversation flowed very easily. She was surprised and a little disappointed when the clock in the hall chimed the hour.

Nathan raised his head, listening.

'I must go,' he said. 'The Tsar and his sister are engaged to go on to Lady Collingwood's at midnight and I must be there to escort them.' He pulled Felicity to her feet. 'Soon we shall be done with all this pretence. I shall carry you off to Hampshire.' He kissed her and stood for a moment, looking down at her. The look in his eyes sent a pleasurable shiver through Felicity; even her toes curled when he said softly, 'It will be our honeymoon.'

Chapter Ten

Lady Souden's ball was the last event the royal visitors would attend before the Emperor left London at the end of his visit. Nathan was escorting the royal party to Dover and when he returned he would carry Felicity off to Rosthorne Hall. Lydia confessed herself grateful that Felicity would be there to help her through the ordeal.

'Lydia, how can you call your ball an ordeal?' laughed Felicity. 'You love entertaining, you know you do!'

'True, but I have never entertained a grand duchess before, nor had so many crowned heads of Europe in my house!'

'It will not be necessary to introduce me to them all, will it?' asked Felicity, nervously.

'No, no, not unless you wish it,' murmured Lydia, soothingly.

'I do *not* wish it, most decidedly!'

'Then you may remain in the background, but pray do not go too far away from me; James must attend to his guests so I shall feel happier knowing you are there to support me if I need you.'

Something in Lydia's tone made Felicity look closely at her.

'My love, are you unwell?'

'I am perfectly well, thank you.' Lydia laid her hands on her stomach. 'But I *am* increasing, and James is concerned—I think he has passed some of his anxiety on to me.'

Felicity promised to look after her and went up to her room to change into her green satin gown in readiness for the evening. Lady Souden sent her own maid to dress Felicity's hair and to fix around her neck a collar of fine pearls that Sir James and Lydia had given her—'Look upon this as a wedding gift,' Lydia had said when she had presented it to her that morning. 'For soon you will begin your new life as Countess Rosthorne.'

Lydia's words came back to Felicity as she sat before her mirror while the maid's nimble fingers finished their work on her hair. She trembled a little, but with pleasure at the thought of Nathan carrying her away.

'No need to be nervous, miss,' said Janet, misinterpreting her shiver. 'You look as fine as fivepence, if you'll forgive me saying so.'

Felicity stared at her reflection. There was an alarming amount of skin exposed by the low neckline of her gown.

'Is it not a little...revealing?' she murmured when Lydia came to collect her.

'Not at all. It shows off your lovely shoulders and that beautiful, slim neck of yours. You look quite beautiful!'

'I think it would be better if I were to throw a kerchief about my shoulders...'

'No time, love.' Lydia caught her hand. 'We must go down now to welcome our guests!'

An hour later the rooms were so crowded Felicity knew the ball would be hailed a success. The arrangements had been very thorough, and Sir James's staff so well drilled that there was nothing for her to do except move from room to room, keeping a discreet watch upon Lydia. Society had grown accustomed to the sight of Lady Souden's companion, but she was aware of the surprised looks from several of the ladies, as well as admiring glances from the gentlemen. Her chin went up. Let them look and speculate on her improved appearance; in a few days everyone would know the truth. She watched the royal party arrive and was entertained by the jostling that ensued as the guests tried to make sure they were noticed by the

Grand Duchess of Oldenburg or the Emperor. She was surprised and enormously gratified when she saw Nathan making his way over to her.

'I hope I can persuade you to dance with me this evening, Miss Brown,' he said, a smile glinting in his eyes.

'I think not, sir.' Laughter trembled in her voice. 'If I dance with you, my lord, how can I say nay to any other gentleman who asks me?'

The mockery in his eyes deepened. 'Easily. You inform them that you have a jealous lover.' He leaned closer. 'Or tell them you have a husband.'

She brought up her fan and fluttered it nervously. 'My lord, have a care,' she begged him, looking about her.

He laughed. 'There is no one to hear us. But I suppose I must agree with you; if you dance with me and refuse everyone else it might rouse suspicions. Very well, dance with anyone you wish.'

'If I do *that*, sir,' she responded, greatly daring, 'it will only be with you.'

His brows went up, but there was no mistaking the triumphant look in his eyes. He bowed over her hand. 'I am engaged for the first dance with the grand duchess, but after that, I shall seek you out, *Miss Brown*.'

Smiling, Felicity watched him walk away. She did not expect to dance much, and certainly not the first dance, but she hoped that Sir James might ask her to stand up with him, and perhaps one or two of the other gentlemen of her acquaintance. She saw Gerald Appleby striding purposefully towards her until his approach was halted by Lady Charlotte, who took his arm and led him away in the opposite direction. Felicity's smile grew—if only Lady Charlotte knew that she was wasting her efforts.

'So, madam, are you free to dance with me?'

Felicity turned to find Nathan at her side.

'Is that how you invited the grand duchess to stand up with you?'

'No, ma'am, she asked *me*.' He held out his arm. 'Well?'

'Despite your rag-manners, Lord Rosthorne, I will dance with you.'

With a laugh he swept her off to join the set. Once again she knew the exhilaration of dancing with Nathan, the touch of his hand, even though they were both wearing gloves, sending shock-waves through her body. His intimate smile turned her insides to water. When the dance required him to take her left hand his grip on her fingers tightened.

'You are wearing your rings!'

'I thought it was time,' she said.

'And has no one noticed?'

She met his eyes, her own twinkling with mischief.

'It is customary when dancing only to *touch* the tips of your partner's fingers, my lord. *Your* grip is far too familiar!'

He grinned. 'Baggage!' he hissed as the dance separated them once more.

When the music ended he led her off the floor and procured a glass of wine for her.

'Thank you.' She glanced around; there were laughing and chattering groups on all sides, but none close enough to overhear her. 'I received a letter today, from my uncle's lawyer.' She glanced up at him. 'It seems my uncle's legacy has grown into a very useful sum. I have you to thank for that, I think.'

'I sought out the man when I got back from Corunna. I thought you might have contacted him. Once he knew I was your husband he disclosed to me details of your uncle's estate. I advised him to invest it for you.'

'As my husband you could have taken it for your own,' she said carefully, 'to replace the money you had given me.'

'I could, of course, had I wanted to do so.'

She kept her eyes upon the wineglass, held tightly

between her hands. 'You did not think, then, that I had stolen your money?'

'No, I never really thought that of you.'

She gave him a tremulous smile. 'I am very relieved to hear that, my lord,' she murmured, her spirits lifting.

Nathan was in no hurry to move away. Felicity was surprised at how easily they conversed, but eventually she felt obliged to comment.

'We are attracting attention, my lord. You should not be spending so much of your time with…' she hesitated '…Lady Souden's drab little attendant.'

A smile glinted in his eyes. 'Is that what I called you? Damned impudence!'

She laughed. 'It was no more than I deserved. But truly, you should leave me now, sir. People will talk.'

He moved closer. 'Let them talk. In a few days it will not matter.'

A shiver of anticipation ran down her spine.

'There will be waltzing later,' he said. 'Will you stand up with me?'

'Perhaps, my lord, if I am not engaged.'

His eyes narrowed. 'I believe you are laughing at me.'

'Would I dare to do that, my lord?'

'I think in this mood you would dare anything!'

He kissed her hand. 'Tomorrow morning I leave with the Emperor and the grand duchess for Portsmouth. One night there and I take them on to Dover. As soon as they have sailed my duty is done and I shall come for you.' He added quietly, 'I cannot wait to have you to myself again, Fee.'

The blazing look in his eyes set her pulse racing. Such was its intensity that for a moment she thought he might sweep her up and carry her off that very instant. It shocked her to realise how much she wanted him to do just that. He held out his arm to her.

'Would you like me to escort you back to Lady Souden now, Miss Brown?'

Felicity gave herself a mental shake. This was Lady Souden's ball, part of the Prince Regent's Peace Celebrations. Nathan had his duties to attend to, as had she. But soon…

'Ah, there you are, Cos!' Mr Appleby's cheerful voice called out behind them. 'I've been looking for you.'

Impatience flickered over Nathan's face.

'Well, Gerald, now you've found me.'

'Aye. Here's an old friend eager to meet you again,' said Gerald as they turned towards him.

Leaning on Nathan's arm, Felicity felt him tense. There, standing beside Gerald, was Serena Craike.

* * *

Chaotic thoughts reeled through Felicity's mind. What new torment was this? She had helped Lydia write the guest list and had seen all the replies; she would have known if Serena Craike—or Ansell—had been amongst the guests.

'Lady Ansell arrived in town only this morning,' Gerald continued. 'Knowing you were old friends, General Rowland brought her along with him.'

He beamed at them all. The lady gave a soft laugh, released Gerald's arm and stepped forward, holding out her hand.

'Well, Nathan, I can see that I have surprised you into silence. How gratifying.'

Nathan touched the lavender-gloved fingers and bowed over them. 'Ma'am. What brings you to town?'

Another of those soft, seductive laughs. 'Oh, boredom, and a desire to seek out old friends.' She spread her hands. 'As you can see I am still in mourning.'

The lady's gown of silver-grey silk was cut very low at the neck and very high at the waist, making the most of her ample bosom, while the thin skirts clung to her shapely legs. Felicity thought she had rarely seen anything less suited to a widow. No wonder then that Gerald could not take his eyes off her.

'Lady Ansell,' said Gerald, 'you will not know Miss Brown. Let me present you.'

Felicity froze. The widow subjected her to no more than a cursory glance. There was no sign of recognition, but Felicity's relief was tinged with anger when she realised that she was being dismissed as being of little importance. Lady Ansell lost no time in turning her limpid gaze back to Nathan. Gerald immediately began to chatter again.

'Well, well, I am sure you would like to catch up on old times. Miss Brown, this is our dance, I think...'

He was holding out his hand to her, but Felicity did not know if she dared let go of Nathan's arm. She hesitated, but found Nathan lifting her fingers from his sleeve and handing her to his cousin, saying, 'Yes, thank you for your company, Miss Brown, but I must not monopolise you.'

Felicity allowed Gerald to lead her away and as she did so she was aware of the widow stepping up, taking her place at Nathan's side, her voice almost purring as she said, 'Well now, my lord, let us find somewhere we can be private...'

'Up to your old tricks, Serena?' asked Nathan, gently removing her hand from his sleeve.

'I have no idea what you mean.' When he made

no reply she pouted and once more tucked her hand in his arm. 'What, still sulking with me because I preferred Adam Elliston to you?'

'I was never one of your admirers, Serena, you know that.'

He was aware of heads turning in their direction and his irritation grew. The knowing looks being cast towards them showed that many of the guests were drawing their own conclusions about his relationship with Serena Ansell. Thank heaven Gerald had taken Felicity away. He did not want Serena to destroy the fragile trust he was building there. The widow gave a little sigh.

'My period of mourning is almost over; I think I might risk dancing with you.'

'But first you must wait to be asked,' he replied.

She laughed gently. 'Oh, how ungallant, my lord! Well, at least escort me down to supper, Nathan.'

'I regret that is not possible. I am required to attend the grand duchess this evening.'

'That did not prevent you from dancing with the little chit who's just walked off with your cousin.'

'No, but I promised to return directly, which I am now going to do. I suggest you go back to General Rowland and let him escort you.' He disengaged himself once more, gave her a quick nod and walked away, leaving the widow staring at his retreating back.

* * *

'Do you…do you know Lady Ansell well?'

Felicity's voice sounded very odd, but Gerald did not seem to notice.

'Lord, no, never met her before tonight. Heard of her, though.'

They took their places in the set and Felicity hoped she would remember the steps. Her mind seemed to be working very sluggishly. For the first few minutes she concentrated on the dance. When she closed with Gerald she could smell the wine on his breath. That was why he was so garrulous. She thought she could use it to her advantage.

'What have you heard of her?' she asked.

'Oh, things. Not really fit for a lady's ears.'

She gave him what she hoped was an encouraging smile. 'Surely you can tell *me*.'

'Oh, very well.' He lowered his voice a little. 'She has a bit of a past.' He mouthed the next word, *lovers*, and winked at Felicity. 'I shouldn't be surprised if Rosthorne had an interest there at one time.' A sly grin curled his mouth. 'Perhaps she's come back to rekindle an old flame. There's no doubt that she is a dashed attractive woman. That glorious hair and those green eyes—irresistible combination!'

Felicity did not reply. The light-heartedness that had been growing within her was now replaced by a lead weight. She declined a second dance with Gerald, pleading a headache, and as he led her off the floor she looked around for Nathan, but he and Serena had disappeared. An ice-cold hand clutched at her heart. Gerald obviously believed that no red-blooded male could resist the luscious beauty of Serena Ansell.

And Nathan was every inch a red-blooded male.

There was a sudden flurry of movement in the corner of the room. A lady had fainted, a common occurrence in hot and overcrowded ballrooms. As she crossed the room to see if she could help, Felicity caught a glimpse of rose-pink skirts and a tremor of alarm ran through her as she pushed her way through the crowds. Her fears were realised—it was Lydia. She was lying back in a chair, her eyelids fluttering as someone waved smelling salts beneath her nose. Felicity rushed forward.

'What happened?'

'Is that you, Fee?' Lydia put out a trembling hand. 'I am a little faint. Perhaps you could help me to my room?' As Felicity helped her to her feet, Lydia smiled at the crowd around her. 'No need for this fuss. Pray continue to enjoy yourselves; I shall be better in a little while.'

'We should find Sir James—' said a voice in the crowd.

Lydia waved her hand. 'No, he is busy with our guests. Miss Brown will look after me.'

While Janet put her mistress to bed, Felicity sent a footman running to fetch the doctor. She returned to find Lydia lying back against her pillows. She was alarmingly pale, but gave a wan smile when she saw Felicity.

'A lot of fuss about nothing,' she murmured.

'Not at all. We have to look after you and the baby. I shall sit with you until the doctor comes.'

Felicity pulled a chair beside the bed and reached for her hand. Lydia sighed and closed her eyes. After a few moments her steady breathing indicated she had fallen asleep. As the silence settled around them, Felicity was left with nothing to do but to think back to the last time she had seen Serena.

Felicity had stood in the mirador, her hands pressed against the glass as she watched Nathan ride away to join his regiment. She was determined not to cry, but loneliness pressed in upon her, and after a restless night she knew she must find some activity to fill the long days until she heard from Nathan. She remembered the kindness of Colonel McTernon's wife at her wedding and decided to seek her out. She was about to put on her warm pelisse when the little Spanish housemaid knocked on the door and announced a visitor.

Serena Craike sailed into the room in a cloud of olive-green velvet, her hands buried in a swansdown muff.

'Ah, my dear, I thought I should come and see how you go on.'

'I was about to go out,' Felicity greeted her shyly, indicating the pelisse thrown over her arm. 'I thought I might visit Mrs McTernon…'

'Oh, it is far too early for that; she will not yet have broken her fast.' Mrs Craike laughed gently. 'I can see that you are not yet used to our ways, Miss…I mean, *Mrs* Carraway.'

Felicity turned to put her pelisse over a chair. 'Will you not sit down, Mrs Craike?'

'Thank you, but I can only stay a moment. I thought I might drop a little word of warning in your ear.'

'Warning?'

'With our menfolk gone we shall be left to entertain ourselves, and when ladies get together there is nothing they like better than gossip.'

'Oh? How does that affect me?'

Serena gave another soft laugh. 'Bless you, my dear, you must know that your marriage is quite the *on dit* of our little circle.'

Felicity shifted uncomfortably. She did not want to talk about her marriage.

After a minute or two Serena continued. 'Yes, when the handsome Major Carraway suddenly announces that he will marry, you can imagine the speculation.'

'But there is no secret about it. My circumstances—'

'Yes, that must be very hard for you, my dear.'

'Why should it be?'

Serena's smile was all sympathy. 'To know he married you out of pity. Oh, there is no need to colour up, child. I am sure Mrs McTernon and her circle think that he acted most honourably by you, but you must be prepared for a little talk.'

'Talk, madam?' Felicity shook her head. 'I cannot think why—'

'Can you not?' Serena's green eyes were fixed on her face. 'But everyone knows Nathan is desperately in love with *me*.'

Felicity was stunned. She felt as if she had been hit by one of the huge white waves she had seen rolling on to the beach. Fearing she might faint, she sat down on a chair, but not for a moment did she take her eyes from her visitor. Serena Craike regarded her with a mixture of amusement and sympathy.

'Did he not tell you? Perhaps he thought you knew of it already.'

'I do not believe you.' She remembered Nathan's words when he first told her of Serena—*Adam is not the first man to fall under her spell.* Dear heaven, did he mean himself? Trying to fight off the thoughts and images that crowded in upon her, she muttered, 'It is not true.'

'I thought you might say that.' Serena pulled a letter from her muff and held it out. 'You will recognise the writing. Nathan gave it to me yesterday.' Her smile grew. 'Did he not tell you? He came to see me, shortly after he had left you.'

With trembling fingers Felicity took the folded paper. It was a single sheet and covered with Nathan's familiar black writing. The words danced on the page and she was obliged to blink several times before she could make sense of it. My Passion. The very first words cut into her heart. She forced herself to read on. Nathan had not used the word love, but it was apparent in every line. Felicity's eyes filled with tears.

'No.' She shook her head. There must be some other explanation, although her poor brain could think of none. She turned the paper over. 'There is no name on this. It is not addressed to you.'

She raised her eyes. Serena met her challenging look with a contemptuous smile.

'He did not need to address it; he gave it to me personally.' She pulled off her glove and held out her hand. 'With this.' A black cloak of unhappiness wrapped itself around Felicity. There, on Serena's slim finger, was a thin gold band engraved with thorns.

In the ballroom, Nathan looked in vain for Felicity. If she did not appear soon it would be too late to join the dancers gathering for the waltz. He recalled hearing someone say that Lady Souden had fainted, so perhaps Felicity was looking after her. His jaw tightened. His wife should not be playing nursemaid to anyone. The sooner he restored her to her rightful place the better! He heard a heavily accented voice behind him, and turned to find the Emperor approaching with Serena Ansell on his arm.

'Ah, Lord Rosthorne, the man for whom we look.' The Emperor beamed at him. 'Lady Ansell, she wishes to dance the waltz. Myself, I would escort her, but we have already danced twice tonight and the tongues, they will wag, no?'

'Majesty, I regret…' Nathan paused, casting one more look about the room. Still no sign of Felicity. He turned back and bowed, trying to ignore the triumph in Serena's cat-like eyes. 'Majesty, it would be my pleasure to dance with Lady Ansell.'

* * *

Felicity wiped away a tear. So Serena had come back. To rekindle an old flame, Gerald had said. As the maid opened the door she could hear the orchestra striking up in the ballroom. They were playing a waltz. Nathan had asked her to dance a waltz with him. Lydia stirred.

'I am glad I have not broken up the party,' she muttered. 'You should go downstairs, Fee.'

'Yes, yes, I will, if I may. Just—just for a few moments.'

She sped out of the room and down the stairs, pausing halfway down to look across to where the double doors stood wide. Just in time to see Nathan whirling by with Serena Ansell in his arms.

She gripped the handrail, afraid that her knees might give way. Then she turned and made her way back up to Lydia's room.

'Back so soon?' Lydia murmured. 'There is no need, Fee. I shall be perfectly safe with Janet to look after me.'

'No, I shall stay with you, Lydia, until the doctor comes.' Felicity dragged up a smile that went slightly awry. 'There is nothing for me downstairs.'

Chapter Eleven

The night was giving way to a clear dawn when Felicity finally left Lydia's bedchamber. The doctor had come and gone and Felicity had stayed with Lydia, holding her hand until she had fallen asleep, by which time the orchestra had finished playing and the last guests were leaving the house.

Felicity decided against going back downstairs. She was desperately tired. The re-appearance of Serena had awakened all her old anxieties. Gerald's words echoed in her brain and her last image of Nathan waltzing with Serena did nothing to convince her that he was impervious to the widow's obvious charms. She thought that the little bubble of happiness growing within her must have been made of glass, for now that it had fractured, the sharp pain of her disappointment was unbearable.

* * *

It was a week later when Nathan returned to London and he made his way directly to Berkeley Square. There had been no opportunity to speak to Felicity before he left the Soudens' ball. Understandable, of course, with Lady Souden being carried off to her room, but he was anxious now to see her again.

'So,' said Sir James, when Nathan was shown into the study, 'your royal charge has left England.'

'Yes, Sir James. We stopped off at Portsmouth where there were sufficient cheering crowds and 21-gun salutes to please his Highness, then on the Saturday morning the Emperor and the Prussian royals breakfasted with the Duke of Clarence before leaving for Dover where, thank heaven, the weather was favourable and nothing delayed their departure.' Nathan drained his glass. 'And now I am back, and wish to see my wife.'

There was the slightest of pauses.

'Ah.'

Nathan watched Sir James get up and refill the glasses.

'Is something amiss?' He was suddenly tense. 'Is Felicity ill?'

'No, no, your wife is very well, Lord Rosthorne.' Sir James handed Nathan his glass and returned to his seat. 'You may recall that Lady Souden was taken ill on the night of the ball.'

'Of course. I trust she is now recovered?'

'Unfortunately, no.' Sir James's face was unusually solemn. 'We feared she might lose the baby, but that has not happened. However, her doctor prescribes complete bed-rest. I wanted to take her back to Souden, but she is too ill to be moved.'

'I am very sorry to hear it.'

'Thank you. Your wife has been a great support during this time—you will know that Lydia had asked her cousin to come and live with her, but unfortunately the woman broke her leg and is now tied to her own house. And even if she was available—' Sir James broke off, sombrely regarding his glass. At last he looked up, his grey eyes meeting Nathan's. 'My wife needs peace of mind, Rosthorne; Dr Scott insists that she must not be upset or disturbed in any way. You know the bond that exists between your wife and mine; I very much fear that if Lady Rosthorne was to leave now, it would distress Lydia greatly. I would therefore ask if you would spare her to us for a little longer.' He put up his hand. 'I can see by your face that you are minded to refuse, and you have every right to do so. Felicity is your legal wife. But I would ask you, as a friend, to let her stay.'

Closing his lips tightly against any unwary comment, Nathan jumped up. 'And what does Felicity say about this?'

'Lady Rosthorne is anxious not to do anything that could endanger Lydia's health.'

After a few hasty turns about the room Nathan found himself by the window and paused there, staring out. 'Another delay—how long could this last?'

'Possibly until October, when the baby is due.' Sir James came to stand beside him at the window. 'We might lose the child. If that is the case, then so be it, but my concern is Lydia. I will do everything in my power to save my wife.'

Nathan looked at the older man. He noted the sadness in his eyes, the lines of worry etched upon his face. It shocked him to realise that Sir James was so desperately concerned for his wife. This man, this great diplomat who had the ear of princes, who consorted with royalty and advised the government, was actually begging him not to take Felicity away. With a sigh Nathan turned again to look out of the window. The bright sun was still shining down, the day was as full of promise as it had been when he had arrived, but not for him.

'I would do the same, in your place,' he said quietly. Sir James placed his hand on his shoulder, his touch eloquent of relief, gratitude and a measure of sympathy. 'I would like to see my wife for a few moments, if that is possible.'

'Of course. I will send her down to you.'

* * *

Felicity entered the study. Nathan was standing at the window, staring out into the street.

'I am glad you are back safely, my lord.'

'Are you?' He turned and crossed the room to greet her. He kissed her hand and would have kissed her cheek, but she drew back with a tiny gesture of denial.

'I cannot stay long,' she said quickly. 'Lydia becomes very restless when I am away from her.'

His hand cupped her chin. 'Are you in constant attendance upon Lady Souden? Poor Fee—that would explain the dark shadows beneath your eyes.'

Forcing a little smile, she freed herself from his grasp. 'Yes, that would be it. Sir James has told you—explained…'

'Yes. I was hoping to take you into Hampshire tomorrow. I have already written to my mother—she is eager to meet you—but it seems that that meeting will have to be postponed.'

'I am very sorry.'

'So too am I. Perhaps I should stay in London. I could take you to the town house tonight—'

'No. Lydia often needs me during the night.'

His brows drew together. 'I am beginning to think you are trying to fob me off.'

'That is not so, my lord. Lady Souden is ill, she needs my attention.'

'Perhaps you should consider devoting some attention to your husband!'

She put her hands together. 'And I *will*, I give you my word, as soon as I can safely leave Lydia.' She looked down, conscious of his frowning stare.

He said quietly, 'What is it, Fee? What makes it so important that you stay here?'

'Lydia must have love and comfort and careful nursing, all the things that—that a new mother needs if she is to have a healthy baby.'

'I suppose it is no good suggesting that she could find these things elsewhere.'

'She could, of course, but…it is important to *me* to help her through this ordeal.'

'And why is that?'

'She…is my friend, and I will do everything in my power to make sure she does not suffer the agony of losing a child.'

Nathan fixed his eyes upon Felicity. She stood before him, eyes downcast and looking distinctly uncomfortable. There was something she was not telling him. She was removed, distant, no longer the delightful companion he remembered from their last meeting.

He wanted to take her arms and shake her, but that would not release the lively, loving creature he knew was inside her. It might drive her even further from him. He decided to change tactics. 'Then you had best remain here.'

Felicity did not know whether to be most relieved or disappointed at his calm acceptance.

'It seems our marriage must wait a little longer, my dear. I will go down to Rosthorne and set everything in readiness for you.' He took her hand again. 'I will let you get back to your patient. Write to me; let me know as soon as you can be spared.'

'I will, my lord.'

His hand tightened on her fingers. 'So formal? I would rather you called me by my name. Can you do that?'

'Of course…Nathan.'

Gently he drew her into his arms, placing two fingers beneath her chin to tilt her face up for a brief, gentle kiss. Her heart cried out against such restraint. She wanted him to crush her to him, to override her sensible arguments and carry her off to his town house. She thought she would happily do without sleep if she could spend a few hours each day with Nathan.

'So, madam, will you miss me?'

This was her chance—she could ask him to stay, tell him how much his presence would support her, but even as the words formed on her tongue the vision of Serena's green eyes and flaming curls intruded. She would not demean herself by admitting her need when he was besotted by another woman. So she summoned up a bright smile and stepped away from the comfort of his arms.

'Of course, my lord, but I am so very busy it is best if you are not here to distract me. But... the Peace Celebrations are to continue for some months yet—do you not wish to stay in town for that?'

He grimaced. 'I have had enough of crowds and spectacle. There is plenty of work to be done at Rosthorne.'

'And you will set out for Hampshire tomorrow?'

He nodded. 'As soon as it is light.' He paused. 'If there is nothing more to say then I shall leave you now.'

'No,' she said brightly. 'I wish you a safe journey, my lord.'

His gaze rested upon her for a long moment and it was as much as Felicity could do to maintain her cheerful countenance. Then, with a word and a nod, he was gone. Felicity ran to the window and peeped out. A groom was walking Nathan's great black horse up and down the road. As she watched, he turned quickly and brought the animal back to the door just as Nathan appeared. He mounted effortlessly into the saddle and exchanged a few brief words with his groom as he gathered up the reins. Felicity drew back quickly as Nathan cast a last, unsmiling look at the house before he turned his mount and trotted away.

'Fee? What are you doing?'

Felicity looked up. 'Oh, are you awake, Lydia? Janet and I thought you might sleep for an hour or so, yet.'

'No, dearest, I have been lying here watching you. Are you writing to Rosthorne?'

Felicity put down her pen and walked across to the huge bed, where Lydia lay propped up against a bank of snowy white pillows.

'I am, but it can wait. Shall I draw the curtains? The afternoon sun is very bright—'

'No matter, I like to see the sun shining.' Lydia patted her hand invitingly. 'Come and sit on the bed and tell me all that you are writing to him.'

'Well, he asks after your health, so I have said that Dr Scott is very pleased with you, and that you now spend a little time each day on the daybed by an open window.'

Lydia placed her hands on her swollen belly and chuckled. 'Did you also tell him that I am becoming grossly fat?'

'Of course not! I described you as being in high bloom now.'

'Did you? Then he will be demanding that you leave me.'

Felicity's smiled slipped a little. 'Not for a while yet; his letter said that he is off to Yorkshire for a few weeks, to visit his estates there.'

'No word of his coming to town?'

'No. Lydia, do not look at me in that way. It was agreed that I should stay here with you for as long as you need me.'

'And I *do* need you, love. With James obliged to spend so much time dancing attendance on the Prince Regent I should be moped to death here without you.'

Felicity smiled. 'How can you say that when every post brings you a shower of letters and we are forever taking in flowers from your friends? Even Lady Charlotte sent a bouquet.'

'Lord, yes, I was surprised to see she was still in town. Keeping an eye upon her son, I think.' Lydia chuckled. 'I hear he is very taken with the red-haired widow, Lady Ansell. Lady Charlotte will wish to squash *that* connection.'

Felicity tried to smile. She wondered if she should tell Lydia about Serena, but decided against it. Lydia stirred restlessly.

'I am most disappointed in Rosthorne,' she complained. 'I thought he was very much in love with you, but if that was so I wonder that he has stayed away from town for so long.'

'Clearly he was not so besotted as you thought,' returned Felicity, trying to keep her voice light.

'Oh, Fee, I am sorry—if I had not been ill you would have been happily settled with your earl by this time.'

Felicity shrugged, sadness squeezing at her heart. What happiness could there be for her if Nathan was still in love with Serena Ansell?

The months dragged on: the hot summer days gave way to the cooler mists and rain of autumn and still Nathan did not come to London. He wrote several times to Felicity, his letters polite, friendly even, but with no hint of the lover in their tone and Felicity resolutely buried the hopes that had burgeoned so strongly at the beginning of the summer. She would do her duty, when the time came, but before that there were nervous weeks ahead as the time drew near for Lydia's confinement.

It was the news Nathan had been waiting for. The brief note from Sir James informed him that Lady Souden had been safely delivered of a strong, healthy girl. Mother and baby were both doing well, Dr Scott was confident that there was no risk now of childbed fever and declared that they would both be well enough to travel to Souden at the end of October.

Nathan penned a short message of congratulations to Sir James and his lady, and an even shorter one to Felicity, informing her that he would be in London by the end of the week and requesting that she should be ready on the Friday morning to travel with him to Hampshire. As he fixed the seal to this second missive, he thought over all the frustrations of the past few months, when he had thrown himself into the business of his estates rather than giving in to the urge to post up to town. He was surprised how much he had missed her; it was a physical pain and now that the waiting was almost over he allowed himself to think of her again, to remember her shy smile, which would light up a room for him, and the mischievous twinkle he would sometimes surprise in her eyes. He had been very forbearing; she had said she did not want him there to distract her so he had kept away, but now, climbing into his travelling carriage on a misty October morning, he was returning to claim his wife.

Chapter Twelve

'Of all the arrogant, unfeeling—!' Felicity almost stamped her foot as she read Nathan's hasty scrawl.

'What is it, Fee?' Lydia, with a sleeping baby in her arms, did not look up.

'This note from Rosthorne. He informs me I am to leave here tomorrow morning, without so much as a by your leave!' With a little huff of frustration she twisted the paper between her hands and hurled it across the room.

Lydia merely smiled. 'He has been very patient, my dear, and I cannot keep you with me for ever, much as I would like to, for you are so good with your little god-daughter.'

Felicity's anger drained away as she regarded the mother and child. 'Baby Elizabeth is so good, it is not difficult to love her.'

'She *is* a darling, isn't she? But you have such

a way with you.' Lydia twinkled up at her. 'I find it hard to believe you have no experience in the nursery.'

Felicity gazed for a long moment at the baby. She had to breathe deeply to remove the constriction in her throat.

'No,' she said at last, and with perfect truth. 'No, I have never held a baby before.'

'Well, once you are back with your husband I am sure it will not be very long before you have a family of your own—'

'Oh, Lydia, pray do not go on!'

'Darling Fee! What is it?'

Felicity hesitated, then with a sob she threw herself on her knees beside Lydia's chair. 'I am afraid,' she confessed, resting her head against Lydia's knee.

'Frightened of the bedroom? I am sure there is not the least need...'

Felicity blushed. 'No, it is not that. It is Nathan.' She searched for her handkerchief. 'I am not sure of him. I—I do not think I know him any more...'

Lydia, still euphoric after the worries of the past few months, merely smiled and laid a gentle hand on Felicity's head. 'This is nothing more than nerves, Fee. You love him, do you not?'

Felicity sighed. 'Yes,' she whispered. 'That is, I *did*, but he is so different now.'

'You are both different—five years older, for one thing. I have seen the earl's face when he looks at you. He desires you, Felicity.'

'But does he *love* me?' she persisted, wiping her eyes.

Lydia smiled. 'For gentlemen, love and desire are very closely linked,' she said softly. 'With James, one followed the other, and look how happy we are now.' She gave Felicity a little push. 'Go and pack your bags, my dear, and consider your good fortune: Rosthorne is a kind and honourable man. He is also very rich and exceedingly attractive, despite the scar across his brow. I vow if I was not head over heels in love with James I would set my cap at him myself!'

Nervously, Felicity tied the ribbons of her bonnet. She had seen the handsome travelling carriage pull up outside the house and had received a message that Lord Rosthorne was awaiting her below. A glance out of the window showed her that even now the servants were carrying her trunk out of the house.

Sir James was standing with the earl in the hall and both men turned as Felicity made her way down the stairs. Her new pelisse and bonnet were a present from Lydia, who had insisted that the soft sage-green colour suited her very well and would boost her confidence. Very necessary, she thought, as she met the earl's unsmiling look.

Felicity dropped a curtsy. 'My lord.'

He bowed. Sir James stepped forward.

'Well, Lady Rosthorne, we must say goodbye to you.' He reached for her hand and kissed her fingers. 'My wife has already told you how grateful we are to you?'

'Yes, sir. I have just left her bedchamber.'

'Then it only remains for me to say goodbye and to wish you and Lord Rosthorne every happiness.'

Nathan held out his arm to her. 'Shall we be on our way, ma'am?' She met his eyes and observed the glint of amusement there. He knew how much she wanted to turn and run. But his look was not unkind. He said gently, 'Come, my lady.'

Felicity gave him her hand and he led her to the waiting carriage. She had time for one final, smiling wave to Sir James before they were away, clattering out of London. She was very aware of the earl, sitting in one corner of the coach. He was watching her and his gaze made her spine tingle. She had the impression that he could see every curve of her body, despite the jaconet muslin pelisse that enveloped her. She did not know whether she was most alarmed or excited by the thought. Excited, she admitted to herself. She had certainly missed him.

'I was surprised to receive the letter from Sir James,' remarked Nathan. 'I thought perhaps you might write first, to tell me the good news.'

Felicity cleared her throat. 'I—I was waiting, to be sure...'

'Putting off the evil day?' His dry tone sent the blood rushing to her cheeks.

'Not *evil*, my lord.' She risked a quick glance at him and observed that he was smiling. She was emboldened to add, 'I confess I am a little appre-hensive.'

'There is no need.'

'No? The tone of your note was very peremp-tory, and we left Berkeley Square so quickly this morning...'

'I am sorry to rush you away from your friends,' he replied. 'Naturally I am anxious for you to assume your role as my wife, but there is another reason I wish to be at Rosthorne in good time today. My mother is expecting us and she keeps early hours—her health is not good, you see. She injured her hip in a riding accident years ago and it has never healed properly. She tires very easily.'

'Oh, I am sorry for that,' Felicity responded with ready sympathy. 'How far is Rosthorne?'

'A little over fifty miles. It is just west of Petersfield,

near the village of Hazelford. It is not the biggest of my houses—judicious marriages by my ancestors added a couple of substantial properties in the north—but it is the one I use most.'

'And Mrs Carraway lives there?'

'Yes, she has her own apartments in the east wing.'

'I am looking forward to meeting her.'

With nothing more to say, she turned her head to gaze once more out of the carriage window. She heard Nathan shift his position, felt his thigh against hers.

He said softly, 'Don't be afraid of me, Felicity.'

She did not move. His fingers were playing idly with the curls at the back of her neck, causing a sensation akin to ice trickling down her back.

'I—I am not afraid,' she stammered, fighting the desire to lean back against his hand.

'Good. I would not have you afraid.' She could feel his breath on her cheek. 'We could deal very well together, if you would only trust me.'

She remained perfectly still, her eyes fixed on the landscape flying past them. 'I do, Nathan. I do trust you.'

His lips brushed her neck. She trembled, her breath exhaled in a tiny moan. Nathan put his hands on her shoulders and turned her towards him, his lips seeking hers. The next moment she was locked in his arms and he was kissing her, tenderly at first, but with increasing passion. Her arms crept around his neck. She was aware of his fingers unbuttoning her pelisse, exposing the soft column of her throat to his caresses.

Nathan's pulse leapt erratically when she responded to his kiss. She pressed against him, her fingers tangling gently in his hair. Her touch excited him and he felt the latent passion behind her hesitant, tentative responses. He drew back, suppressing his desire to lose himself in her soft, innocent beauty. He kept one hand on her neck, his thumb tracing the fine line of her jaw. She gazed at him, her eyes dark beneath half-closed lids and her reddened lips parted slightly, inviting him in. It was irresistible. He kissed her again, then gently put her away from him.

'You are too tempting, madam wife. I will have to move back into my corner before I forget myself.' He saw the flash in her eyes, half-surprise, half-pleasure, and he laughed. 'You do not realise just how bewitching you are, do you?'

The blush in her cheeks deepened. 'Am I, truly?'

'Yes, *truly*.' He lifted her hand, turning it to place a kiss on the exposed skin of her inner wrist, between the edge of her glove and the lace cuff of her sleeve. She did not pull away and he saw that she was watching him, a soft glow in her eyes. What he read there sent his heart soaring. He placed her hand back in her lap and released it.

'Compose yourself, madam. We shall be stopping soon for a change of horses and some refreshment. I shall not be able to leave the carriage if you continue to look at me in that way.'

Felicity flushed, laughed and looked away, inordinately pleased with the effect she was having upon her husband.

The coach rolled on, the bustling, dirty streets and the acrid smell from the coal fires were soon left behind and they were rattling through towns and villages where small children stared in open-mouthed wonder and labourers in the fields straightened their backs to watch them go past.

Felicity gazed at everything with interest, especially when they reached Hampshire and Nathan pointed out the rich pastures and thickly wooded slopes of his estate.

'When shall we see the house?' she asked him, glancing up at the sun, low on the horizon. 'Shall we be there before dark?'

'Yes, we are nearly there now. Rosthorne Hall is too well screened to be seen from the road. You must wait until we are in the park.'

Even as he spoke the carriage slowed. A sharp blast of the horn brought the lodge-keeper hurrying out to throw open the gates leading to a tree-lined drive. Nathan let down the window to exchange a few words with the man as they drove past then sat back, reaching for Felicity's hand.

'Welcome to Rosthorne, my lady.'

Even as he spoke the carriage emerged from the belt of trees and Felicity had her first glimpse of her new home. The sun, which had been fitfully breaking through the clouds all day, now made a final, blazing appearance, as if determined to present Rosthorne Hall at its best.

The house stood on a slight rise. It was built of red brick and creamy stonework with three rows of windows that gleamed in the evening sunlight. A stone pediment containing the Rosthorne coat of arms stood over a central doorway, which opened on to a set of shallow stone steps. From the neat square windows of the semi-basement to the hipped roof with its dormer windows and tall chimney stacks, the whole house had such symmetry that Felicity thought it quite perfect.

'You like it, I am glad,' said Nathan, when she had voiced her opinion. 'There have been some alterations and redecoration to the interior—for one thing the dining room is now much closer to the kitchens, so the food arrives hot at the table, but the outside is very much as it was when the house was built more than a century ago.'

As the carriage came to a halt, a crowd of servants came running out and lined up on the steps. Anxiety fluttered through Felicity and must have shown in her countenance because Nathan grinned at her.

'They wish to welcome their new mistress,' he explained as he helped her to alight. 'You need only smile at them for now, my dear—Mrs Mercer will introduce them all to you tomorrow, isn't that so, Mercer?'

The stately butler waiting at the door to receive them allowed himself a fatherly smile.

'Indeed it is, my lord. Mrs Carraway has given instructions that dinner should be put back an hour and has requested that you join her in the little drawing room, if you are not too exhausted from your journey.'

Nathan looked a question at Felicity. She nodded and they followed the butler into the hall where Nathan tossed his hat and gloves on to a console table and a wooden-faced footman waited for Felicity to divest herself of her bonnet and pelisse. She tried not to cling to Nathan's arm, but as he led her into the little drawing room her heart was beating a rapid and nervous tattoo against her ribs.

The likeness between mother and son was very marked. They shared the same keen brown eyes and both had an abundance of brown hair tinted with reddish-gold, although the lady's was also sprinkled liberally with grey. Mrs Carraway was sitting in a wing chair beside one of the room's long windows, an embroidery frame between her hands. A tall, thin woman in an iron-grey gown with hair to match was sitting opposite, reading to her in a low voice. As they entered she stopped reading and looked up. A rather overweight spaniel emerged from behind the sofa and ran forward, barking. Mrs Carraway put down her embroidery and held out her hands to Nathan, smiling.

'So you are here, and in good time, too. Norton said you would be, but I did not look to see you before dark.'

Nathan bent to make a fuss of the spaniel gambolling around his ankles, then went forward to take her hands, kissing each one in turn and then her cheek. 'Mama! I promised we would be here in time for dinner. Mrs Norton knows I am true to my word.' He paused to acknowledge her companion. 'The roads were clear; there was nothing to delay us. And how are you, Mama? Well, I hope?'

'I am very well, now you are come.'

Felicity hung back, watching this interchange while the red-and-white spaniel snuffled around her feet.

'You see, Mama, I have at last brought my wife home.'

Felicity curtsied. 'How do you do, ma'am?'

Mrs Carraway held her hand out to her. 'You must forgive me for not getting up. I am sure Nathan has told you I have a tiresome problem with my hip. Don't mind Bella, she will soon lose interest in you once she knows you have no food for her.'

'I do not mind her at all, ma'am,' murmured Felicity, stooping to fondle the spaniel's ears.

'Well, that is fortunate,' murmured Nathan, smiling, 'because Bella has the run of the house.' He clicked his fingers and the little dog ran over to him, gazing up adoringly with her big brown eyes while he scratched her head. 'I bought her for Mama when I first joined up. Thought they would be company for each other.'

'And she has been with me ever since,' nodded Mrs Carraway. 'She is very old now, of course. She has almost no sense of smell, and her eyes are growing weaker, but she is still my constant companion. Bella rarely leaves my side.'

'Because you spoil her, Mama.' He gave the dog a final pat and straightened. 'You feed her far too many titbits.'

'Perhaps I do, but I will not quarrel with you over that today, Nathan. I want to talk to your wife.

Come along, my dear; come and sit over here where I can see you.' She smiled as Felicity perched nervously on the edge of a chair. 'Norton, I would be obliged if you would order refreshments to be sent up. And then you may take Bella out for her walk while I talk to Lady Rosthorne. That is, if you are not too tired after your long journey?'

Felicity knew a craven impulse to say she was exhausted, but she suppressed it. In a very short time a jug of raspberry shrub had been provided for the ladies and Mrs Carraway ordered Nathan to go away and drink a tankard of ale with his steward, who had a mountain of notes to discuss with him.

When she and Felicity were alone, Mrs Carraway fixed her dark eyes upon her guest and said gently, 'Well, my dear, you have led my son a merry dance, have you not?'

'Indeed, I am sorry for it, ma'am. I never intended to cause so much trouble.' Felicity stared down at the cloudy liquid in her glass. 'You have every right to condemn me.'

Mrs Carraway was silent for a moment. 'Any mother will tell you,' she said at last, 'that it is very hard to forgive an injury to one's child. But I promised myself I would not judge you until I had met you. You have your chance to explain it all to me now, my dear. Nathan has, of course, told me his version of events, but only the barest details.'

'Did he tell you I stole his money?' asked Felicity bluntly.

'He was very careful *not* to say so.'

'I am no fortune hunter, ma'am, I assure you. I left him because…because he did not love me.'

'Odd, then, that he should marry you.'

'It was an act of chivalry, ma'am. He was in love with someone else. A—a married woman. When I found out, I was determined to go away. I needed the money he gave me to get to England and then…I was very ill for a while, you see, and there were doctors to be paid. I thought he would forget me.'

'I thought he had,' returned Mrs Carraway. 'His attempts to find you evoked little interest and when he was obliged to return to the Peninsula, having heard nothing from you, I was more than happy to allow the matter to rest. After all, I had no real desire to find the woman who had deserted my son.'

Felicity closed her eyes. 'I am so sorry,' she whispered.

'The matter was forgotten. By the time Nathan became earl it was as if your marriage had never happened. Nathan never mentioned you, until a few months ago, when he came to tell me that you were alive and living in town.'

'Was he…' Felicity ran her tongue over her dry lips '…was he pleased to have found me?'

'Perplexed, I think,' Mrs Carraway said at last. 'But he is determined to honour his obligations.'

'Oh.' That did not sound very encouraging. 'I never meant for him to find me again, only…'

'Only?'

The gentle understanding in the lady's countenance invited Felicity to confide. She said, 'Lady Souden took me to London with her and once I had seen Nathan, I…I could not help myself. I wanted to see him again and again. I knew it was dangerous, that I should go away, but I could not resist. It was inevitable, I suppose, that he should discover me.' She spread her hands. 'And here I am.'

'Yes, here you are,' agreed Mrs Carraway. 'You love him very much, do you not?'

Felicity gave a little sigh. 'Yes, I do. Very much indeed.' She leaned forward, saying earnestly, 'Oh, ma'am, if only he will let me, I mean to be a good wife to him. It was very foolish of me to run away, but now I really do want to make him happy.'

Mrs Carraway watched her and after a long moment she nodded, apparently satisfied. 'Yes, my dear, I think I believe you.'

There was a soft knock on the door.

'May I come in?' Nathan hovered in the door-way. 'Collins has nothing for me that cannot wait until the morrow.'

'Then by all means join us, Nathan.' Mrs Carraway looked at the clock. 'I was about to summon Norton to take me to my room, and you two must change for dinner. I told Mercer to lay covers on the table in the small parlour,' she added. 'Much cosier for just two of you.'

'Oh, will you not be joining us, ma'am?' asked Felicity.

'Not tonight, my dear. I am a little tired, so Norton will bring my supper to my room. Besides, I think the two of you should have some time alone.'

Chapter Thirteen

The dining table in the small parlour was capable of seating only four couples in comfort but to Felicity, entering the room upon her husband's arm, there seemed a vast expanse of white linen between the two places set at each end of the table. There was also an inordinate amount of silver on display, including an oversize salt cellar and mustard pot, a pair of bell-shaped goblets, a variety of candlesticks and a very ornate wine cooler.

Nathan's lips twitched and his glance flickered over Felicity. He turned to address the butler.

'Are you trying to impress Lady Rosthorne with all this magnificence?' He murmured a few brief instructions before leading Felicity back to the drawing room.

'Is that your normal style of dining?' asked Felicity, looking up at him with eyes that were at once apprehensive and wondering. Nathan was quick to reassure her.

'When we have visitors of consequence, perhaps, but they would be entertained in the dining room, not the little parlour.' He chuckled. 'Poor Mercer. He was here in my uncle's day, and the late earl enjoyed a great deal more ceremony than I care for. I am sorry to delay your dinner, my dear, but I think you will find it much more comfortable once Mercer has carried out my orders.'

When they returned to the parlour a short while later, the table had been transformed. Most of the gleaming silver had been cleared away and the covers had been laid at one end of the table only with a place for Felicity set on Nathan's right hand. A cheerful fire crackled in the hearth and instead of the glare of dozens of candles, the room was illuminated only by those in the gilded girandoles on the walls and one carefully placed branched candlestick on the table.

'That is much better,' Nathan approved.

He led Felicity forward and held her chair for her himself before taking his place at the head of the table. After the soup she took a little of the fish and allowed Nathan to carve her a few slices of chicken. At first she was too nervous to eat more than a few mouthfuls from the array of dishes spread out on the table, but Nathan's quiet attentions and gentle manner soon put her at her ease. She refused a second glass of wine, in favour of a glass of water, but when the dishes for the second course appeared she took a small helping of the fricassee and a little of the plum pudding.

Conversation was desultory. Nathan was very aware of Mercer's silent presence behind him at the sideboard. Ostensibly the butler was polishing glasses, but Nathan knew he was listening attentively to every word that was spoken.

'We must hold a ball, my dear, to introduce you to the neighbourhood, but I would as lief wait a little while, until we are more settled.

'There must be an announcement, of course; I shall send something to the London newspapers and journals tomorrow, but I see no reason for any formal entertaining until the new year.'

'As you wish, my lord.'

'Of course, it may be impossible to keep my aunt Appleby away,' he mused. 'She lives not twenty miles from here and will insist upon driving over to hear the whole story for herself.' He laughed. 'Do not look so horrified, I shall not allow her to bully you.' He reached out and covered her hand with his own. 'I shall not allow anyone to hurt you.'

The sudden change in tone and the warm grasp of

his fingers brought the blood rushing to Felicity's cheeks. She raised her eyes to his but looked away immediately, for the intense glow in his eyes made her suddenly very shy. Nathan squeezed her hand before releasing her and they sat in silence while the covers were removed to reveal the highly polished mahogany table. A number of pretty little sweetmeat dishes were placed on its gleaming surface. Nathan raised his hand and signalled to the butler.

'Leave the wines and glasses on the table, if you please. I will serve my lady. You may go now; I shall not need you again tonight.'

Perhaps it was the removal of the snow-white linen that made the room seem smaller, and a little darker, but there was a different atmosphere in the parlour once she and Nathan were alone. She was intensely aware of him sitting beside her. She need only reach out her hand and she could touch him.

She felt a sudden rush of affection for him. He was her husband, and he was exerting himself so much for her comfort.

This is my life now, she thought. Serena Ansell and all the problems of the summer seemed as distant as the moon.

He pulled one of the little dishes closer. 'These confits are made by a French émigré in London. I

have them sent down for my mother, she is especially fond of them.'

Felicity shook her head. 'I do not think…'

He reached out and picked up a small shell-shape
between his long fingers. 'Try it.' He held it up to
her mouth. 'It is chocolate.'

Felicity's lips parted and he slid the small, fra-
grant sweetmeat into her mouth.

'There,' he said, smiling. 'Do you like it?'

She could only nod, her mouth still full of the
rich, velvety confection.

'Good. Now let me find you a little wine to
follow it. Which shall it be, the claret, port, or…?'
He reached out for one of the decanters. 'Madeira,
I think.'

Felicity watched him pour the wine into two
glasses. 'I have never tried that,' she admitted.

'Then you shall do so now, and we shall drink a
toast, to many such nights as this.' He handed her
a glass and she sipped at it, enjoying the slightly
nutty flavour and warmth in her throat as she swallowed. Nathan was watching her, waiting for her
opinion.

'I like it, sir. Very much.'

Nathan smiled, the slow curving of his lips
drawing an answering smile from Felicity.

Sitting within the golden glow of the candlelight,
they began to talk. In response to Nathan's gentle

questions she found herself telling him about her years with Lady Souden, describing the joys and frustrations of life as a governess, albeit a well-loved one. She was encouraged by his mellow mood to ask Nathan about his work on the estates. She sipped at her wine and listened attentively as he talked to her of his various houses and the improvements he had put in progress. His deep voice flowed over and around her, smooth as the chocolate he had given her. She watched him, observing the animation with which he spoke of his plans for new building works, better drainage and crop rotation.

'I think you love your role as Earl Rosthorne,' she ventured when he paused to refill their glasses.

'It was a little daunting at first, but I have some good people around me, like Collins, my steward here. There is much to be done, it is a lifetime's work.' He met her eyes. 'And you can help me, Fee, and you will.'

She returned his look, her spirits singing.

'There is nothing I should like more, Nathan.'

'Good. Then you must come riding with me—get to know the land and the people. That is the first step.'

She sipped at her Madeira. A warm glow was spreading through her, making her feel comfortable, and happy and…reckless. Nathan gestured towards the sweetmeats.

'Would my lady care for another?'

'No.' She put down her glass. 'It is my turn.'

She selected a sugared plum and held it out to him. Smiling, Nathan opened his mouth. Her eyes widened as his teeth closed gently on her finger. He reached up to capture her hand and with infinite care he began to press kisses on her palm. Slowly he moved his mouth to the inside of her wrist, then placed a series of butterfly-light kisses along her arm towards the hinge of her elbow.

Felicity stilled. She caught her bottom lip between her teeth and tried not to move. The touch of his mouth on her skin was sending little shocks through her. A pleasurable lightness was pooling in her belly. She fixed her eyes upon him. The candlelight reflected in the red-gold tints in his hair and enhanced the strong lines of his countenance. She marvelled at the concentration on his face as he gave his attention to the soft white skin of her arm.

'Oh, heavens,' she whispered, unable to contain herself.

Immediately he looked up. 'Do you not like that?'

'No—yes,' she confessed. 'Too much.'

To her disappointment he released her hand.

'I should go,' she said, her voice not quite steady. 'It is time for me to retire to the drawing room.'

'What, would you leave me here in solitary splendour to enjoy my brandy?'

'It is the custom, my lord.'

'In general, of course, but not tonight.'

'N-no?'

The warmth was spreading through her again, but this time it was caused not by the wine but by the look in Nathan's eyes. He rose and held out his hand to her. Silently she gave him her own and his fingers closed around it, safe. Secure. She followed him out of the room and up the dark stairs, the only light coming from the bedroom candle that Nathan picked up from the hall table as he passed. Her heart was hammering hard against her ribs. It was five long years since she had been in Nathan's bed. Then he had been very patient with her. What would he expect of her now? She knew so little, she might as well be his bride of five days rather than five years.

In the main bedchamber they found the candles burning on the mantelshelf and Nathan's man on his knees before the fire, coaxing it into a blaze. He jumped to his feet as they entered.

'It's good to see you again, my lady,' he said with a little bow. 'Welcome to Rosthorne Hall.'

'Thank you, Sam.'

He gave her a quick smile, half-saluted Nathan and went quickly to the door.

'Sam.' Nathan's one quiet word halted him. 'Find my lady's maid and tell her she may go to bed. She will not be needed again tonight.'

With a nod he was gone, and they were alone.

'Very cavalier of you, my lord,' said Felicity, trying to conceal her nerves with a flippant remark.

He looked down at her, his eyes glinting. 'Do you think I cannot undress you? Come here.'

She walked towards him and he put his hands on her shoulders, drawing her closer. His kiss was slow and thorough and Felicity's senses took flight. She was no longer nervous but eager now for him to make love to her. The memory of their wedding night, a memory that she had suppressed for so long, flooded into her mind and she wanted to feel again the soaring, intense pleasure of his body against hers. She put her arms about him, hugging him close while his own hands loosened the thin drawstrings that fastened the little puff sleeves of her gown. Then they slid around her back to tease open the hooks. When Nathan raised his head and gently pulled away from her, Felicity felt bereft. She wanted only to be back in his arms, to be kissing him once more.

The little part of her brain that was still working registered some satisfaction at his laboured breathing and the way his hands trembled as they moved up over her arms and pushed the gown off her shoulders. It fell to the floor with a whisper. Her chemise followed swiftly and he turned her around, pressing kisses on the back of her neck while he drew the laces from the confining corset that imprisoned her. But even as the linen and whalebone stays fell away she was imprisoned again as Nathan's hands slid around to cup her breasts. With a little moan of frustration she turned within the circle of his arms, pulling his face down to hers, seeking his mouth. Impatiently she began to tear at his clothes. Jacket and waistcoat were quickly discarded, shirt and breeches followed. He swept her up and carried her to the huge tester bed.

Nathan laid her down gently on the covers, deep in shadow, and she reached for him, eager for his touch. He obliged with kisses and caresses that sent her spirits soaring. She responded with caresses of her own, revelling in his closeness, the feel of his skin against hers. She was like a flower, unfurling in the heat of his sun, opening up, offering herself with an abandon that shocked her. Their coupling was wild and urgent. They rolled together in a tangle of limbs, crying out as excitement surged through them until at length they fell back on the covers, spent and exhausted.

A warm sense of well-being had settled over Felicity. She put her hand up to Nathan's face, her fingers moving up the soft ridge of scar, following it from his cheek to his temple. He covered her fingers with his own.

He said with difficulty, 'This—disfigurement. Does it—do you find it…repellent?'

'No,' she said softly. 'It is part of you—it is what makes you who you are.' She drew his head down and placed her lips gently against the mark.

With a sigh he caught her against him, burying his face in her hair. Felicity wrapped herself about him and allowed him to possess her once more, before finally succumbing to a deep, contented sleep.

Felicity awoke to find herself alone. She sat up when she heard the soft creak of the door as her maid peeped into the room.

'Ooh, I beg your pardon, my lady, did I wake you?'

'No, Martha. Where is the earl?'

'His lordship is already gone out riding, my lady. He left orders that you was to be allowed to sleep on and he will join you for breakfast.'

Felicity threw back the bedcovers.

'Then you had best help me to get dressed.'

* * *

It was an hour later when Nathan returned. Bella heard his approach; she was sitting at Felicity's feet under the breakfast table but came out and uttered a joyful bark as Nathan appeared in the doorway. Felicity was every bit as happy to see him as the little spaniel, but she contented herself with a wide smile. He was dressed for riding in jacket, topboots and tight-fitting buckskins. She thought how well he looked as a country gentleman. He was relaxed, his complexion still glowing from his early morning exercise, and he sat down beside Felicity, eager to discuss his plans for her entertainment. After listening to him for a full five minutes she put up her hands, laughing.

'Enough, my lord,' she said. 'Much as I would enjoy visiting all your neighbours and attending the local assembly you must remember that I have very few gowns suitable for a countess.'

He poured himself a cup of coffee. 'It is not the gowns but what is underneath that is important.' He turned his head towards her, his eyes glinting. 'And what is beneath your gowns is *very* suitable for a countess, my lady.'

She flushed scarlet and was thankful they were alone in the room. She said seriously, 'I would not wish to embarrass you, my lord.'

He took her hand and kissed it. 'You could never embarrass me but you are quite right, we did not buy you a trousseau. Shall we post back to London and open up the town house? Or will you put yourself in my mother's hands? She rarely leaves Rosthorne and has local dressmakers and milliners that attend her here.'

'I would rather not return to town, sir, and would gladly talk to your mama,' replied Felicity. 'An excellent solution.'

After breakfast Nathan took Felicity along to Mrs Carraway's apartments. She was only too pleased to help.

'In general I use Jannine, in Winchester. She has a sister in town who is very useful for providing details of the latest fashions. I shall write to her immediately and explain that we need pattern books and fabrics sent here as soon as possible. I shall tell her that you need a complete wardrobe: walking dresses, morning gowns, pelisses, spencers—and we shall need a milliner, too...'

'Dear ma'am, you must not overtax yourself,' cried Felicity, alarmed. 'I had not thought to give you so much work!'

Mrs Carraway brushed aside her concerns.

'Norton and I will positively enjoy being involved in such a task. Of course, the decisions on styles and fabrics must be yours, my dear, but I do hope you will allow us to help you.'

Felicity's response was heartfelt. 'I do not know quite where I should begin, ma'am, and should be very glad of your assistance.' She added hesitantly, 'My Uncle Philip did not approve of elegant clothes. He thought they were the trappings of the devil.'

'Then he was wrong,' replied Mrs Carraway robustly. 'They are the trappings of your position as Rosthorne's countess. Nathan is lord of the manor here, and as his consort people will expect you to dress accordingly.'

Thus it was that within a few days an army of seamstresses and dressmakers descended upon Rosthorne Hall together with ells of muslin, chintz and silks in a bewildering assortment of patterns and colours. Felicity allowed herself to be pinned, prodded and measured, but her reward was to slip away every morning to ride out with Nathan. Her riding habit was serviceable rather than elegant, but the blue jacket showed her neat figure to advantage and Nathan announced that it was perfectly suitable for riding around the estate.

He introduced her to the tenants and lodge-keepers, gardeners and gamekeepers that they met during these rides, and on one particularly sunny day when they had reached the limits of the Rosthorne land he suggested riding a little further.

'That is, unless you have to get back to the house.'

'To be stitched into even more gowns?' she laughed at him. 'No, I thank you!'

'I thought you would enjoy buying new clothes.'

'I do, but not all at once! Mama Carraway has been so good as to take charge of the sewing room. I have only to choose the fabric and the pattern and she does all the rest. I am very grateful to her.'

'And I am grateful to *you*,' he responded promptly. 'You have provided my mother with a new interest and she is greatly enjoying herself.'

'I am glad. Your mama has been very kind to me.' She paused, then added haltingly, 'I thought, at first, that she might not like me—and she had every right—I behaved abominably to you.'

He reached out for her hand. 'No, she likes you, very much.'

'Thank you,' whispered Felicity. She blinked rapidly and said after a moment, 'Well, my lord? Where are we going now?'

'To West Meon, no more than a few miles away. Adam Elliston's parents live in the village—I should like to make you known to them.' Felicity did not reply immediately; the mention of Nathan's friend brought back vivid memories of Corunna. Nathan said quickly, 'Perhaps it is too much to ask of you, after all we have been riding for—'

'No, no,' she interrupted him, smiling. 'I should be very happy—honoured—to meet them, if you do not think me too shabbily dressed for the visit?'

'No. You have a little mud on your cheek, but if we remove that I think you will pass muster.'

'Mud? Where?'

Nathan brought his horse closer. 'Keep still and I will deal with it.' He pulled off his glove and took her handkerchief from her fingers. 'You did the same for me, in Green Park, do you remember?'

She shivered. 'How could I forget? Have there been any more attacks since you left town?'

'No, none. So you see, there is no grand plan to dispose of me.' He cupped her chin with one hand while he wiped the mud from her cheek. 'There, you are respectable again.' Felicity remained very still, gazing into his face. Nathan's mouth curved upwards in a tantalising smile. 'What say you we postpone our visit to the Ellistons? We could dismount here and—ah—take a stroll in the woods.'

Her heart began to race. She could not mistake his meaning, nor the warm look in his eyes. It was an outrageous suggestion, but she was not at all shocked by it, only by her own impulse to agree. She swallowed convulsively and said in a rallying tone, 'If we do that, my lord, I shall certainly not be fit to be seen!'

He laughed. 'No, you are right, we must go on to West Meon.' He released her, sighing. 'Pity…'

A chuckle escaped Felicity, but she said severely, 'Fie, my lord. Let us ride on; you must attend to your duty.'

'That is what I was planning to do.'

She choked, decided it would be unwise to try to respond and instead she spurred her horse on, hoping that she would regain her composure before they reached their destination.

'So Nathan has been introducing you to our neighbours.'

Mrs Carraway joined them for dinner, and they were seated within the candles' glow in the small parlour.

'He took me to West Meon today to meet Mr and Mrs Elliston, and their daughter,' replied Felicity. 'They send their regards to you, and Mrs Elliston promised to call very soon.'

Mrs Carraway nodded.

'A delightful couple, and their daughter Judith is a lovely girl. She has been their sole comfort since they lost Adam—such a good-natured boy. I felt for them most deeply when I learned of his death.' She added, her voice breaking, 'And I feel my own good fortune even more.'

Nathan reached across the table for her hand. 'So, too, do I, Mama. But let us not dwell on the past—tell me how you have gone on today. Have you been busy with the dressmakers all day?'

'No, for Mrs Orr, the vicar's wife, came to take tea with me. A pleasant woman, but addicted to gossip.' Mrs Carraway smiled at Felicity. 'I think her object in calling was to find out all about you, my dear. You need not be anxious, I told her only that you had been living quietly with friends in London until Nathan could bring you home. She thought it very romantical! Everyone is eagerly awaiting your appearance at church tomorrow.'

'Good heavens,' exclaimed Nathan, startled. 'Do we have to go? You will remember how they stared the first time we came here, as if I were a prize exhibit!'

'Of course you must go, my son! It is most important that you and your wife are seen abroad, and you know that they will soon grow tired of staring at you.' She reached out and lifted a chocolate shell from the sweetmeat dish in front of her. 'And Felicity will not be the only new face for the congregation to gape at. Mrs Orr tells me Godfrey Park is let.'

'I had not heard that. Godfrey Park is a neat little property about three miles north of here,' Nathan told Felicity. 'We passed it on our way here from town. So, Mama, who are our new neighbours?'

'Well, according to the agent—and he should know the facts, should he not?—it is a widow. The relict of a wealthy gentleman from Somerset. A Lady Ansell.'

Chapter Fourteen

The warmth and contentment Felicity had been feeling vanished in an instant. Her eyes flew to Nathan. He was very still, looking at Mrs Carraway.

'Ansell? Formerly married to Colonel Craike?'

'That I do not know, only that she is a wealthy widow.'

'Well, we shall find out soon enough,' Nathan responded coolly. 'Did I mention that I have given instructions for the track through the Home Wood to be cleared? It has become sadly overgrown this summer…'

Lady Ansell's name was not mentioned again, but Felicity felt her presence like a cloud over her own happiness.

As she made her way upstairs to their bedchamber that night she resolved to say something to Nathan. She was at her dressing table, brushing out her hair, when he came in. Even in the candlelight the colourful pattern on his heavy silk banyan was garishly bright.

'You are the devil of a time about your undressing,' he told her.

Felicity dismissed her maid.

'I have been looking at my new gowns; two of them are ready and I have been trying to decide which one I shall wear tomorrow. If Mama Carraway is correct we shall be under scrutiny when we go to church.'

He came up behind her and placed his hands on her shoulders, meeting her eyes in the mirror. 'It is only natural that everyone will want to see my new countess.'

She smiled a little, and looked away, idly straightening the glass pots on the table. 'They will also wish to see the new tenant of Godfrey Park.' She risked a fleeting look up. 'I wonder what brings her to Hampshire?'

'I have no idea.'

Words filled Felicity's head, but they would not be spoken—she wanted to ask Nathan is he still loved Serena, if he had invited her to be near him. If she was his mistress. She knew such arrangements were not uncommon and the questions battered at her head, even as Nathan pulled her up into his arms. *Ask him*, the voice inside her screamed. *Ask him to tell you the truth, now.* But as Nathan swept her up and carried her into the bedroom, she buried her head in his shoulder and quelled the nagging demon inside her, wretchedly acknowledging that she would not ask the questions, because she was too afraid of the answers.

The dawning of a bright and warm Sunday morning did much to restore Felicity's spirits and her confidence was greatly increased by Nathan's look of admiration when she presented herself in a new flounced gown of white muslin with an olive-green velvet spencer and matching high-poke bonnet.

'Well, my lord, will I do?' she asked shyly, fingering the green ribbons of her bonnet.

'Admirably.' He held out his arm to her. 'Shall we go?'

They found Mrs Carraway waiting for them in the carriage, the faithful Norton at her side.

'Well now, you make a very handsome couple,' she declared as Nathan handed Felicity into the carriage. 'Just one thing, if you will permit me, my dear. Norton, re-tie the ribbons of Lady Rosthorne's bonnet, if you please. Yes, that's it—a large bow, just beneath her ear.'

As Mrs Carraway's companion sat back to admire her handiwork, Felicity cast an anxious glance at Nathan. He was grinning at her.

'Very dashing.'

'Oh,' she said, daunted. 'Not *too* dashing for a Sunday?'

'Not at all, my love,' declared Mrs Carraway. 'It is perfect for a young bride, as is the colour in your pretty cheek. Give the driver the word, Nathan, we do not want to be late.'

The little church in Hazelford village was crowded and Felicity was glad of Nathan's arm as he escorted her to family's box pew below the pulpit. The congregation stared at her with unashamed curiosity and she guessed that many of them had come especially to see the new Lady Rosthorne.

'Well, Mr Orr's sermon was not too long, thank heaven,' muttered Mrs Carraway as they prepared to leave the church after the service. 'Now, my son, you must take your countess outside, and face the dragons!'

Felicity accompanied Nathan out of the church, blinking in the sunlight, and was confronted by a bewildering number of strangers, all wishing to be presented to her. With Nathan beside her she smiled and said all that was proper. From the corner of her eye she saw Norton escorting Mrs Carraway to the carriage; another few moments, she thought, and they could drive away, back to the peace and privacy of Rosthorne.

'Ah, my lord—' the vicar's blustering tones shattered her hopes '—we cannot let you and your good lady leave without introducing another new member of our congregation.'

Felicity turned to find Serena standing before her, tall and beautiful in a lavender carriage dress, a single ostrich feather curling around the edge of her bonnet and framing her perfect features.

'The earl and I were in Corunna together,' Serena told the beaming vicar.

Felicity bridled at the implication of her words.

'I knew him even before he married.' She turned to Felicity with the merest hint of a curtsy. 'But you were only Mrs Carraway then, my lady.'

'Yes, of course.' Felicity was surprised that her voice did not shake. 'And you were Mrs Craike.'

'I was. Poor Craike, it was such a long time ago.' The widow sighed and turned her gaze upon Nathan. 'My congratulations, my lord. You must be very happy to have found your bride again.'

'Thank you, ma'am. I am very happy.' Nathan's attention was sought by the vicar and he turned away, leaving Felicity alone with Serena Ansell.

'So—' the widow was smiling but there was no warmth in her green eyes '—you could not resist the idea of being a countess.'

Felicity's lip curled. 'Think that, if you will.' She was determined not to be intimidated by this woman. She turned and began to walk towards the carriage. Serena followed her.

'It is what everyone will think when they know the truth.'

'Why should they? I have merely been living quietly with friends.'

'Using an assumed name.'

Felicity shrugged. 'I did not wish to draw attention to my situation.'

'And just what is your situation now, my lady?' purred Serena. 'Does Nathan know why you left him in Spain?'

'Yes.' Felicity stopped. 'What happened five years ago is no longer of interest.'

Serena's brows rose. 'Are you quite sure?'

Felicity drew herself up. 'I will acknowledge you as an acquaintance, madam, but nothing more.'

'And I will acknowledge *you* as Nathan's wife in name, but nothing more.' Serena glared at her, all pretence of friendliness gone. 'I will allow you your title, Lady Rosthorne,' she said contemptuously. 'But do you think someone as innocent, as unskilled as you can keep the man?'

'I intend to try,' retorted Felicity, thoroughly angry. 'And if you still have his ring, I think it is time it was returned.'

There was an arrested look in the widow's face.

'Well, madam,' said Felicity coldly, 'Do you still have it?'

'Why, I…it may well be in my jewel case,' came the careless reply.

Felicity's indignation swelled. If Nathan have given *her* such a token she would cherish it. Serena was watching her, a cold little smile playing around her lips.

'You never told him of our final meeting, did you?' she said softly. 'You never challenged him.' When Felicity did not reply the widow gave a soft laugh. 'No, you did not dare. And even now, you will not confront him.' She leaned closer. 'You poor fool, you were a nobody that Nathan plucked from the streets of Corunna—you know you can never be worthy of him!'

Felicity stared at her, inwardly flinching as Serena put into words her own deepest fears. Before she could summon a suitable retort, Nathan came striding up.

'I beg your pardon, my dear, I never intended you leave you alone.' He placed his hand under her elbow.

'Your wife and I have been getting better acquainted,' said Serena, smoothly. 'It is such a comfort to know I have such good friends living nearby.'

With a final smile she turned and walked away.

Silently Felicity accompanied Nathan to the carriage where Mrs Carraway was waiting for them.

'You look pale, my dear,' she observed as Nathan handed Felicity into the carriage. 'Such an ordeal for you, to meet so many new people.'

'Is that it, Fee?' asked Nathan, regarding her closely. 'I trust Lady Ansell said nothing to overset you?'

Felicity knew that even if she had wanted to tell him everything Serena had said, she could not do so here, in front of his mother. So she shook her head and disclaimed, dismally ashamed at her own cowardice.

'I admit I am intrigued by our new neighbour,' mused Mrs Carraway as the carriage rattled its way back to Rosthorne Hall. 'Very beautiful, of course. One wonders why she has decided to bury herself away here in Hampshire? Perhaps we should call—'

'No!' Felicity's involuntary gasp caught Nathan's attention.

'I pray you will not seek for too close an acquaintance with Lady Ansell, Mama,' he said.

'Oho,' cried his mama, her eyes twinkling. 'I smell some story here, Norton! Well, my son, are you going to tell us what is so very bad about the widow?'

'Certainly not,' returned Nathan, smiling faintly. 'I abhor gossip. Suffice to say that I knew the lady in Corunna, and she is not good *ton*.'

'But we cannot ignore her. Such a wealthy widow—she will be invited everywhere.'

'But not into my house. Is that what was worrying you, Fee?' He took her hand and squeezed it. 'Serena Ansell has her place, but it is not at Rosthorne Hall.'

Felicity sank back into her corner, deriving some small measure of comfort from his words.

When they arrived back at Rosthorne, Mrs Carraway went off to her apartment with her companion. As soon as Felicity had divested herself of her bonnet and spencer, Nathan escorted her to the drawing room.

'Well, that is the biggest ordeal over,' he remarked. 'To be obliged to sit in church while every man and his dog gawps open-mouthed—'

'It was not so very bad,' she said, preceding him into the room. 'I had your mama there to support me.'

He reached for her hand and pulled her down on to the sofa. 'They were very taken with you.' He raised her fingers to his lips. 'I was told several times how lucky I am to have found such a wife.'

'Nathan.' She clung to his hand. 'You never told

me what happened to your ring, the one engraved with the rose thorns that you wore on your little finger.'

'I told you it was lost during the war. There is nothing else to know.'

Felicity screwed up her courage. 'Did you…did you give it away?'

Gently he removed his fingers from her grasp. 'It was a long time ago, Fee. We will forget it, if you please.' He rose. 'Collins tells me they have now finished clearing the path through the Home Wood. I was going to ride out there later—would you care to join me?'

His face was impassive, but there was a hardness about his eyes, a look that told her not to ask more questions. She capitulated.

'Yes,' she said. 'I would very much like to ride out with you.'

Let him keep his secrets, she thought, *and I will keep mine!*

Felicity settled into her new home. She enjoyed the companionship of her mama-in-law and fell ever deeper in love with her husband. He encouraged her interest in the estate, was always kind and attentive, yet doubts continued to haunt her. She longed for the courage to talk to him, to confide her fears, but she could not bring herself to risk their new-found happiness.

Mrs Carraway's excellent dressmaker delivered another selection of gowns in time for the Hazelford Assembly and Felicity spent a pleasant afternoon choosing just what she would wear.

'You will be the first in consequence there so it is important that you are looking your best,' Mrs Carraway told her when Felicity asked for her opinion.

They were in the large sunny apartment that was designated as the countess's dressing room and Felicity was trying on her new muslin evening dress. It was a very pale cream decorated at the neck, sleeves and hem with exquisite green-and-gold embroidery.

'I am aware that every eye will be upon me when I walk in,' murmured Felicity. 'I shall be so nervous.'

'Just be yourself and everyone will love you.' Mrs Carraway turned in her chair. 'Martha, my dear, run along to my room and ask Norton to look out my gold shawl.'

'Oh, please, no, you have done so much for me already,' cried Felicity, dismayed, as her maid ran off on her errand.

'Heavens, why should I not? You are my daughter now.' She held out her hands. 'What is there in that to overset you?'

Felicity went to her and dropped down on her knees beside her chair. 'You are so generous, and since I have been at Rosthorne everyone has been so kind…I do not feel that I deserve it—I came here with so little.'

'Now enough of this foolish talk. You have won all our hearts and that is all that signifies.' She put her hand under Felicity's chin and turned her face up, smiling down into her eyes. 'Have a little more confidence in yourself, my love, and you will do very well.'

The words echoed in Felicity's head as she entered the ballroom at the Swan Inn that evening. With her hand securely on Nathan's arm, she thought it was easy to be confident. Easy to convince herself that they could be happy together. A quick glance at him made her heart swell with pride. She had seen Mr Brummell in London and knew that Nathan followed his precepts, but privately she thought her husband looked much more handsome than the arbiter of fashion himself. His tall figure and broad shoulders were ideally suited to the superbly cut evening coat and tight-fitting knee-breeches he was wearing that evening. The snowy whiteness of his intricately tied cravat accentuated his dark face, tanned by years of soldiering in Spain and France, but Felicity much preferred this to the ruddy cheeks and bushy side-whiskers of the other gentlemen present.

Nathan glanced down at the silent little figure beside him. He knew how nervous she must be to be opening the dancing in a crowded room full of near-strangers and her quiet dignity impressed him. A number of gentlemen were already heading towards the card room, but he decided he would not leave Felicity until he was sure she was more comfortable.

'I insist upon at least the first two dances with you,' he told her and was inordinately pleased at the way her face lit up. Even now, after a month together, desire stirred his bones whenever she smiled like that.

As they danced together he found he had eyes for no one else. He enjoyed watching the way she moved to the music, taking in every graceful step. He wanted to draw her aside and plant kisses on the delicate curve of her neck, but that must wait. He could not even dance with her again, at least not yet; having brought his new countess to the assembly, he could not monopolise her. Seeing his cousin as they left the dance floor, he buried his frustration and hailed him cheerfully.

'Gerald, well met, Cos! I thought you would still be in town.'

Mr Appleby came up, grinning. 'So I would be, but when Mama received your letter she insisted upon posting down here immediately.'

'Ah, I see.' Nathan looked down at Felicity. 'My dear, may I present to you my cousin, Mr Gerald Appleby?'

Gerald grinned as he took Felicity's outstretched hand.

'Well, well, Lady Rosthorne, you fooled us all very neatly! When Nathan wrote to explain that you had been living in town all this summer, under our very noses, I could scarcely believe it! Mama was for once almost speechless when she realised that little Miss Brown was in fact Nathan's wife! Depend upon it, I told her, the whole charade was a scheme concocted by Lady Souden to keep you out of the public eye while Nathan here prepared Rosthorne for his countess. Am I right?'

'Y-yes.' Felicity cast a laughing glance up at her husband, who grinned.

'Very acute of you, Gerald.'

Mr Appleby nodded. 'There is a rumour running around town that my cousin had lost you, Lady Rosthorne. I can only say that it was incredibly careless of Nathan. I hope he means to take better care of you in future!'

Felicity blushed and murmured something incoherent.

'Forgive my cousin's attempts at humour,' retorted Nathan, smiling in spite of himself. 'Is Lady Charlotte with you tonight?'

'No, we only arrived at Appleby Manor this afternoon and she was too exhausted to come here. I, on the other hand, was eager to meet my new cousin.' He turned again to Felicity. 'If you are not engaged, madam, would you honour me with the next dance?'

Nathan was aware of Felicity's hesitation. He gave her a reassuring look and a slight nod. Immediately she smiled.

'I shall be delighted to dance with you, Mr Appleby.'

'Capital! I shall return to claim my prize,' exclaimed Gerald, adding irrepressibly, 'I charge you not to lose her before then, Cousin!'

'What a pleasant young man he is,' murmured Felicity, as Gerald lounged away. 'He was always very attentive when I was in town.'

'I am aware,' growled Nathan. 'Insolent puppy!'

She laughed at that. 'He was merely being kind to Lady Souden's impoverished companion.'

'Aye, and putting me to shame. I paid you very little attention.'

'If you had done so, I should have been obliged to retire from society rather than risk discovery.'

He stopped and turned towards her.

'And now?' he asked. 'Are you sorry that I discovered you?'

A faint blush mantled her cheeks. She did not look up, but he saw the slight shake of her head. Surrounded by the noise and chatter of the room, he had to bend his head to catch her words.

'No, I am not sorry.'

His heart swelled with pleasure. He hoped he was not strutting like some arrogant coxcomb as they continued their perambulation of the room.

Felicity was enjoying herself. Nathan's obvious approval did much to calm her nerves and she almost skipped off to dance with his cousin. After that her hand was solicited by any number of gentlemen, including Mr Elliston, who had arrived with his wife and daughter while she was dancing with Gerald.

They were talking with Nathan when Mr Appleby escorted her back after their dance.

'Ah, here is that lovely wife of yours, Rosthorne!' cried Mr Elliston, in great good humour. 'Good evening to you, Lady Rosthorne. We were just saying what a blessing it is that Rosthorne here is no longer in the army.'

'I count myself very fortunate, sir,' replied Felicity, smiling up at her husband.

'But what if Boney should get free?' put in Gerald. 'What then?'

'If he posed a threat to England then I suppose I might be called upon to join up again,' said Nathan.

Mr Elliston cocked an eyebrow. 'And what would you say to that, Lady Rosthorne?

Felicity smiled. 'If my lord considers it his duty to go and fight then naturally I should support him. And I think I might best do that by staying here and looking after his estates.'

'A truly excellent answer, my love, thank you.' Nathan picked up her hand and kissed it. He smiled into her eyes. 'I knew you would make me a perfect wife.'

Later, when Nathan asked Miss Elliston to stand up with him, her father turned a kindly smile towards Felicity.

'I'd be honoured to tread a country measure with you, Lady Rosthorne, if your husband will allow it.'

'With pleasure, sir, if your *wife* will allow it,' responded Felicity, twinkling.

'Away with you both,' laughed Mrs Elliston. 'I

shall take myself over there to enjoy a comfortable gossip with my friends!'

Two lively country dances left Felicity and her partner breathless but upon excellent terms, and Mr Elliston took her off in search of refreshment in the supper room.

'If you will forgive me for saying so, ma'am, it does my heart good to see Nathan in such spirits,' he told her as he handed her a glass of punch. 'The war took its toll of him, you see. Losing so many comrades.'

'Including your son,' she ventured, shyly.

'Aye. That shook him badly. Even now he don't like to talk of it and shies away from any mention of Adam. Feels he is somehow to blame, you see, because Adam followed him into the army. He came to see us, you know, as soon as he could get leave. Brought back Adam's effects, such as they were. They were like brothers, growing up, and Nathan is like a second son to us.' Mr Elliston shook his head. 'I don't say it didn't break our hearts to lose our boy, but it was some consolation that Nathan survived the war, albeit marked. It don't frighten you, that scar down his face?' he shot at her.

Felicity smiled. 'I do not notice it.'

The old man beamed. 'That's the spirit! Now, I suppose I had better return you to his lordship, before he thinks I have run off with you!'

* * *

Nathan observed Felicity going down to supper with Mr Elliston as he returned Judith Elliston to her mama, where she was immediately carried off by Gerald Appleby to dance again. Nathan made his way to the card room, satisfied that Felicity would not need his company for a while. However, he found he could not settle to picquet or whist and it was not long before he was heading towards the ballroom once more to look for his wife. As he crossed the deserted landing he heard his name and stopped. Lady Ansell was coming up the stairs.

'I am very late—have I missed all the dancing?'

'Not quite, the orchestra will play for another hour yet.'

'I suppose it is useless to expect you to partner me.'

He returned her speculative look with a bland one of his own. 'It is.'

'Ah well, then you can at least escort me to the ballroom.'

He made no move to offer her his arm. 'Why have you come here, Serena?'

'Why, to dance, of course.'

'I meant why have you chosen to settle in Hazelford?'

'Do you not know, Nathan?' she murmured, looking up at him from under her lashes.

'Should I?'

She laughed and waved her hand dismissively. 'I have been invited to go to Bath at Christmas,' she told him, straightening her long silk gloves. 'I have family there. But I can easily cry off, if you would like me to stay.'

'Your actions are of no interest to me, madam.'

'No?'

'Not in the least.' He held her eyes. 'You are wasting your time with me, madam.'

'Am I?' She stepped close, sliding her fingers over his chest and on to his shoulders. 'Are you not just a little bit tempted?' Her voice was warm and inviting. She was leaning into him, so close that he could smell the heady perfume of the flowers pinned to her corsage. 'I liked you well enough in Corunna,' she murmured, 'but Adam Elliston was before you and you had such *chivalrous* ideas about not stealing his lover. Besides, *then* you were only a boy. Now I would like to try the man...'

She reached up, brushing her lips against his. For a moment he did not move, but allowed her to kiss him. Her hands slid up and around his neck, but her touch awoke no answering spark in him. He placed his hands on her waist and gently but firmly detached himself.

'Enough, madam. Man or boy I never was, nor ever will be, for you.'

He saw the flash of anger in her eyes. It was gone in an instant, and she was smiling again. She shrugged.

'I suppose it is still honeymoon for you and that innocent little bride of yours. But when the novelty wears off, I shall be waiting for you.'

Without a word Nathan turned away. Her self-assurance was incomprehensible. As he walked back into the ballroom, his uppermost emotion for Serena Ansell was pity.

Chapter Fifteen

'Well, upon my soul!'

It was only the briefest moment before Mr Elliston whisked Felicity back into the ballroom, but the vision was imprinted upon her brain: Serena with her arms around Nathan's neck, *his* hands placed possessively upon her waist.

'Really, I would not have expected such behaviour from Rosthorne!' muttered Mr Elliston, distressed.

'Y-you misunderstand, sir,' replied Felicity. 'The earl has known the lady for many years. I am sure it was no more than a friendly greeting.'

The words sounded hollow, even to herself. She had gone happily with Mr Elliston when he had suggested they should look for Nathan in the card room, but as they stepped out of the ballroom there had been no avoiding the sight of the earl locked in a passionate embrace with Serena Ansell. This was no friendly greeting—she and Mr Elliston both knew that.

'By Gad, I wish we had not walked away,' declared her partner. 'I wish I had told him then just what I think of such outrageous behaviour! When I see him—'

'No!' Felicity stopped. 'I pray you, Mr Elliston, please, for my sake, say nothing of what we have just seen.'

'But it is scandalous! I had not thought it of Nathan.'

'Then pray do not think it now,' she begged him. 'Please, let us go and find Mrs Elliston, and forget the last few minutes.'

Mr Elliston puffed out his cheeks and stood, frowning down at her. Felicity looked up at him imploringly and gave his arm a little shake.

'Please, sir. For my sake.'

He let his breath go in a long, disapproving sigh. 'Very well, my dear, if that is what you wish. But it goes very much against the grain. And it has destroyed all my pleasure in this evening.'

'Yes.' Felicity nodded sadly. 'So, too, has it destroyed mine.'

Mr Elliston guided Felicity back to his wife, who was watching Judith Elliston dancing with Gerald Appleby. Felicity was content to join her, a fixed smile upon her face while inside her heart was breaking. She glimpsed Nathan through the crowd, but made no attempt to attract his attention and it was some time before he found her. As he approached, Felicity cast an anguished looked at Mr Elliston, who was visibly bristling. Reading the entreaty in her eyes, the old man harrumphed and walked off with barely a nod towards the Earl as they passed.

'So there you are. I thought I should find you wearing out your slippers on the dance floor.'

Nathan's smile roused Felicity to a speechless rage. How dare he act so unconcerned, when only moments ago he was locked in the arms of his mistress! Felicity was pleased when Mrs Elliston answered for her.

'I think it is the Countess who is worn out,' she told him, smiling. 'The poor child has been sitting here this past half-hour and spoken barely a word!'

'I am a little tired,' admitted Felicity, unable to meet Nathan's eyes.

'Then I shall take you home.' He reached out for her hand and pulled her to her feet. 'No one will miss us if we slip away now.'

'Yes, yes, take her home and cosset her,' cried Mrs Elliston. 'Goodnight to you, my dear. I shall call in a few days to see how you go on.'

Felicity kept her head high as she accompanied Nathan out of the building. She had come in so full of hope and happiness and was leaving now enclosed by a fog of misery. She wanted very much to burst into tears, but that would not do: she was the Countess of Rosthorne and must keep her smile in place. As they left the room they passed Lady Ansell, surrounded by a group of laughing gentlemen. She looked up as they passed and her smile reminded Felicity of nothing less than a cat that had lapped a whole pot of cream.

The carriage was blessedly dark and Felicity could stop smiling. Anger still simmered inside her. Should she confront Nathan? Would he admit his involvement with Serena or would he perhaps tell her it was none of her business? She remembered his words that night in Berkeley Square, when she had first challenged him: *'What did it matter if I had a whole string of mistresses?'*

She stifled a sigh. Her knowledge of men was woefully inadequate. Apart from Sir James Souden, who was a most devoted husband, the only other man with whom she had any close acquaintance was her late uncle, Philip Bourne, and she had learned very quickly that any attempt to confront or question his authority resulted in physical punishment. She did not think that Nathan would actually harm her, but the thought of hearing from his own lips that Serena Ansell was his mistress and that she must accept the fact was worse by far than any beating.

Nathan tucked a carriage rug around her knees and climbed into the coach beside her.

'There…' he reached for her hand. 'Was it the noise and the heat that overset you?'

'I think so.' She hesitated. 'Lady Ansell came in very late. She is very popular with the gentlemen.'

'It has always been the same.'

'Mr and Mrs Elliston do not know she was…acquainted with Adam?'

'No.'

'Should—should they not be told?'

Nathan put his head back against the squabs and exhaled slowly. 'Why rake up old coals?' he said at last. 'It would only cause them distress. Besides, I do not think she means them any harm.'

Felicity bit her lip.

She could readily believe that Serena had no interest in the Ellistons—she had her sights fixed on another prey entirely.

Felicity retired as soon as they arrived at Rosthorne, but she did not sleep. Every time she closed her eyes she saw Serena Ansell clasped in Nathan's arms and the image had her fighting to wake up. She lay very still when Nathan came to bed, hardly daring to breathe when he leaned over her and dropped a gentle kiss on her neck. She heard him sigh and turn away, but did not stir until his regular breathing told her that he at least was at rest.

She used the same tactics the following morning, waiting until Nathan had left their chamber before she sent word that she was too tired to join him for their usual morning ride, and when at last she did appear in the breakfast room she looked so haggard that Mrs Carraway insisted upon sending for the doctor.

Nathan knew nothing of this until he returned from the stables to find the house in uproar and a message from his mother to attend her immediately.

'Well, Mama, what have you done to set the house by the ears?' Nathan strode into her sitting room, his riding crop and hat still in his hand.

She smiled up at him, accepting his kiss upon her cheek. 'Doctor Farnham has called to see Felicity.'

'The devil he has!'

'No need for alarm, love.' She gestured to him to sit down. 'She was looking so worn down and tearful this morning that I asked him to look in. He thinks it is nothing more than an irritation of the nerves. He has bled her, and she is quieter now.' She studied the rings on her fingers. 'He recommends separate bedchambers.'

'*What?*'

'Pray, do not look so black, Nathan. You know that the old earl and his wife always maintained their own rooms.'

'Of course I know that! It was I who ordered one of them to be redecorated as the countess's dressing room.'

'Yes, well, Mercer is organising for a bed to be made up in there for Felicity. It is only a temporary measure,' she added quickly. 'Doctor Farnham thinks her recovery will be swifter if she is allowed to rest.

With a smothered oath Nathan got up and began to prowl about the room. 'Is Farnham saying it is my fault? That somehow I—'

'No, no, love. Many young brides find the transition to married life difficult, and you must admit that the circumstances of your marriage are a little…unusual.'

Nathan shook his head. He walked over to the window and looked out. The view was a particularly fine one, stretching out over the formal gardens and to the park beyond, but today Nathan saw nothing of its beauty. He thought only of his wife.

'I must see her.'

'Of course.'

Felicity lay in the great bed, her head and shoulders supported on soft white pillows. Doctor Farnham had been very kind, telling her cheerfully that her spirits were a little disordered, but it was nothing that rest would not cure. When he had suggested she should have her own room she had agreed to it, although with a little anxiety as to Nathan's reaction. But now, with the doctor gone and only her maid bustling quietly about the room, she felt too tired to be anxious about anything.

She opened her eyes when she heard the door open. Nathan came in. He was still wearing his riding jacket and topboots and when he came closer she saw the tiny furrow in his brow. He dismissed her maid and smiled at her.

'Now then, Fee, what's all this?'

The concern in his voice nearly overset her.

'I am a little out of sorts, but I shall be better directly, if I rest.'

He sat on the edge of the bed and took her hand. 'Will you tell me what is the matter?'

His gentle tone brought the tears welling up, clogging her throat. She gave the tiniest shake of her head. Muted thuds and bangs could be heard coming from the adjoining room.

'So, madam, you intend to abandon me again—' He broke off when she gave a little sob. 'Ah, love, I did not mean to make you cry, I was merely teasing you.' His brows contracted. He said quietly, 'Is that it? Have I frightened you with my love-making?'

Her cheeks flamed and she covered them with her handkerchief. 'No, no,' she said, her voice muffled. 'You have been so kind, so gentle…'

'There was nothing gentle about our first night in this bed,' he said drily. 'Nor when I threatened to carry you off by force from Souden House! But you may rest easy, love—I shall not touch you again until you command it and I will not enter your bedroom uninvited, I give you my word.' He leaned forward and kissed her forehead. 'I shall leave you to sleep now.'

He was gone as swiftly as he had come and Felicity was left staring at the closed door. He had not countermanded the doctor's orders; she was to have her own apartment, her own bed. With a heavy heart Felicity could not help thinking that she was driving him even more surely into the arms of Serena Ansell.

It was not to be supposed that Felicity's youthful spirits could stay at low ebb for very long. The following day she left her bed, and by the end of the week she was well enough to venture out of doors, although she declined Nathan's suggestion that she should join him once again on his morning ride. She thought a little innocuous conversation over breakfast and again at the dinner table when Mrs Carraway was present was far less dangerous than being alone with Nathan. And for the rest of her day there was plenty to occupy her: the final fittings for her new wardrobe, gentle drives with Mrs Carraway as well as receiving morning callers. Mrs Elliston and her daughter were regular visitors and very welcome, unlike the appearance of Lady Charlotte Appleby.

'I vow,' said Mrs Carraway, when her sister-in-law had departed, 'she came with no other purpose than to see what changes you have put in place and to criticise them! I begin to wish that we had not invited her and Gerald to stay at Christmas, I swear we shall come to cuffs!'

Nathan laughed. 'Nonsense, Mama, you never fight with anyone. You are far too sweet-natured, just like Fee.' His eyes rested upon his wife, who was picking at her dinner. 'Were you subjected to my aunt's caustic tongue, my dear?'

She glanced up, a distracted, unhappy shadow in her eyes. He wished he knew how to banish it.

'Only a very little, my lord.' She tried to smile.

'I was very properly engaged with my embroidery when she arrived, and apart from telling me that the new curtains in the morning room are entirely the wrong colour, she was more aggrieved that you were not there to greet her.'

'But I had no idea she was coming!'

'That is no excuse, Nathan,' said Mrs Carraway, chuckling. 'My sister-in-law expects the world to wait upon her pleasure! However, I told her that since she chose to call before noon there was little chance of finding you at home, since you spend every morning on estate business, usually riding here, there and everywhere!'

'Well, I am very glad I missed her,' declared Nathan. 'But talking of riding—the weather looks set to be fine tomorrow morning. Felicity, would you like me to have your mare saddled up for you?'

'Th-thank you, that is very kind, but, no, I think not.'

Nathan bit back his disappointment. He said coolly, 'Just as you please, my dear. But if you change your mind, you only have to send a note to the stables.'

Felicity remembered his words when she awoke the next morning to find the sun streaming in through her window. When she heard the door open she looked up hopefully, but it was only her maid bringing in her morning cup of hot chocolate.

'It is very quiet next door, Martha. Is the master sleeping late?'

'No, my lady. He was on his way out o' doors when I came up to you.'

The disappointment was severe. Now the opportunity was lost, Felicity realised how much she would have liked to go out riding with Nathan. But the sunny weather was having its effect upon her spirits. Suddenly she wanted to be up and doing something. She threw back the bedcovers.

'Find my walking dress for me, if you please, Martha. I am going out!'

Despite the sunshine there was a chill in the air as Felicity set out to walk across the park, but she strode on, conscious that her mood was lifting. She stopped and looked about her. The park stretched away in every direction with avenues of sycamore and lime leading the eye beyond the palings to where the Rosthorne estate continued in the form of meadows, pastures and forests as far as the horizon.

'I am mistress of all this,' she murmured and her heart swelled with a curious mixture of wonder, apprehension and pleasure.

Nathan was fond of her, she did not doubt that. He might not love her, but he was kind and generous; other women managed with far less. She quickly buried the thought that she did not deserve his regard; she would earn it. The past was over; it was time to make amends. A few nights sleeping alone had convinced her that she no longer wanted to keep him at a distance—she missed him too much. And if she had to share him with a mistress—or even a whole string of mistresses—then so be it. She turned her head to look at the trees on the southern horizon, their autumn leaves blazing yellow, gold and brown in the sunlight. The route around the estate might change, but she knew that on his return Nathan always rode through the Home Wood. There were several footpaths through the trees, but only one track suitable for riders. She turned her footsteps in the direction of the wood. She would cut through to the bridleway and meet him.

Twenty minutes of brisk walking brought her to the edge of the wood and she plunged in, following the leaf-strewn path that meandered through the undergrowth. She did not slow her pace, for she was eager to reach the bridleway to meet Nathan, who would be approaching from the opposite direction. The wood was dappled with shade and she picked her way through the drying leaves and felled branches that littered the path. There was no wind to stir the trees and disturb the peacefulness. A tiny doubt disturbed her— what if Nathan had already passed this way? She quickened her step; she did not want to miss him and have to walk back to Rosthorne alone. She was just beginning to wonder if perhaps she had taken the wrong path when her ears caught the soft drumming of hoofbeats somewhere ahead of her. Relieved, she quickened her pace. The steady drumming was growing nearer. He was moving fast; she recalled following Nathan through the wood, always at a canter. Suddenly horse and rider were visible through the branches, one huge dark shape surging along the track. Then the regular thudding stopped, there was a shrieking neigh from a horse, a crash, then silence.

Her heart in her mouth, Felicity raced the last few yards to the bridleway. The big black hunter was standing riderless, trembling and snorting nervously. She looked around, a giddying wave of nausea sweeping over her when she saw Nathan lying motionless on the ground.

'Nathan!' She ran forward and dropped to her knees beside him. He was very pale, but she noted with relief that a pulse throbbed steadily in his neck. Her instinct was to call for help, but the wood seemed unnaturally quiet now. Frighteningly so. She looked around. There was something lying on the path: a length of thin cord, snaking amongst the fallen leaves. Intrigued, Felicity walked across and picked up the end. The cord pulled taut across the bridleway, just level with the horse's knees. A cold chill scurried down her back. She dropped the cord and swung round, her frightened eyes searching the trees. She could see no one, but she picked up a stout stick and kept circling, ears straining for any little noise. She did not know whether to be frightened or relieved when she heard another horse approaching. An instant later the Earl's steward trotted into view.

'Collins! Thank heavens!' cried Felicity. 'You must help me—my lord is hurt!'

The steward threw himself from the saddle and followed her to where Lord Rosthorne was lying. She dropped to her knees again and dashed away a tear. She must try to think clearly.

'We must get him back to Rosthorne. Ride to the house, Collins. Fetch some men, and a carriage—'

'Wait, my lady. He's coming round.'

Even as the steward spoke, Nathan's eyelids fluttered.

'Oh, thank God!' whispered Felicity. She reached

for his hand. 'Do not try to move, sir, until you are sure nothing is broken.'

'Only my pride,' he muttered, struggling to sit up. 'I shall have a few bruises tomorrow, no doubt. Heaven knows what caused Jet to stumble—'

'He didn't stumble, my lord,' growled Collins, who was examining the hunter's legs. 'He was brought down. There's some nasty gashes here.'

'There is a rope across the path,' added Felicity.

Nathan stared at her and raised one hand to his head. She said quietly, 'This time there can be no question. Someone deliberately tried to harm you.'

'We must get you home, my lord,' said Collins brusquely. 'If my lady will stay here with you, I'll ride on to the Hall and fetch a carriage.'

'You had best have some of the men search the woods and park, too,' said Nathan. 'Although I have no doubt the attacker is long gone. And send a boy to walk Jet back to the stables.' He waited until the steward had ridden away before fixing his gaze upon Felicity once more. The scar across his eye was very noticeable, enhanced by the bruise beginning to form on his cheekbone. His eyes fell upon the stick lying beside her.

'What is that? Did you mean to cudgel me to death while I lay helpless on the ground?'

'Pray do not joke, sir. I picked it up for protection.'

'Hmm.' He put a hand to his head, wincing. 'What were you doing in the wood?'

'I walked out to meet you. I regretted not riding out with you this morning.'

'Tell me what you saw.'

'Nothing, my lord. I was approaching the track when I heard your horse fall. I ran here and... found you.'

'And you saw no one?'

'No.' She pointed towards the cord, still lying across the path. 'Whoever was holding the rope was on the far side of the path. They were gone by the time I came up.' She shivered and looked around apprehensively. 'It is another attempt upon your life, Nathan. This time you cannot deny it.'

'No. I shall take care not to ride out alone again.'

'Good.'

'You must come with me, for my own protection.'

That drew a reluctant smile from her. 'I will, my lord, gladly, but my presence is not sufficient.'

He waved his hand towards the discarded cord. 'I beg to differ. Whoever is trying to kill me is very keen not to be detected.'

'I disagree, my lord. I—'

Nathan held up his hand. 'Enough.'

He struggled to his feet. Felicity jumped up, putting her arm about him as he swayed.

'You are still dizzy, you must not stand.'

'Neither can I remain on that damp earth.'

She guided him to a fallen tree and sat down beside him. She shivered.

'Are you cold, Fee?'

'No. A little frightened, perhaps. Your attacker might return.'

'I doubt it.' He took her hand and squeezed it. 'Not with you beside me.'

Their companionable silence lasted no more than five minutes before Nathan exclaimed, 'Oh to the devil with this sitting about! We will walk on and meet the carriage.'

'But, Nathan—'

'I am not an invalid,' he retorted, getting up and walking towards his horse. 'If you would kindly pick up my hat for me, it is better for us to be moving than to grow chilled to the bone sitting here. Come along.'

He held out his hand to her. Felicity took it and, with Jet hobbling along behind them, they made their way slowly out of the woods.

Word of the attack spread quickly. Nathan met with neighbouring landowners and extensive searches were made of the surrounding area. When it was known that it was not the first time someone had tried to kill the Earl, patrols were organised to keep watch on the local roads and fields. Gerald Appleby was one of those who volunteered for this duty.

'I thought you were off to London,' remarked Nathan, surprised.

Gerald merely grinned at him. 'I have no intention of returning to town when there is such excitement going on here,' he said.

Despite all the activity, Felicity remained anxious and could not relax until Nathan was safely returned to the house every evening. However, there was one piece of news that cheered her— she learned that Serena Ansell had left Hampshire and would not be returning until the spring.

Mrs Elliston conveyed these tidings when she came to visit Felicity and Mrs Carraway just days after the attack.

Mrs Carraway, who had not taken to the widow on the few occasions they had met, proposed her own theory for Lady Ansell's departure.

'You do not suppose that she was responsible, and has gone away until the dust has settled?'

Felicity was immediately upon the alert. 'What makes you say that, ma'am?'

'I have seen the way she looks at my son.'

Mrs Elliston gave a very girlish giggle. 'Do you think he spurned her advances? A woman scorned, as they say...'

Felicity hurriedly changed the subject. 'S-several of our neighbours have left Hampshire,' she observed. 'Do you plan to remain at Hazelford for the Christmas period, Mrs Elliston?'

'Yes, we always spend Christmas very quietly at home. Judith is making her annual visit to her aunt in Bedfordshire, but once she returns we shall not stir again until the new year. And you, ma'am? The neighbourhood will be expecting grand entertainments here, now that Rosthorne has a new mistress.'

Felicity was at a loss to answer and it was Mrs Carraway who replied quietly, 'Not this year. We shall keep the season very quietly. However, I hope you can be persuaded to join us for dinner one evening. Lady Charlotte and her son will be staying with us for a few days and I know they would be very happy to see you both—and your daughter, of course.'

'We shall be delighted,' replied Mrs Elliston. 'Judith and Mr Appleby were getting along famously at the assembly the other week, and I have no objection to continuing the acquaintance.' She added, with a touch of defiance, 'Though I doubt Lady Charlotte will be quite so sanguine about her son's friendship with a mere *Miss* Elliston, being herself, as she never fails to remind us, the daughter of an earl!'

Chapter Sixteen

'We will soon be back at the Hall now, my lord.'

Nathan heard a hint of relief in his steward's voice. They had ridden out to look at the plantation Nathan had established the previous year and the short December day had closed in upon them very rapidly. Collins still insisted upon accompanying the Earl whenever he rode on the estate, even though there had been no sightings of any strangers in the area and the regular patrols set up after the attack had ceased. Felicity, too, colluded with his staff to make sure Nathan was never alone.

He thought of his wife as he rode through the gates and into the park for the final part of his journey. She was so anxious for his safety, yet she still kept him at a distance. They had resumed riding together every morning and during the day she would be friendly, affectionate even, but she resisted his every attempt at intimacy, putting up an invisible barrier between them. He was careful not to allow his impatience to show, but he wondered how long he could continue before his resolve snapped and he broke his promise not to enter her bedchamber.

The icy December wind cut at his cheeks and the scar over his eye throbbed in the cold. A good thing, he thought bitterly. It took his mind off the ache in his loins.

They clattered into the stable yard, where a large, old-fashioned travelling carriage was being manoeuvred into one corner.

'Lady Charlotte has arrived, sir,' observed Collins.

'Oh lord,' he muttered ruefully, 'I had forgotten she was coming today.' He jumped down and handed the mare's reins to his groom. 'Take a look at her left hind fetlock, Pat, I fear it might be sprained.'

A shorter, thickset figure came running out of the stable, tugging at his forelock.

'Will 'ee let me take 'er, Mr Patrick? I'll look at 'er.'

Patrick handed over the reins and turned back to Nathan with a slightly apologetic smile.

'It's Harris, my lord. Lady Charlotte's man,' he explained as they watched the man lead the horse into the stable. 'He's a half-wit, but a natural healer. He seems to know just what to do with animals.'

Nathan nodded. 'Very well, if you are sure, Patrick. Report back to me later.' He turned and saw Felicity coming across the yard to meet him, a paisley shawl pulled tight about her shoulders and Bella trotting at her heels.

'I was watching out for you, my lord; you are very late.'

'I beg your pardon. My mare went lame and I didn't want to push her.' Her anxious eyes flew to his face and he shook his head, smiling a little. 'It is all perfectly innocent; with Jet's knees not fully healed I have been riding Juniper a little hard lately.' He put his hand on her elbow. 'Shall we go indoors, out of this biting wind?

'Where is my aunt?' he asked as they walked through the flagged passage leading to the hall.

'Your mama is entertaining Lady Charlotte and Mr Appleby in the drawing room.' She glanced up. 'You are cold, sir. I had Sam build up the fire in your dressing room; you will need to change.'

'Should I not make my apologies to my aunt first?'

She chuckled. 'I fear that whatever you do, you will be in the wrong. It is her way. Go upstairs, sir. I will make your excuses.' She began to move away, but he caught her hand.

'Shall we leave my mother to look after our guests?' he murmured, drawing her into his arms. 'You could come upstairs with me and help me out of my muddy clothes...'

The light in the passage was very poor, but he thought he saw a sudden longing in her eyes. A swift flash of desire. It was gone in an instant, replaced by the wary, anxious look she wore so often these days. He ran his hands gently up and down her arms. 'What is it, my dear? What is worrying you?'

'W-worrying me?' She gave a nervous little laugh. 'Why, nothing, my lord, only the thought of entertaining Lady Charlotte. I have already had to bring Bella away, because she objects to dogs in the drawing room...'

Felicity looked past Nathan towards the hall, then down at the little spaniel, anywhere rather than into Nathan's face, for there was no mistaking his look and it made her knees grow weak. She wanted so much to give in to him and to her own yearning, but the spectre of Serena Ansell haunted her and she could not rid herself of the conviction that Nathan would always compare her unfavourably with the beautiful widow. Her thoughts returned to their first meeting at Souden House, when he had swept her up, intending to carry her off with him. If only he would show the same forcefulness now. If only…

Nathan's hands fell away from her shoulders. 'Of course. Take Bella to my mother's apartment, Norton will look after her. Then go back to your guests and I will join you as soon as I may.'

Felicity watched him stride away. Bella scampered after him, but a curt word sent her back to Felicity, her ears flattened.

Since neither Mrs Carraway nor Lady Charlotte kept late hours, the evening came to an end before midnight.

'I hope that was not too intolerable for you,' said Nathan as he escorted Felicity to her room. 'My aunt is not the most amenable of guests. Her comments concerning the attack in Home Wood were outrageous. I hope you did not take her seriously.'

'No, indeed. Do you…?' She hesitated. 'Does she *truly* think I tried to murder you?'

'My aunt likes to make mischief, nothing more.'

'But it *is* suspicious! When Mr Collins came up I was holding that stick…'

'Hush now. You have already explained it to me.' They had reached the door of her bedchamber and he stopped, turning to look down at her. 'When I came round to find you bending over me, the look in your eyes was not that of a murderer.'

'It—it wasn't?' Felicity gazed up at him. She suddenly felt very short of breath.

'No.' He lowered his head until his lips were just touching hers. She put her fingers against his chest and grasped the lapels of his evening coat. Smiling, he captured one hand and turned it.

'Remember,' he said softly, pressing a kiss into her palm, 'I am in the next room if you want me. You only have to walk through the door.'

'I—I—'

He dropped a light, butterfly kiss on her forehead and walked away. A moment later she heard the soft click of his door closing.

Sam was laying out his master's nightgown and banyan when he entered the room. With a word Nathan dismissed his valet and stood, head bowed, straining his ears against the silence. He heard Felicity go into her room, the soft pad of feet across the boards, the murmur of voices. She was not indifferent to him, he would swear to it. He had noted her relief when he had arrived that evening, seen the shy longing in her eyes, felt her cling to him when he had kissed her goodnight. He could have taken her then, swept her into his room, into his bed and kissed her into submission. She would respond to him, he was certain of it, but he wanted more from his wife. He wanted her to come to *him*. Nathan walked across to the adjoining door and rested his shoulder against the wall, staring at the door handle, willing it to turn, willing Felicity to come in.

But the door between them remained resolutely closed.

Christmas Eve dawned grey and windy, the blustery weather reflecting Felicity's restless mood. Lady Charlotte was a difficult houseguest, but Felicity was determined not to be intimidated by her autocratic manner, nor her constant references to the way Rosthorne used to be run. Her courage dipped a little when she found only Gerald and his mother at the breakfast table, but she scarcely had time to say good morning before Mrs Carraway came in, leaning on Nathan's arm.

Gerald, pouring coffee for his mother, bade them all good morning and offered to fill their cups.

'Yes, thank you.' Mrs Carraway took her seat beside Felicity. 'I have given Norton a holiday to visit her family in Petersfield, so Nathan came to fetch me for breakfast.'

'Then do not hesitate to tell me, ma'am, if there is anything I can do for you today,' put in Felicity.

'Must we have that animal in here?' demanded Lady Charlotte, frowning at Bella who was capering around Gerald's feet, her paws pattering and skidding on the polished boards.

'I am afraid so, Aunt,' said Nathan cheerfully. 'She is used to having the run of the house in the mornings. But you need not worry; we never feed her from the table. She merely waits for any scraps that might fall.'

'And saves the servants the trouble of sweeping up.' Gerald grinned, still wielding the coffee pot.

'Exactly. No coffee for me, thank you.' Nathan picked up the ale-jug from the sideboard and filled a pewter tankard. 'This is one of the old earl's customs that I *have* continued,' he said, a smile glinting in his eyes.

Gerald looked towards the window, where the rain had started to drum against the glass.

'We must entertain ourselves indoors today,' he remarked. 'What time did you say the Ellistons were coming?'

'We expect them before dark,' said Felicity, 'unless the storm persuades them to cry off.'

Nathan shook his head. 'It is only a few miles and Elliston is not one to fight shy of a little bad weather.'

Gerald walked over to the window. 'When I saw them at the assembly, Mrs Elliston gave me permission to call at any time; I could always ride over and escort them.'

'By all means,' said Nathan, 'if you think it necessary.'

'I do not see the least need for such a thing,' stated Lady Charlotte. 'Indeed, if the weather remains inclement this afternoon, I shall want you here to entertain me.'

Felicity's lips twitched.

'We must not expect the gentlemen to wait on us the whole day, ma'am. I am sure we shall be able to entertain ourselves. We might play at battledore in the long gallery, or charades.'

Gerald chuckled. 'Mama's idea of entertainment is to have someone read to her while she sleeps on her daybed.'

'Then I shall be very happy to do that,' declared Felicity gallantly. 'In fact, Lydia—Lady Souden—has sent me a copy of *Waverley*. I was going to share it with Mama Carraway, but I can easily read it to you both!'

With Lady Charlotte's entertainment organised, Gerald went off to order his horse, and when breakfast was over Mrs Carraway took her sister-in-law away to the morning room. Nathan detained Felicity as she was about to follow them.

'It is very good of you to give up your time.'

Felicity was warmed by his compliment; suddenly the day seemed much brighter. 'Nonsense, I am only being a good hostess. I very much wish to read *Waverley,* so it will be no hardship for me.' She chuckled. 'I hope it is sufficiently diverting to keep Lady Charlotte happy throughout the day, and then perhaps she will behave herself this evening.'

In the event Felicity's hopes were realised, for Lady Charlotte was at her most gracious during dinner. She greeted Mr and Mrs Elliston with a condescension that made Mr Elliston's eyes twinkle and proceeded to dominate the conversation.

'She behaves as if she were the hostess here,' murmured Mrs Carraway as she and Felicity led the ladies to the drawing room after dinner.

'As long as she refrains from making any of her more outrageous remarks, I am very happy with that,' returned Felicity, a glimmer of a smile in her eyes.

The evening was going much better than she had expected; Mr Elliston had been a little brusque with his host at first, but he observed Felicity's anxious look and soon took the opportunity to reassure her.

'No need to make yourself uncomfortable, ma'am,' he muttered, during one of Lady Charlotte's many reminiscences of how past Earls of Rosthorne had been wont to celebrate Christmas. 'Much as I would like to take Nathan to task for his dastardly behaviour at the assembly, I gave you my word and we will say no more about it.'

Her only other concern was that Lady Charlotte might take exception to her son's attentions towards Miss Elliston, but although her cold stare rested upon the young couple several times during the evening, she made no comment, and even expressed mild disappointment that the party was such a small one.

'When I was young the events at Rosthorne Hall were on a much grander scale,' she stated, fixing Nathan with an accusing stare. 'All the principal rooms would be opened up and the house would be full of guests. Although I admit that this year the country is exceedingly thin of company. If Lady Ansell had been in residence you could have invited her.'

'No, ma'am, I could not,' retorted Felicity. She added, aware of the surprised glances of her guests, 'I am not well acquainted with the lady.'

'No more are we,' put in Mrs Elliston. 'My husband does not wish for the connection. The lady has a reputation for being rather *fast*.'

'Is that so, Rosthorne?' demanded Lady Charlotte. 'I believe you knew Lady Ansell when you were in the Peninsula.'

Felicity risked a quick glance in Nathan's direction. His face was quite impassive.

'Yes, she was in Corunna.' Nathan's tone was slightly bored. 'She was Mrs Craike then, but I believe she was quite a favourite with the officers.'

'I wonder that she should choose to live here,' mused Mrs Carraway. 'Hazelford is very quiet, and there are few enough single gentlemen to attract her interest.'

'Perhaps it is not a *single* gentleman who interests her,' muttered Felicity.

Nathan's head came up. 'Would you care to explain that remark, my dear?'

She flushed under his searching gaze and was relieved that her mother-in-law had not noticed the interruption and was continuing with her own conjectures.

'I do not like to think that any gentleman of our acquaintance would set up such a liaison.' Mrs Carraway laughed. 'Imagine respectable Dr Farnham being caught in her web, or even the vicar!'

Mr Elliston harrumphed in disapproval and stalked away.

'You may rest easy, then,' replied Gerald, smiling. 'Your speculation is very wide of the mark— Mama had a letter from Lady Ansell to say she is not returning to Godfrey Park, but means to remain in Bath.'

'Which is very inconvenient,' announced Lady Charlotte. 'There are few enough families of note in this area with whom one can dine.'

Mr Elliston, who was standing at the unshuttered window, announced that he was anxious to set off in good time for West Meon.

'This wind shows no sign of abating,' he said, 'and I fear there may be a few trees blown down before morning.'

A particularly fierce gust of wind rattled the window at that moment, giving substance to his argument, and the party broke up shortly afterwards, with Gerald escorting the ladies to their coach.

'I was tempted to saddle up and ride back with them,' he said, coming back into the drawing room. 'I would like to be sure they have a safe journey.'

'Their way lies mainly through the valley, which will afford them some shelter,' said Nathan. He raised his head as a door slammed somewhere in the house. 'I will have Mercer check all the shutters tonight.'

'Yes, please do.' Lady Charlotte beckoned to her son. 'Give me your company to my door, please, Gerald. These stormy nights are very alarming.'

'I did not think that anything could alarm

Lady Charlotte,' remarked Felicity, when Mr Appleby had escorted his mother away.

Mrs Carraway chuckled. 'Nor does it. The woman has nerves of steel.' She struggled to her feet, leaning heavily upon her stick. 'I think I shall retire now.'

Felicity jumped up. 'Then let me give you my arm, ma'am,' she said. 'We will leave Nathan to make sure the house is secure.'

Walking back a short time later, Felicity was obliged to use her hand to shield the flame of her bedroom candle, for the howling wind seeped into the house and whined along the dark corridors. She was relieved when she reached her own chamber and lost no time getting into bed and blowing out her candle. She lay tense and nervous under the covers, listening to the storm battering the house. There was a crash as something smashed on the terrace below her window and a growl of thunder added its own menace to the darkness. Felicity curled herself into a ball and snuggled down beneath the bedcovers. Finally, she fell into an uneasy sleep.

Once he had make a last tour of the house, Nathan too retired, but sleep eluded him. He tossed restlessly in his bed. The storm would almost certainly do some damage. He had already heard the sounds of a pot or a tile shattering on the terrace and he hoped the young trees on his plantation would survive. He turned over. He could do nothing about it until it was daylight.

A sudden cry caught his attention. He sat up. The sound had come from Felicity's room. He heard her cry out again. Reaching for his tinder box, he fumbled to light his candle, then, pulling on his dressing gown, he went across to the connecting door. As he stepped into the room the door from the corridor opened and the maid appeared, holding aloft her candle with a shaking hand.

'Ooh, excuse me, m'lord, I heard m'lady calling out...'

They both looked towards the shadowed bed where Felicity lay restlessly muttering.

'It is all right, Martha,' said Nathan quietly. 'I will look after my lady.'

With a little curtsy the maid withdrew. A sudden gust of wind rattled the window shutters and the flame of his candle flickered wildly. Felicity muttered and gave another anguished sob. Nathan moved towards the bed.

'Felicity.'

Nathan put the candle down beside the bed. Her eyes were closed and she thrashed out, throwing off the covers.

'No, no. Leave me alone—*Déjeme*!'

She was crying out in Spanish, just as she had done five years ago when he had rescued her from the robbers in Corunna. And just as he had done five years ago, Nathan climbed on to the bed and took her in his arms. She fought against him, but he held her close, muttering soothing words. She began to cry.

'I have lost everything! There's nothing left, nothing!'

'Hush now.' He stroked her head. 'We can buy you new things.'

'No, no, I have lost him!' She was rambling wildly. 'It is God's punishment! Why must I live...?'

'It is only a dream, Felicity. Wake up.'

'It's too late. I have lost him! If only God would let me die...'

Nathan's arms tightened about her. He said sharply, '*I* won't let you die! Wake up, Felicity!' She stopped fighting and he felt her flutter, like a little bird in his arms. 'You are safe now, Fee,' he murmured the words into her hair. 'You are with me.'

'I am so sorry, so sorry.' She sobbed into his chest. 'Don't leave me!'

Nathan settled himself more comfortably on the bed and pulled her against him. 'Hush now. I will never leave you.'

She continued to cry, great, wrenching sobs that racked her body. Nathan felt powerless to do anything but hold her. He pulled the covers over her shoulders to ward off the cold night air and remained there, cradling her in his arms while the storm raged at the windows.

The candle had burned itself out before Felicity finally grew calm. She lay quietly in the darkness, her head resting against his heart. Nathan felt her stir.

'Nathan?'

'I'm here.'

She pulled the sheet up to wipe her eyes. 'I don't deserve you,' she murmured. 'You have been so forbearing with me. I wish I knew why you are so good to me.'

'You are my countess.'

'I don't deserve you,' she said again, sleepily. 'I don't know why you should want me.'

He smiled to himself.

'Because you are irreplaceable,' he murmured. 'God knows I tried! All those stories they tell of me, the women, the broken hearts that litter Europe; I was trying to forget you, to prove to myself that you did not matter to me. But you do, Fee.' He kissed her hair. 'You matter very, very much.'

She did not reply but lay against him, her breathing deep and regular.

She was asleep.

Chapter Seventeen

Felicity did not wake up until Martha came into the room to open the shutters. The storm had blown itself out and bright sunlight flooded the room. She stretched.

'Is it very late? I had such dreams!'

'The master said not to wake you early, m'lady.'

'Oh, he was here?' Felicity pulled the sheets around her. She remembered him holding her, but she had thought it part of her dream.

'Yes, m'lady. He came in last night, when you was crying in your sleep. Terrible dreams you must have had, ma'am.'

'Yes.' Strangely, the horror of the night was gone and Felicity remembered only feeling safe and secure in Nathan's arms.

Martha stood beside the bed, smiling at her. 'The master sends his compliments, madam, and says he will escort you down to breakfast in half an hour.'

'Heavens, then we must be quick!'

Felicity scrambled out of bed, bubbling with an equal measure of happiness and alarm. She was inordinately pleased that Nathan should want to attend her, but a nervousness remained about what she might have cried out during the night.

When Nathan knocked at her door some thirty minutes later, Felicity was ready for him.

'I fear I disturbed your sleep last night, my lord.'

He took her hand. 'Nigtmares,' he said. 'You were very distressed.'

'And you stayed with me. I thank you for that.' She gave him a smile.

'Do you often have such bad dreams?'

'No, not now. I think it was the storm that disturbed me.' She hesitated, then said shyly, 'I am very glad you were there, Nathan.'

He squeezed her hand. 'I shall always be there for you.'

She accompanied Nathan down the stairs.

'We are exceedingly late, sir. And it is Christmas Day—I very much fear we shall miss the morning service.'

'I am certain of it.' Nathan grinned at her. 'I do not doubt that my mother has gone on without us, but we shall not be missed; my very regal Aunt

Charlotte will more than make up for our absence!' As they reached the hall Nathan paused. 'You go on, my dear; I will slip down and speak to Collins. I want to know if there was much damage last night.'

He strode off in the direction of the servants' wing and Felicity made her way into the breakfast room. Bella came dashing up and Felicity bent to make a fuss of her.

'So where have you escaped from?' she murmured, fondling the spaniel's soft ears. 'Have they all gone off to church and left you here? Never mind, I will take you for a walk later.'

Felicity straightened and went into the breakfast room with Bella capering around her. The room was empty, but even before she had taken her seat Mercer entered with a fresh pot of coffee. She had just filled her cup when Nathan came in. His warm smile made her toes curl with pleasure.

A young footman hurried in with a plate of hot toast which he placed on the table.

'Coffee, my lord?' he asked reaching for the pot.

'No, no, Toby, bring me some ale, if you please.' Nathan sat down beside Felicity. 'The crash we heard last night was one of the pots from the balcony shattering on the terrace. The shrub had grown too large and the wind caught it. Collins has already ridden over the park; we have lost a couple of trees but nothing more serious. I shall go out later, to check the damage for myself. Perhaps you would care to come with me?'

'But, our guests...'

'I think they can spare you to me for an hour.'

'Then, yes, thank you. I should very much like to come with you.'

Her eyes fell on Bella, who was scampering about the room. She opened her mouth to utter a warning, but it was too late—the footman was carrying Nathan's tankard of ale upon a tray and did not see the little dog under his feet. Servant, tray and tankard crashed to the ground and Bella, delighted with the chaos she had created, hurried to lap up the frothing ale that was spilled on the floor.

'Never mind, never mind.' Nathan waved away the lackey's anguished apologies. 'Just go and find a cloth to mop up this mess. Leave that, Bella!' He looked at Felicity and said severely, 'And I would be obliged, madam, if you would refrain from laughing at my servant's misfortune.'

Felicity was not deceived; she saw the smile tugging at the corners of his mouth and took her hands away from her own.

'I should not, I know, and I shall be sober again by the time the poor man returns, I give you my word.'

With a laugh Nathan took her face between his hands. 'I love to see you so happy. I have missed your smiles.' He kissed her, then sat back, glancing down at Bella.

'Hmm, by the time Toby returns I think that damned dog may have licked the floor clean.' He picked up his tankard from the floor and wiped the edge of it with his napkin. 'I had best fetch my own ale while Bella is preoccupied.'

Still glowing from his kiss, Felicity began to butter a piece of toast.

'Thank goodness Lady Charlotte was not here to witness the accident,' she remarked. 'She would want poor Bella banned from the house! What a poor start to Christmas Day, I feel sure your mama will ring a peel over us when she—oh heavens—*Nathan*!'

Felicity jumped to her feet, sending her chair toppling backwards. Nathan had just finished filling his tankard. He looked around. Felicity struggled to speak.

'Look—Bella—' She turned her horrified gaze towards the little dog, who was staggering across the floor, her legs giving way beneath her.

'Nathan, what is it?' whispered Felicity.

The dog had collapsed on her side, her breathing laboured.

'I'm not sure.' He picked up the tankard and sniffed at it, frowning. 'Poison. In the ale.'

Nathan crossed the room to Bella in a couple of strides. Felicity looked down at the spaniel, who stared up at her with wide, frightened eyes. She put her hands to her mouth.

'Is there nothing we can do?'

'I have heard that coffee sometimes works.'

Felicity reached for the coffee pot on the table, then put it down again. 'This one will be better, it is cold,' she said, running to the sideboard and picking up another silver pot.

'Quickly then.' Nathan cradled the little dog, forcing open her mouth while Felicity gently poured the coffee down her throat.

Bella struggled, but Nathan held her firm.

'I hope that's a good sign,' he muttered. 'Try a little more.'

'There is no more,' she said, her voice breaking. 'Shall I fetch the other pot?'

'No, wait.' Nathan released the spaniel and moved away a little as she vomited.

The footman, returning at that moment with a mop and bucket, stopped in the doorway, staring open mouthed at the scene before him.

'Will she be all right?' asked Felicity as Bella lay on the floor, panting heavily.

'I cannot say.' Nathan lifted Bella carefully into

his arms. 'I shall take her down to the stables. Patrick will know better than I how to doctor her.' He turned to the servant. 'Pick up my lady's chair, if you please, and clear up the mess on the floor, but on no account allow anything else in the room to be touched.'

Felicity started forward. 'I shall come with you.'

'No, I would prefer you to stay here and make sure no one comes into the breakfast room.'

When Nathan had gone, Felicity sat back down at the table. Her appetite had quite disappeared; in fact, she felt a little sick, but she fought against it, and when the servant had gone she remained staring fixedly out through the open door, waiting for Nathan to return.

The chimes of the long-case clock in the hall told Felicity that she had been sitting alone for only a half-hour, but it seemed a lifetime before Nathan came striding back towards her. He looked very grim, and her heart turned over.

'Well?' she said, hardly daring to breath.

Nathan shifted his eyes to her face, as if recalled to the present and his frown lifted a little.

'Patrick is hopeful she will recover. It seems we did the right thing.'

'Thank heavens.' She watched him pick up the

jug of ale and pour a little into a clean water glass. He lifted it up to the light, then sniffed at it cautiously.

'What is it, my lord?'

He held the glass out to her. 'What can you smell?'

'I am not sure. Hops, perhaps...' she wrinkled her nose '...and a faint, unpleasant odour...like mice.'

'Quite.' He put the glass back on the sideboard. 'Hemlock, but the smell is so faint that anyone might quaff half a tankard before becoming aware of it. And poor old Bella, as we know, has very little sense of smell these days.'

Felicity put her hands to her mouth. 'If you had drunk it...' she whispered, growing cold at the thought. 'Who would do such a thing?'

He took her hands and sat down beside her.

'There is a bottle of hemlock tincture in the stables,' he said slowly. 'You will recall my mare sprained a fetlock; Patrick used the tincture in the poultice he applied to bring down the swelling.'

'Oh, dear heaven! Has the bottle disappeared?'

'No, but Patrick thinks some of it may have been used. However, he cannot be sure.'

'But who would want to do such a thing?' she repeated.

'Who would have the opportunity to put the

hemlock into the ale?' he countered. 'I stopped at the kitchens on the way back and spoke to Mercer. He tells me he drew off some of the ale for himself this morning and he also filled the jug and carried it here. My mother and Lady Charlotte were already at breakfast when he brought it in.'

'And the other servants?'

He shook his head. 'They are all local people and have worked here since they were children. I shall have to question them, but I cannot believe that any of them would be capable of such a trick.'

'But if it is not a servant…' She left the sentence unfinished and stared at him in horror. Nathan held her gaze.

'Who was in this room when you came down this morning, Fee? Think carefully.'

She frowned.

'No one,' she said. 'Mercer followed me in with the coffee pot and placed it directly on the table, but he touched nothing on the sideboard.'

'Then it is possible that someone put the hemlock into the ale while the room was empty, knowing I had not yet broken my fast.'

She clung to his hand. 'Oh, Nathan, I do not like to think of someone here in this house, wishing you harm.'

'No more do I.' He smiled slightly. 'But despite everything, we must eat, you know. I shall call

Mercer. He will have everything cleared away from here and bring us a fresh breakfast in the morning room.'

Felicity could not enjoy her food, despite Mercer's earnest assurances that he had watched every stage of its preparation. However, she admitted she felt better for having eaten something and was able to await the church party's return with tolerable equanimity. Their shock and horror when they discovered what had happened was understandable, but Felicity found the repeated questions and conjecture distressing and made her excuses to slip away. As hostess she knew she could not absent herself for very long and after a suitable period she went back to join her guests. The short December day was overcast and the house was very gloomy. In the drawing room everyone was gathered about the hearth, where the light from the blazing fire combined with the candle flames to provide a comforting glow around the little party.

Felicity entered unnoticed and she was still in the shadows when Lady Charlotte said emphatically, 'Look at the facts, Rosthorne; she had every opportunity to slip something into the ale. And it would not be the first time—was she not in the wood when you came off your horse? And I had not been in the house five minutes before I could see that you and that wife or yours are estranged.'

The little group became aware of Felicity's presence. All eyes turned to her as she emerged from the shadows, the damning words hanging in the air around them. Felicity looked at Nathan. She prayed for him to defend her, but it was Mrs Carraway who said with a touch of asperity,

'That is utter nonsense, Charlotte. I would ask you not to repeat such foolishness! Felicity, my dear, pray you come and sit here by me. You must not take any notice; we are all a little upset. Nathan has asked Mercer to gather all the staff together in the servants' hall and he will speak to them all, but I cannot think that any of our regular people would do such a thing. They have worked here for generations and have nothing to gain from such a trick.'

'What about the stable hands?' asked Gerald, pouring a glass of wine for Felicity.

Nathan shook his head. 'I questioned them when I took Bella down to the yard.'

'I trust you did not trouble Harris with your questions,' put in Lady Charlotte. 'You know that he is very simple, and as like to tell you a lie if he thinks it is what you wish to hear.'

'No, ma'am, I did not question him. He came forward immediately to help Patrick look after

Bella. He was overwrought when he saw her; I do not see him harming anyone.'

Felicity hardly heard them. She was still staring at Nathan, wanting some sign of reassurance, but he avoided her eyes. Surely he could not think that she had tried to poison him?

'If you will excuse me,' said Nathan, rising, 'I will go and talk to the servants now.'

'And I think we would all do well to rest before dinner,' said Mrs Carraway. 'Felicity, would you give me your arm, please?

'My sister-in-law grows ever more eccentric,' she murmured as Felicity accompanied her along the darkened corridors to her apartment. 'We do not heed her, I promise you.'

'But it is true, ma'am, that I was alone in the breakfast room for some time before Nathan joined me.'

'And he told us you warned him not to drink the ale. Nathan has had a trying day, my dear, but he would be a fool indeed if he did not know that you would never do such a thing.'

Felicity took some comfort from Mama Carraway's words, but the memory of Nathan's cool, unsmiling look would not go away.

Once she had settled Mrs Carraway in her room Felicity made her way back towards her own bed-chamber. She ran up the back stairs and along the corridor that looked down on the stable yard. The short winter's day had already ended and in the corridor the feeble light of the candles in their wall brackets was enhanced by the glow from the braziers burning in the yard below. Felicity glanced out of the windows as she passed. Harris was coming out of one of the stalls and she heard someone hail him. Gerald Appleby crossed the yard and put his arm about the groom's shoulders, engaging him in earnest conversation. Felicity watched them for a long moment, a slight frown between her brows, then she turned and made her way slowly to her room.

When Felicity came downstairs nearly an hour later she found there was an unusual amount of activity in the hall. Footmen were carrying a number of corded trunks out of the door. Gerald Appleby was standing to one side, talking with Nathan, but when he saw Felicity he came across to her, a rueful smile on his lips.

'My dear Lady Rosthorne, what can I say? How can I apologise? I was just telling Nathan that Mama is rather overcome by the events here and wishes to return to Appleby Manor.' He lifted his hand. 'No, no, ma'am, I know you would protest that the Christmas dinner is almost on the table, and that it is very dark, but I am afraid Mama is adamant that she wishes to leave immediately, so we do our best to accommodate her.'

Felicity, who had not intended saying anything at all, merely nodded and walked across the hall to stand beside Nathan as Lady Charlotte came down the stairs, leaning on her dresser's arm.

'I have never been in favour of allowing animals to roam loose in the house, and look what comes of it.' Lady Charlotte's clear, uncompromising tones preceded her.

Felicity stiffened indignantly. She looked up at Nathan, but there was no reading anything from his impassive countenance.

'Well, we must hope the little dog makes a full recovery and no harm done,' put in Gerald, stepping forward. 'Come, Mama, let me escort you to your carriage.'

'My compliments to your mother, Rosthorne,' announced Lady Charlotte as she walked slowly towards the door. 'She will be sorry I am cutting short my visit.'

'I have already explained everything to Lord and Lady Rosthorne, Mama.' Gerald flashed a quick, apologetic smile towards them. 'And I have sent Harris on ahead to Appleby Manor so I hope that when we arrive everything will be in readiness for you. It is a clear sky, and the moon is already rising, so I think we shall make good time.'

Nathan and Felicity walked to the door and watched as Gerald ushered his mother into the coach. Lady Charlotte's dresser climbed in and while the two ladies made themselves comfortable Gerald ran quickly back up the steps.

'Goodbye, Nathan.' He held out his hand. 'I do hope Bella recovers; I dare say you will be glad to have us out of the way at this time.' He gripped Nathan's hand, gave a quick nod to Felicity and ran back down the steps to the coach.

Nathan watched the carriage drive away, but his thoughts were elsewhere, going over and over the events of the day. After questioning the servants he could not bring himself to believe that any one of them had put the hemlock into the jug, but if that was so, then he had to face an even more unwelcome thought. Beside him Felicity shivered and pulled her shawl a little closer about her. Nathan put his hand under her elbow.

'There is a chill wind blowing. We should go in. There is a good fire in the drawing room, and Mama will join you soon.'

'You are not coming in?'

He looked away, not wanting her to guess at the turmoil in his mind. 'Not yet. I have some work to complete in my study.'

'Then I shall come with you, for I need to speak with you, alone.'

'As you wish.'

His heart sank. At any other time he would have welcomed her confidences, but now he needed to be alone, to think through the events of the day. He ushered her into his study and closed the door. Candles were already burning around the room and after the chill of the night air the blazing fire was a welcome sight.

'You were working here, perhaps, when you heard that Lady Charlotte and Mr Appleby were leaving?'

'I was.'

'Their departure is very sudden.'

'Yes, it was a surprise to me. I would have sent for you to bid them adieu but Gerald begged me not to disturb you.'

Nathan sat down and idly shifted the papers on the desk while Felicity paced the room.

'Nathan.' She stopped in front of his desk. 'I think your cousin knows something of this attempt to poison you.' Her words were rushed rather than considered.

'And why should that be?'

His voice was harsher than he had intended and she hesitated before continuing. 'I saw him talking with his mother's groom.'

'When was this?'

'After I had taken Mama Carraway to her room. I was on my way to my own chamber and saw them in the stable yard. It did not look as if Mr Appleby was giving Harris any ordinary instructions,' she added quickly, 'I thought they looked more…secretive.'

'It is most likely that he was giving him his orders to quit Rosthorne.'

'I do not think so.' She shook her head. 'The groom was looking very frightened.'

'Harris is simple. You heard Lady Charlotte say so.'

'Yes, but he could have fetched the hemlock from the stable if Mr Appleby asked him.' He watched her as she considered this. 'You sent word that you would be late,' she said slowly. 'Gerald could have returned to the breakfast room when it was empty and put the poison into the ale. Nathan, he must be involved.'

'No, you are mistaken.'

'How can you be so sure?'

'Never mind that for now—'

'Never mind!' she exclaimed, an angry flush on her cheeks. 'You would prefer to think that *I* poisoned you!'

'Of course not!'

'Then tell me what you suspect.'

'At this moment I would rather not—'

'No, of course,' she said bitterly. 'It is easier to think ill of me than of your own family!'

'Now you are being foolish!'

'Am I? Would you not be pleased to have some excuse to be rid of me?'

Nathan's brows snapped together. 'Now what the devil are you talking about?'

'I know you would like to put Serena Ansell in my place.'

'*What?*'

Felicity dashed a hand across her eyes. 'She is the wife you really want, is she not? I saw you, at the assembly—embracing!'

'That was *not* what you saw! Felicity, listen—'

She put up her hand. 'You need not deny that you love her, she told me of it herself.'

Nathan stared at her, frowning. He forced himself to speak quietly. 'And just when did she tell you that?'

Felicity sank down on to a chair and pressed her fingers to her temples. 'In Corunna, just after you had left town. She came to tell me that you were in love with her.'

'And you believed it?'

Felicity threw up her head. 'Why not, when she had your letter and your ring to prove it?'

'Impossible.'

'How can you deny it?'

'I *do* deny it.' He sat back, arms folded. 'And this was your reason for leaving me? Upon the word of a woman with the morals of an alley cat?'

'She had *proof*!'

'Preposterous. I have never written to her.' Her look of disbelief angered him. 'Damnation, Felicity, after five years, how am I supposed to convince you?'

She turned away. 'There is no need,' she said dully. 'You said yourself the past is over.'

With a smothered oath he jumped up from his chair and reached out, grabbing her wrist.

'Well, I was wrong! There is very clearly a need to talk about the past! We must clear this up now, Fee, or every time we have a disagreement it will be there, between us.'

She glared at him, her grey eyes positively smouldering. There was no shuttered look in them now.

'Sit down, Fee. It is time we were done with any secrets.'

He gently pushed her down into a chair and took another for himself, turning it to face her, so that when he sat down their knees were almost touching.

'Very well, Fee, let me tell you the truth now. Serena *did* kiss me at the assembly, but if you had stayed another minute you would have seen me push her away. The woman delights in making trouble. When we were in Corunna she liked to think that every man would fall at her feet. I never did, but I do not think she understood that. I can believe she told you some fairy tale to drive you away from me.' He rubbed his temple, his fingers coming to rest on the ridge of his scar. 'Perhaps I should have warned you about her, but she was Adam's mistress; foolishly I thought that was enough for her. As for writing to her—no, I never did that.'

Felicity stared down at her hands clasped tightly in her lap. Perhaps she had been foolish; she had not wanted to believe Serena, but...

'She had your ring, Nathan. The band engraved with thorns, I could not mistake it.'

She risked a glance at his face. She knew him well enough now to realise that although his eyes rested on her, his thoughts were far away.

'I gave that ring to Adam Elliston,' he said at last.

'To Adam? But why did you not tell me so, when I asked you about your ring?'

He rubbed his chin. 'I find it...very hard to talk about Adam. When he died it was like losing part of my soul. We were neither of us rich, but when we arrived in Corunna he spent all his money on

Serena, every last groat. It is possible, I suppose, that he loaned her the ring. After all he was quite besotted with the woman. But he had it later, I know, for I saw it. He wanted to give it back to me, but I told him to keep it, for good luck...' He dragged himself back to the present and looked at her. 'If only you had stayed, Fee, we could have put this to rights in a few minutes.'

She did not answer. If only she had stayed.

'I understand why you wanted to get away from me,' Nathan said. 'I realise you must have been hurt and angry, but later, when you had time to think, why did you not contact me? Why hide yourself away for so long?'

He leaned forward, his eyes fixed upon her. 'Well, Fee?'

Silence stretched between them. Felicity stared at the floor, her arms wrapped across her stomach.

'When I arrived in Portsmouth I was still intent on disappearing, but I had been violently ill during the sea voyage and could do no more than find myself safe lodgings, calling myself Mrs Brown, the name I had used on board ship. Then, I realised my condition. I was carrying your child.' She began to rock herself on the chair. 'I wish I could explain to you that first, joyous realisation: suddenly anything seemed possible. I decided I should move closer to London, where I would be within reach of the best doctors. I reasoned you could not object to me spending your money to protect the baby.

'My landlady had a sister in Camberwell with a lodging house and she recommended me to her.' Felicity stopped rocking and glanced up at him. 'Since she knew me as Mrs Brown I did not like to confess the truth, lest she thought me not respectable enough for her house, but I thought that once the baby was born I would write to you and try to effect a reconciliation.' She shivered. 'Then the sickness returned. I gave money to my landlady to engage a good doctor. Unfortunately, not all his skill or the careful nursing of my landlady proved effective. The baby—a little boy—was born three months early and died within a few hours. I did not even hold him.'

Felicity blinked hard, and stared at the Turkey rug beneath her feet. She would finish this now.

'It was then that I regretted being introduced into such an honest household; all I wanted then was to sink into oblivion. It would have been so easy for the landlady to let me die and keep my money for herself. Instead she paid the doctor to visit me regularly and undertook to nurse me back to health. Gradually, I recovered my strength and from somewhere came the will to live again.

'I saw a notice in the London papers, announcing

my friend Lydia's marriage to Sir James Souden. I decided to write to her and ask for her help.'

'Why did you not write to me?'

She gave the slightest shake of her head. 'I buried all hopes of resuming my life with you when I buried my baby. I thought it was a punishment. Y-you see, when my uncle had died, I felt no grief, no remorse, only relief that I was free of him. Then, when you rescued me in Corunna, it seemed too good to be true, such happiness could not come without a price.

'It was at this time that I read your notice, seeking information about me. Of course no one in Camberwell knew who I was, so I was able to ignore it. I saw one or two more notices, but then they stopped and I learned that the Guards had returned to the Peninsula.' She lifted her head to look at him, her eyes swimming with tears. 'I lost the baby, Nathan. *Our* baby. How could I expect you to forgive that, since I could not forgive myself?'

Nathan put a hand up to his eyes. So many thoughts battered him; he grew cold at the thought of her being so alone. Now he could understand why she had been so determined to stay with Lydia this summer.

Felicity gave a little sob. 'I beg your pardon—pray tell your mama that I, too, am overset by the events of today and I will not dine with you!'

She was at the door before Nathan could collect his scattered thoughts.

'Fee, wait!'

By the time he reached the study door she had disappeared. His mother was standing in the hall, staring into the darkness of the upper landing and without a word he dashed past her and up the stairs.

Five minutes later he came back down to find Mrs Carraway waiting for him.

'Felicity was crying,' she said. 'Have you quarrelled?'

'No, Mama, not exactly, but she is upset.'

'Then should you not go to her?'

'I tried, but she has locked her door. She does not want to talk to me.' Nathan's chin went up. 'I am not such a monster that I would force myself upon her.'

His hand was gripping the carved handrail and she covered it with her own.

'Do you want to tell me, my son?'

He rubbed his eyes. 'Later, perhaps, when I have made sense of it all myself.'

Chapter Eighteen

A prolonged bout of tears left Felicity drained and exhausted, but when she had cried herself out and could think rationally, she found she was not sorry that she had told Nathan about the baby. She had no secrets from Nathan now. Her maid arrived at the door, saying that the master had sent her up with a dish of hot soup for m'lady's supper and Felicity's spirits rallied a little. Tomorrow, she told herself, tomorrow we will start afresh.

She rose early the following morning and dressed with care before going down to the breakfast room, only to have her burgeoning hopes dashed when Mercer informed her that the earl had already breakfasted and gone out riding.

'He is not alone?' she said anxiously.

'No, my lady, Patrick is with him.'

With this she had to be satisfied, but she had

no inclination for a solitary breakfast and went in search of Mrs Carraway.

She found her mama-in-law sitting in her sunny morning room, writing letters.

'Do come in, my dear, these can wait.'

'Thank you.' Felicity stooped to fondle Bella's ears when the spaniel came up to say hello to her. 'She seems fully recovered now, Mama Carraway,'

'I believe she is, and Nathan tells me he is inclined to believe he was mistaken, that there was no poison in the ale.'

'But Bella—'

'She is an old dog and may well have suffered a slight stroke. She would have recovered even without Nathan's pouring coffee down her throat.' The older woman sighed. 'We must hope that is the case, for I cannot bear to think that anyone wishes to harm my son.'

'Nor I, ma'am,' added Felicity earnestly. 'But can he really believe this was not another attempt on his life? I cannot credit it.'

'Nathan and I discussed it last night. He says it is all coincidence and conjecture. He was at pains to assure me that he does not think his life is in danger.'

'Well, ma'am, I wish he had been at pains to reassure *me*.'

'That is difficult, of course, when you lock yourself away.'

Felicity flushed at the gentle rebuke in the words. She said quietly, 'We quarrelled last night. Did he tell you?'

'No.' Mrs Carraway moved over to the sofa and beckoned Felicity to join her. 'Nathan has never worn his heart on his sleeve. He does not readily discuss the things that matter most to him.'

Felicity clasped and unclasped her hands nervously. She took a deep breath. 'Then, I think *I* should tell you. Everything, ma'am.'

Haltingly, and with a few tears, Felicity told her story. She blushed when she spoke of mistresses and hesitated before voicing her suspicions about Gerald Appleby, but Mrs Carraway was not shocked, and merely patted her hands when she had finished.

'Thank you for your honesty, my dear; I may live retired here at Rosthorne, but my friends keep me well informed about the ways of the world. I do not think you need worry about Lady Ansell. I recognised her as a schemer almost at once, and you may be sure that Nathan knows it, too.'

'But what of his cousin, Mama Carraway?' Felicity twisted her hands together. 'I believe Nathan is in danger and—'

'I have never thought Gerald anxious to inherit

the title. However, I am sure Nathan would not dismiss your suspicions without good reason.' She smiled. 'I will talk to him when he comes home. For now, I think we should—' She broke off as the door opened and Mrs Norton came in carrying a letter.

'Excuse me, madam, this has just arrived for you. From the earl.'

Felicity did not need to hear the last few words, she recognised the heavy black writing immediately. With a word of thanks Mrs Carraway broke open the seal and unfolded the crackling paper.

'Oh,' she said. 'He is on his way to Bath.'

A cold, hard hand clutched at Felicity's heart. 'Was there a message for me, Mrs Norton?' she asked.

'No, my lady. Patrick brought only two notes, the other being for Lord Rosthorne's valet. Patrick is having the horses put to the earl's travelling carriage and plans to join him again tonight. It would appear his lordship intends to be away for some time.'

'Yes, it does, Norton. Thank you, that will be all.' Mrs Carraway waited until her companion had retired before turning her attention again to the letter.

'He is going to Lady Ansell,' muttered Felicity. 'You see, ma'am, I have driven him away.'

'Well, it is Nathan's usual untidy scrawl,' said Mrs Carraway, not noticeably disheartened. 'But he wrote this from Appleby Manor. So *that* is why he went out so early this morning.'

'Do you think he went to confront his cousin?' asked Felicity.

'He does not say so, merely that he is accompanying Gerald and Lady Charlotte to Bath.' Mrs Carraway looked up, a decided twinkle in her eyes. 'That does not sound to me like a man going off to seek his lover.' She folded the letter. 'It does seem odd that they should set off today. I suggest you pen a note for Patrick to take back to his master, requesting an explanation. After that, you should put it from your mind, for it is Boxing Day, and we have work to do!'

Felicity made an effort to smile as she carried out her duties as mistress of Rosthorne, distributing the Christmas boxes to the servants and taking baskets of food to the poorest villagers. Somehow she managed to get through the day, but despite her resolve not to allow herself to fall prey to useless conjecture, when she retired to her bed that night her dreams were disturbed by images of Nathan whirling around the dance floor with Serena Ansell in his arms.

* * *

'Three days and still no word from Nathan, save a short scrawl to say he has arrived safely and is staying at the York,' remarked Mrs Carraway as they sat down to breakfast. 'One would have thought he might by now have written to explain just exactly why he went to Bath.' She looked over the rim of her coffee cup at Felicity. 'Did you write to him as I suggested?'

'No, Mama Carraway, I did not. I have tried his patience too far—Lord Rosthorne is no longer interested in me.'

'Oh, my dear, that is not true!'

'No?' Felicity put up her chin. 'When he did not have the courtesy to write to tell me he was going away?' She pushed back her chair. 'If you will excuse me, I think I shall take Bella for a walk. I feel in need of a little fresh air.'

She took the little dog out into the park and while Bella spent a happy hour snuffling around the trees and bushes, Felicity wondered how on earth she was going to survive the rest of her life. It was her own fault. Perhaps if she had not told Nathan about the baby he might have forgiven her for running away from him, but they had agreed, no secrets. She had kept to that, but now Nathan had gone to Bath without any word at all to her.

She blinked rapidly. She would not cry, that

would do no good. She must make a life for herself as mistress of Rosthorne. It was not so very bad, she told herself—she had a comfortable home and could command almost any luxury. She had every reason to be happy.

Except one.

Nathan did not love her.

Felicity returned to the house quietly resolved to do her duty. She spoke to the gardener about the spring planting for the gardens then went off to see Mrs Mercer to discuss menus for the week. With such activities she was determined to keep herself busy but when the stable clock chimed the hour she realised with dismay that it was still only noon. The rest of her day stretched interminably before her, and with a feeling of despondency she sank down on the sofa in the morning room and wept.

'My dear girl, whatever is the matter?'

Mrs Carraway's concerned voice brought Felicity to her feet.

'Oh, it is n-nothing, ma'am! A mere irritation of the nerves, that is all...'

Felicity went to the window to wipe her eyes. Knowing signs of her distress would still be in her face, she kept her back to the room as she heard her mother-in-law murmuring instructions to a servant.

'Come and sit down by me, Felicity.'

Slowly she returned to the sofa. 'Oh, ma'am, you must think me so foolish,' she muttered, kneading her handkerchief between her fingers. 'Nathan should never have married me, and now—'

'Hush.' Mrs Carraway patted her hands. 'I think you and Nathan are both a pair of very silly children.' She looked up as the door opened. 'Ah, Norton. You have brought the box? Bless you, my dear. Put it here, on the sofa between us—thank you.' She waited until they were alone again, then she put her hand on the box and said quietly, 'I think it is time I shared this with you.

'Nathan brought this box home with him from the Peninsula and gave it to me for safe keeping. It contains his most precious mementos: the miniatures of myself and his father; letters from me and from his friends.' She opened the lid and sifted through the papers. 'And this.' She lifted a folded paper and handed it to Felicity. 'It is a letter he wrote to Adam Elliston the day he marched out of Corunna. I think you should read it, because it mentions you.' Felicity took it and stared at the heavy black letters of the inscription. Mrs Carraway continued, 'I know you are convinced that Nathan married you merely to protect you, but I think this tells a very different story.'

Felicity unfolded the two sheets of stiff paper. She began to read.

Adam

Forgive this hurried scrawl and God grant that you read this before you leave Corunna. My orders have arrived. We march today and I know that you will not be far behind us. It was our intention that we should drink a toast together before setting off to join up with Moore's army marching north from Portugal, but the usual confusions of providing food and billets for so large a force as this, added to the delays and frustrations of our disembarking here, have made it all but impossible to do more than snatch a few moments with you. And of course there is my dear wife now to consider, but you will not begrudge me any time I have spent with her, for you know that she has stolen my heart. Felicity—aptly named indeed, for she has become my Life,

As she came to the end of the first page Felicity gave a little sob and put a hand to her mouth.

'Oh,' she breathed. 'I never knew.'

'No,' murmured Mrs Carraway, smiling. 'And

Nathan never told you. You had best read on, although the rest of the letter may not concern you quite so much.'

'Oh, but it does,' murmured Felicity, turning to the second page. 'This concerns me very much indeed!' Her heart thudding in her chest, Felicity realised she had seen this page before, but not in this context.

my Passion.

You will understand how it is, a new husband has his duties. This unforeseen marriage has made demands upon my purse as well as my time, so I am unable to leave you any coin, but to ease my conscience at abandoning you at this time I enclose my ring, an infinitesimal token of my regard. Wear it for me—or if circumstances dictate and you are in dire need, pray sell it, I know you would only do so out of the greatest necessity and I shall never reproach you for it.

Yours etc, as ever

Nathan C.

'Adam died in Spain in the year '11,' said Mrs Carraway, when Felicity had finished reading. 'Nathan told me that he was charged with returning Adam's personal effect to his parents, and this letter was amongst them.'

Felicity handed the letter back to Mrs Carraway. 'I believe Serena read this letter before Adam saw it. She used the letter and the ring to trick me!'

And Serena was now in Bath. With Nathan.

'So, my dear...' Mrs Carraway carefully folded the letter and placed it back in the box. 'He did love you, and loves you still, I think. Will you not write to him, before it is too late?'

Felicity sighed. She *could* write to Nathan, but a piece of paper seemed poor defence against the wiles of Serena Ansell.

'No,' she said slowly. 'I shall not write to him.' She turned to Mrs Carraway, a determined tilt to her chin. 'I shall go to Bath,' she announced. 'This time I am going to fight!'

As Nathan strode away from Bladud Buildings, he thought there was no more dismal place than Bath on a winter's afternoon. It was no longer raining, but there was a chilly dampness in the air that crept into one's bones. He longed to be back at Rosthorne, sitting with Felicity in front of a roaring fire. Dear Fee. He had spent most of the night writing a long letter to her and sent it off express. He hoped, once she had read it, that she would understand why he had been obliged to post off to Bath so urgently.

Gerald pounced upon him as soon as he entered the house in Laura Place.

'Well?'

Nathan shook his head. 'Doctor Thomas is not expected back until tonight.' He let out an exasperated sigh. 'Surely there is another physician we could consult.'

Gerald drew him into the morning room and shut the door. 'I would prefer to wait for Dr Thomas. He has been Mama's physician for years. She will be less suspicious if he comes to see her.'

'Very well, I will call again tomorrow morning.'

'I will come with you,' said Gerald, 'and we won't leave Bladud Buildings until we have seen him!' He put a hand on his shoulder. 'I am very grateful to you for coming with me, Cos. There was no one else I could trust with this. I have not even told the servants here the true state of affairs, only that Mama is not well.'

'Is that wise? Surely it would be better to bring in a nurse—'

'As soon as Dr Thomas has examined her and we have his opinion, then I will hire as many people as I need to look after her,' Gerald interrupted him, looking uncharacteristically grim. 'Until then I do what I can to prevent the news of her...affliction...from spreading.'

'Very well.' Nathan rubbed his chin. 'I can give

you one more day, Gerald, then I must get back to Rosthorne.'

'I understand, and I appreciate all you have done for me.' Gerald raised a smile. 'Will you dine with us?'

Nathan shook his head. 'Thank you, but given my aunt's state of mind I think it would be better if I did not stay. Sir James Souden is in Bath with his wife, and they have invited me to dine with them tonight.'

'Until tomorrow then.'

Nathan gripped his hand. 'Until tomorrow. And let us hope we can get this matter settled quietly!'

It took Felicity two days to reach Bath. The earl having taken his elegant travelling carriage, she had been obliged to use the more elderly barouche and Mrs Carraway's equally elderly coachman, who refused to entertain the countess's suggestion that they should drive through the night.

As they drew up outside the York House Hotel Felicity glanced at her elegant little carriage clock. It was still early and she thought there was a good chance that the earl might not yet have left his rooms. Head high, she sailed through the hotel and up to the earl's apartment. Her spirits dipped a little when Sam opened the door to her and announced that the earl had already gone out.

'He is gone to Laura Place, I believe, m'lady,' said the valet, eyeing the large corded trunk that was being heaved up the stairs under the watchful eye of Felicity's maid.

'Laura Place?'

'To call upon Lady Charlotte.'

Felicity realised she had been holding her breath. She gave a little sigh of relief, but another anxiety quickly crept up on her.

'Oh. And Mr Appleby will be there, I suppose. Has the earl taken Patrick with him?'

'No, ma'am. His lordship was walking, and had no need of his groom.' Sam looked at her closely, then gave a reassuring smile. 'You've no need to worry about Mr Appleby, m'lady. Sound as a gun, he is. Bit of a rattle, but 'tidn't him who means his lordship any harm, if that's what's worrying you.'

She read the understanding in the valet's eyes and allowed herself to relax a little.

'I confess, I was a little anxious,' she said with a rueful smile. 'Thank you, Sam. I shall walk to Laura Place and join the earl, if you will tell me the way.'

Sam grinned at her. 'I think I have a map here somewhere, madam…'

Arriving at Laura Place, Felicity was shown into an over-furnished room while the servant went off to fetch her mistress. Felicity wondered if she had been too impetuous, and if she would have done better to change out of her travelling dress before setting off in search of Nathan. She was sure Lady Charlotte would think so, but Felicity realised with a little kick of pleasure that she did not care what Lady Charlotte thought. A glance in the mirror told her that her hair was still tidily confined beneath her modish bonnet with its swansdown trim and her olive-green pelisse looked surprisingly fresh despite her long journey. Added to this, Nathan had said he liked her in that particular shade of green and that was all that mattered to her. The door opened and she turned with a calm smile to greet her hostess.

'Lady Charlotte. I understood my husband was here.'

'He has gone out with Gerald.' Lady Charlotte regarded her with her cold stare. 'I did not know that you were in Bath. Rosthorne did not say.'

'I arrived this morning.'

'So the earl does not know you are here?'

'No, madam. I walked here with my maid to surprise him.'

Lady Charlotte gave a flicker of a smile. Could it be a little sign of approval at last? wondered Felicity. The old lady's tone was certainly a little warmer when she next spoke.

'The gentlemen are likely to be some time. I wonder, Lady Rosthorne, if you would give me the pleasure of your company in a walk to Sydney Gardens? The sun, you see, is trying to shine, and it would be a pity to miss the best of this short winter day.'

'I should be delighted to come with you, ma'am.'

'Give me a moment, then, to put on my coat.' At the door Lady Charlotte turned. 'Your maid can go back to the hotel, Lady Rosthorne. You will not need her in the Gardens—we will be much more comfortable on our own.'

Felicity waited, smiling to herself. This was a change indeed, if even the proud and haughty Lady Charlotte was warming to her!

Ten minutes later they were at the entrance to the Sydney Gardens. Lady Charlotte had set a surprisingly swift pace, hurrying along Great Pulteney Street with her hands tucked deep inside a huge fur muff.

An icy wind was blowing and Felicity was not surprised to find the gardens almost empty.

'This must be a delightful venue in the summer,' remarked Felicity, looking around her. 'I think, though, we might have the gardens to ourselves today.'

Lady Charlotte did not answer and Felicity

was faintly irritated. Why had Lady Charlotte requested her company if she was not going to talk to her?

They crossed the wide carriage-way that ran around the perimeter of the gardens and followed one of the winding paths into the centre, where the trees and bushes blocked out any sounds from the traffic on Sydney Place. Felicity was about to suggest that it was time they were turning back when Lady Charlotte stopped.

'This will do.'

Felicity looked about her. 'Do for what?' she asked, laughing a little. 'There is nothing here save bushes! Perhaps you could show me the sham castle, or the maze—' She broke off. Lady Charlotte had stepped away from her.

'No, we shall go no further, Lady Rosthorne.' She pulled one hand from the fur muff and levelled a small silver-mounted pistol at Felicity.

'I—I do not understand.'

Lady Charlotte's eyes narrowed. 'I know your little game,' she hissed. 'And you will not succeed. You tricked my nephew into marriage, then left him because he was not rich enough for you. You came back only when he became earl, and now you are determined to deny my son his inheritance.'

'Lady Charlotte, I assure you—'

'You think to secure the title with an heir, do you not? While you and your husband were estranged you did not matter, but now—! Bad enough to have my nephew in the way, but I cannot allow you to give him an heir.'

Felicity saw her raise the pistol. She said quickly, 'I have no wish to deny Gerald the title, ma'am, if you consider it his right.'

'Of course it is his right!' Lady Charlotte's eyes snapped angrily. 'Appleby died soon after Gerald was born and we returned to live with my brother, the earl. Gerald was brought up as one of his own.'

'Nathan told me the old earl was a very kind man…'

'Kindness had nothing to do with it! He wanted Gerald to inherit. Nathan was never his favourite, never!'

Felicity said gently, 'But the old earl had three sons of his own, ma'am, no one could have foreseen—'

'I did.' Lady Charlotte drew herself up. 'When the three boys died, I knew it was meant to be. It was a judgement. Nathan was a soldier; it was only a matter of time before he too perished in battle.'

Felicity fixed her eyes on the old woman's face

and tried not to think about the little pistol pointed at her heart. She must keep her talking.

'But Nathan survived the war and came back to London.'

'Yes, and I knew then what I had to do.'

The cold was eating into Felicity, joining with her fear to make her shiver.

'So it was you behind the attempts to kill Nathan. But how? Did you pay someone?'

Lady Charlotte's lip curled. 'Nothing so vulgar. Harris did it for me.'

'Harris! Your groom?'

'Yes. I have to tell him everything in detail, of course, because he does not have all his wits, but he is devoted to me. Unfortunately he is a poor shot, so his first attempt failed.'

'As did the second,' put in Felicity. 'In Lady Stinchcombe's garden.'

'Yes. I thought he would manage that better. I knew Rosthorne liked to smoke that horrid tobacco so I sent Harris out to the garden. I told him to unlock the garden door to make his escape, but somehow he failed, as he did in Green Park. But you were there, my dear. You were in the park, were you not? You saw him.'

'I did not recognise him.' A faint sound caught Felicity's attention. Voices. Someone was in the gardens. If only she could buy a little more time! 'And was it Harris, too, in the Home Wood?'

'Yes, but you foiled that attempt, did you not? Harris was obliged to flee or risk being recognised. Poor Harris, he came back gibbering about the injury to Rosthorne's horse. That was when I knew I would have to take a hand to do the job myself. Harris brought me the hemlock from the stables and I poured it into the ale. It was very simple.'

'If Bella had not tripped up the footman.'

The voices were growing louder. Felicity longed to cry out, but she knew that as soon as she drew breath to scream Lady Charlotte would shoot. Her hand was so steady Felicity had no doubt she would hit her mark. She raised her voice a little.

'So where is Harris now?'

For the first time Lady Charlotte looked confused. 'Gerald sent him on an errand, before we set off for Bath. He said he would follow us…'

There was a movement in the bushes behind Lady Charlotte. Felicity was aware of several figures moving closer, but she dared not let her eyes wander, she must keep Lady Charlotte's attention fixed upon her.

'Let us return to the house, ma'am. Perhaps Harris has arrived…'

'No!' Those cold eyes narrowed, immediately

suspicious. 'No, we shall finish it now. At least with you dead it will give me time to dispose of my nephew!'

She raised the pistol, taking careful aim. Felicity held her breath. Everything happened at once. Felicity saw Nathan spring from the bushes and launch himself at Lady Charlotte even as her finger closed on the trigger. A shot rang out and something whistled past Felicity's head. She jumped back, her mind whirling as the tension of the past few minutes caught up with her. Suddenly it was all too much and she felt herself falling into blackness.

'What do you think you are doing?' Lady Charlotte's outraged voice made itself heard above the confusion. 'Unhand me at once!'

'It is all right, Mama, I am here.' Gerald came running up. He gently prised the weapon from her fingers.

'Did I kill her? She was in your way, my son. I could not allow that.'

Nathan glanced towards the gentleman in the frock-coat kneeling beside Felicity.

'Doctor?' Anxiety made his voice harsh.

'The bullet missed her, my lord. She is concussed by the fall.'

'Doctor Thomas.' Lady Charlotte stopped struggling with her son and looked across. 'What are you doing here?'

'Why, I came to see you, madam,' said the doctor cheerfully, getting to his feet.

'See to your patient,' muttered Nathan, brushing past him and taking his place beside Felicity's still form. 'I will look after my wife.' He tore off his own gloves and Felicity's and chafed her cold hands. A wave of intense relief washed through him as her eyelids fluttered.

'Where am I? Uncle Philip?' She stared up at him, a slight crease in her brows. Nathan saw the shadow of alarm darken her eyes and she snatched her hand away. 'You are not my uncle. Go away! *Déjeme!*'

'Felicity.' He tried to lift her, but she fought against him wildly.

Dr Thomas hurried over. 'Hysterics,' he muttered, 'brought on by the shock of her ordeal or the blow on the head when she fell. Allow me, my lord.' He bent over and caught Felicity's hands. 'Come along, Lady Rosthorne. No need to be afraid, I am a doctor.'

Nathan watched, helpless, as the doctor raised Felicity to her feet. Her eyes were staring and she continued to ramble.

'He must not find me. I am his wife in name only...

it is a judgement. We can never be happy. Forgive me, Uncle, I did not mean to be so wicked...'

She collapsed again. Nathan looked to the doctor. He was frowning.

'Go and find a cab, my lord. I will attend to Lady Rosthorne and bring her to the entrance of the gardens. Mr Appleby, if you can look after your mother I shall call upon her later.'

Fear gnawed at Nathan as he accompanied Dr Thomas back to the hotel. Felicity was laid in his bed and he could barely contain his impatience until the doctor emerged from the bedroom.

'Is she all right? May I see her?'

'You may go in if you wish, but she is asleep now—I have given her laudanum to help her rest. She has a lump on her head, but I do not think it is anything to worry about.'

'But she was rambling—'

'Her thoughts are scrambled. It means nothing.' He smiled. 'She is young and strong, my lord. She will wake in a few hours none the worse for her ordeal, I am sure. Now if you will excuse me, I shall go back to Laura Place.'

When the doctor had gone Nathan went back into the bedroom. Felicity was lying motionless in the centre of the bed. She looked very frail, her eyes closed and her dark lashes resting against her bloodless cheeks. During all his time as a soldier he had never known such fear as he had experienced when he and Gerald had arrived back at Laura Place with Dr Thomas, only to be told that Lady Charlotte had stepped out some half-hour earlier with Felicity. He had led the way to Sydney Gardens, not caring for the stares of passers-by as he raced along the street and into the trees, expecting at any moment to hear Felicity's screams splitting the silence.

He reached out and placed a gentle hand on her forehead. There was no fever, but her unnatural immobility unnerved him. What if she awoke and did not know him? She had called out for her uncle—what if her mind was trapped in the past, would she not be terrified to find herself being cared for by a stranger?

He jumped up, unable to bear the idleness any longer. With a curt word to Felicity's maid to look to her mistress, he plunged out into the street. Darkness had fallen over the city and a cold drizzle had set in but Nathan did not heed it, nor the surprised look he received from Sir James's butler when he demanded to see Lady Souden.

'I regret my lady is not at home, my lord. Sir James and Lady Souden are dining out and then going on to the ball at the Lower Rooms.'

Nathan found himself back on the street. He

glanced down at his sodden coat and muddy boots. It was not to be expected that he would be allowed into the Assembly Rooms in such a state. Jamming his hat more firmly upon his head, he turned and headed back along the street.

The heavy blackness that engulfed Felicity was lifting. She lay very still, her eyes closed. Something was not right. The bed was very comfortable, but it was not her bed. She was not at Rosthorne. She could hear the steady tick, tick of a clock in the room, and the sound of voices and the occasional rumble of a carriage outside. Perhaps she was in London, at Souden House. Slowly she opened her eyes. The candlelight was too dim for her to see in any great detail, but she was certain she had never seen this room before. She looked at the figure sitting beside the fire and some of her unease drained away.

'Martha.'

Her voice sounded a little strained, but it worked. The maid hurried over, a beaming smile on her face.

'Milady! We've been that worried about you.'

Felicity frowned and closed her eyes. Her memory was trickling back.

'Oh yes, Sydney Gardens.' Slowly she put up

her hand and touched the base of her skull. 'Did someone hit me over the head?'

'No, miss, my lord says you banged your head as you fell. He and the doctor brought you back here.'

'Doctor?'

'Doctor Thomas, my lady.' Martha helped her to sit up. 'I hear he's one of the best in Bath, and Lady Charlotte's physician, too. He left you more laudanum, if you wish to take it madam...'

'No. No, thank you, Martha, just a little water.'

Felicity leaned back against her pillows and tried to think. She felt weak, but apart from a bruise on her head she could feel no other damage. She recalled staring at the black muzzle of the pistol. Lady Charlotte had fired, she was sure of it, but something had happened.

'Where is Lord Rosthorne?'

'That I don't know, m'lady.'

Felicity slid her legs over the edge of the bed. 'I shall get up.'

'Ooh, my lady, I think you should not get out of bed until his lordship returns.'

'And when will that be?' Martha hesitated. 'You do not know that either, I suppose. Well, help me into my wrap.'

Felicity was pleased to find that her legs still

worked. She walked to the door and found Nathan's man tending the fire in the sitting room.

'Where is your master?'

Sam jumped to his feet. 'My lady, you surprised me! I thought you was still asleep.'

'Quite clearly I am not,' retorted Felicity, feeling stronger by the minute. 'Where is Lord Rosthorne?'

'He's gone out, ma'am.'

'Oh. Did he have an engagement?'

'No, madam, not that I know of.'

'And when did he leave?'

Sam looked at the clock. 'About a half-hour since. He said something about a ball at the Lower Rooms, changed into his evening dress, and went out.'

'A ball?' Felicity steadied herself with a hand on the back of a chair. Why would Nathan go to a ball while she was lying unconscious in his bed? Unless… 'A ball at the Lower Rooms would be quite well attended by Bath residents, would it not?'

'I would think so,' replied Sam slowly. 'I believe the entertainments in the Lower Rooms are highly regarded.'

Entertainments. Felicity's fingers dug into the back of the chair. He had left her in a laudanum-induced sleep while he attended an entertainment!

Slowly she turned on her heel and went back into the bedroom, closing the door behind her with a snap.

Bath might believe itself very thin of company, but Nathan considered the three hundred or so people crowded into the Lower Rooms to be far too many. It was almost impossible to find anyone. Suddenly he spotted Sir James Souden and he cut through the crowd to intercept him.

'Well now, Rosthorne.' Sir James stopped, smiling. 'What do you mean, to be scowling so at everyone?'

'Was I scowling?' returned Nathan mildly. 'I was not aware of it.'

'Be damned to you, of course you were scowling,' retorted Sir James. 'Can't say I blame you, either, if it keeps the inquisitive at bay. I can't tell you the number of people who have asked me about this mysterious marriage of yours. It's becoming tedious, my friend!'

'Tell 'em to mind their own business.'

'I do, but it don't stop 'em speculating. Should have brought the lady with you, Nathan. That's the only way to stop the gossip.'

'As a matter of fact, she *is* here, but she is not well. Confined to her room. In fact, I wanted to talk to Lady Souden about her...'

'Here to take the waters, is she? That's precisely why we are in Bath, so that Lydia can regain her strength after her lying in.' Sir James looked past Nathan and smiled. 'Ah, here is my wife now, and Lady Ansell, too. You know her, of course, Rosthorne—she tells me you are neighbours in Hampshire. Servant, ma'am!'

Nathan turned to find Lady Souden approaching with Serena by her side. He swallowed his frustration; he had no intention of mentioning Felicity to anyone but Lydia Souden.

'You are both looking far too serious,' said Lydia, twinkling. 'Lady Ansell suggested we should come over and put an end to that.'

Serena gave them her brilliant smile. 'Good evening, Sir James, and to you, Lord Rosthorne.' Nathan's curt nod had no visible effect. She merely smiled more broadly. 'Do you mean to intimidate me with your severe frown, sir?'

Sir James laughed. 'Just what I was telling Rosthorne, ma'am; his scowls are likely to frighten the ladies.'

'I fear the earl has been too long without company,' murmured Serena.

Nathan met those green eyes and read the blatant invitation in them. 'Thank you, madam, but I am well content.'

'How can one be content at a ball if one does

not dance?' purred Serena. She stepped across to stand beside him, looking up at him under her lashes. 'Come, Nathan—will you not tread one little measure with me?'

'Thank you, but I do not dance tonight.'

'No doubt the earl is missing his wife,' remarked Lady Souden, frowning a little at this exchange. 'Why did you not bring Felicity with you?'

Before Nathan could speak, Serena was taking his arm.

'I found Lady Rosthorne to be very shy,' she murmured, flashing him a conspiratorial smile. 'We do not look to see her in Bath, do we, Nathan?'

He observed Lydia's disapproving look. She began to pull Sir James away towards the supper room. Damnation, Serena was intimating that she was his mistress! He would have to get rid of her before he could go after Lydia and ask her to visit Felicity. Serena turned towards him.

'You are very elusive, Nathan. Did you not receive my note?'

'Yes, but I came to Bath on business, madam.'

'Surely your business cannot take up all your time.' Her voice was very soft, caressing. 'If you cannot visit me, I could come to York House…' He looked down at her and she gave a low laugh. 'You are a fool to resist me, my dear, and for what? A little mouse who is no real wife to you.' Her hand in its silk glove slid over his chest. 'We could… comfort one another.'

He stared down at her, wondering why it was that those perfect features and brilliant green eyes held no allure for him. All he wanted was to have a pair of candid grey eyes smiling at him as if he was their whole delight…

'The Countess of Rosthorne!'

Chapter Nineteen

Nathan's head snapped up as the servant made his announcement. Surely he had misheard?

A hush fell over the ballroom and all eyes turned towards the door. Felicity stood in the doorway, pale and beautiful in rose silk, a shimmering gold scarf across her arms and her hair falling in soft curls around her face. His heart swelled with pride as Mr Guynette, the MC, escorted her across the room towards him.

'Not such a little mouse, madam,' murmured Nathan, detaching himself from Serena's grasp.

He realised he was grinning as Felicity came towards him, her head held high and a confident smile on her lips. Little witch—just when had she turned into such an indomitable woman?

Nathan's look of surprised delight bolstered Felicity's spirits. She was his countess, and he was proud of her—she could read it in his eyes. She was no longer shy little Felicity Bourne, afraid to speak out for fear of reprisals. She was the Countess of Rosthorne! Felicity crossed the room, trying to ignore the fact that everyone was staring at her and her knees were shaking. Mr Guynette was talking to her, but she was not listening. Her whole attention was fixed upon her husband.

'My lord, I regret I could not be here earlier.' Her eyes flickered over Serena Ansell, standing tall and beautiful beside Nathan. She breathed in, pulling herself up another inch as she held out her hand. 'But I am here now, sir, and await your pleasure.'

For a long, long moment everyone in the room seemed to hold their breath, watching the little tableau being acted out before them. It took all Felicity's courage to keep her hand extended and her eyes upon Nathan. Not by so much as the flicker of an eyelid did she reveal the fear that gnawed at her, that he might reject her. Then slowly, she saw Nathan's smile deepen. He walked forward, reaching out to take her hand in his own.

'The pleasure, ma'am, is all mine.'

His words and the look that accompanied them made her heart soar. Nathan tucked her hand into his arm and walked away with her. The ballroom, released from its spell, began to hum again with conversation, the orchestra struck up for the next dance, and everything returned to normal. Except that Felicity and Nathan found themselves almost mobbed by Rosthorne's acquaintances, demanding that he present them to his lady.

It was almost an hour before they could talk together undisturbed. Nathan escorted her to a secluded alcove.

'I thought I should never get you to myself,' he said when at last they were seated. He subjected her to a searching gaze. 'Are you sure you are well enough to be here? I left you sleeping.'

'I am well aware of that, sir, and I took it very ill that you should go out enjoying yourself without me!'

His lips twitched. 'I beg your pardon, madam. I came to find Lady Souden; you did not know me earlier, and I thought that if you were still confused when you woke again you might feel more comfortable if your friend was with you.'

'How thoughtful of you!' Felicity smiled up at him, blinking away a tear. 'You are so *very* good to me!'

A smile glimmered in his eyes. 'I look after my own, madam! But you are very pale. Tell me truthfully, you have no pains, no headache?'

'No, no, I am quite well, now. I was a little dizzy when I first woke up, but that soon passed.'

'Good. Then tell me now how you come to be in Bath.'

'Your second-best travelling carriage, my lord…'

'Yes, yes, saucy Jane, but why?'

'I came to be with you, my lord,' she said simply. 'Mama Carraway and I decided I should follow you. Of course, if I had known about Lady Charlotte I should not have followed you to Laura Place.'

'Imagine my surprise when Gerald and I arrived back there to be told you had walked out with her! I was afraid we would not find you in time—'

'I kept her talking as long as I could.' Felicity shivered. 'She told me *everything*, Nathan. The poor woman is quite deranged.'

'I know. That was why I rode over to Appleby Manor on Boxing Day, to talk to Gerald about it, but he was already making plans to bring her to Bath. He begged me to accompany him. I wrote to you yesterday, explaining everything.'

'Then your letter will be waiting for me when I get back.' She took a deep breath and looked him in the eye. 'I have stopped running, Nathan. I want to be a proper wife, if you will let me.'

'If I will let—oh, my love that is all I ever

wanted!' He reached across the table for her hand. 'In fact, I want to kiss you right now.'

She squeezed his fingers, warmed by the soft look in his eyes. 'I would like that too—but not here...'

'No, of course not.'

He sat back, and she saw the light die out of his face, leaving him looking very serious.

'My dear?' Felicity watched him, a tiny frown creasing her brow. 'Nathan, what is it?'

'Talking to Sir James last night. There are rumours, hints of unrest in France. If that is so, if Bonaparte should rise again—'

She caught his hand. She said quietly, 'If you think it is your duty to rejoin your regiment then I shall not stand in your way, Nathan. But make sure you come back to me, my love.'

He raised her hand to his lips. 'You may be sure of that! Do you know,' he said, gazing deep into her eyes, 'I am suddenly very tired.' The message she read in his eyes made her blush to the roots of her hair. 'Shall we go?'

'Yes,' she whispered, her insides turning to water. 'If you please.'

He rose and held out his hand to her. 'Come along; let us take our leave.'

They walked out through the ballroom where the dancing was still in progress. Felicity saw Lady

Ansell going down the dance with a fair-haired youth. The widow looked up and Felicity met her cold stare with a brief, haughty look of her own before turning away to accompany Nathan across the room to Sir James Souden, who grinned at them.

'Leaving us so early, Rosthorne?'

'It has been an eventful day,' said Nathan. 'Pray give our regards to your wife.'

'She will be sorry she missed you. She is off dancing somewhere.' He shook his head. 'She told me she wanted to come here to take the waters, but there doesn't seem to be much amiss, if she can dance all night the way she does.'

'I wish I could stay and talk to her—' Felicity broke off, aware of Nathan's hand under her elbow. 'But we must leave this instant. Give her my love, Sir James, and tell her I will speak to her tomorrow.'

She turned to accompany Nathan to the door, but they had not gone many paces before Serena Ansell stepped in front of them.

'So your little wife still hangs upon your sleeve,' she sneered. 'Quite the picture of marital harmony. How provincial.'

Felicity stiffened. It was unfortunate that the music had stopped, and Serena's words fell into the sudden quiet. She heard someone close by titter.

'Is it so unfashionable to dote upon one's wife?' returned Nathan.

'You were not always so devoted a husband.'

'Possibly not.' He smiled down at Felicity. 'That was an error and I admit it. But my lady and I have no secrets from each other now.'

Serena looked up at him under her lashes. 'What, none, my lord?'

The meaning was so transparent that Felicity's fingers curled into claws. Nathan put a restraining hand over hers.

'None, Lady Ansell. We have discussed…everything.' He gave a smile as false as her own and turned to leave.

'Then I wish you joy of her, my lord,' Serena called after him. 'Until your countess runs away from you again!'

Felicity gasped. Nathan came to a halt, then slowly he turned back towards Serena.

'Let us speak plainly, madam,' he said coldly. 'And let me correct any misapprehension that others may have. We have never been lovers. I was never susceptible to the charms you offered so freely, and the fact that you were married to my commanding officer and the mistress of my best friend only diminished any regard I might have had for you. You have tried on more than one occasion to make my wife believe that I have an affection for you; I believe you even intercepted my letter to Elliston and used it for your own purposes before passing it on to him. But your stratagems failed, madam. I am happy to state here, quite publicly, that I never was, and never will be, an admirer of yours!'

A look of shock and horror replaced Serena's smile as his voice carried across the room. Others were sniggering now, but Felicity ignored them. She was astonished at Nathan's open avowal and her heart swelled with pride as she realised how difficult it must be for her reserved husband to speak quite so openly.

'Oh, bravo, my lord,' she applauded him as they left the ballroom. 'That will give the Bath tabbies something to talk of.'

'I fear there can be no reconciliation with Lady Ansell.'

Felicity laughed. 'That is one acquaintance I am happy to forgo!' She looked back over her shoulder. 'I wish I had stayed to speak to Lydia. I fear Sir James will think you most boorish to drag me away so intemperately!'

'Souden is too much of a gentleman to think anything so impolite,' murmured Nathan, leading her out of the building. 'I think he is more likely to excuse my conduct as the actions of a man violently in love.'

Felicity stopped. 'Oh. Oh, do you mean that?'

'Mean what?'

She felt herself blushing in the darkness. There was a constriction in her throat, making it difficult to breathe.

'That…that you are in love. Violently.'

He dragged her into his arms. 'Of course I mean it. I am so very much in love with you that I am going to kiss you here. Now. In the street.'

Before she could protest Felicity found herself swept up in a crushing embrace. When at last Nathan lifted his head, her mouth felt bruised from his savage kiss. She heard a discreet cough and realised that the earl's carriage had drawn up beside them and a wooden-faced footman was holding open the door.

'In with you, baggage,' growled Nathan, 'before I forget myself again.'

Felicity sat beside Nathan for the short journey back to the hotel, her head on his shoulder and her hand clasped in his.

'Nathan?'

'Yes, love?'

'What will happen to Lady Charlotte?'

'Gerald will make provision for her to be looked after at Appleby Manor.'

'And her groom, Harris?'

'We have sent him to my estate near Newmarket.'

Felicity sat up. 'But, Nathan, he tried to kill you!'

'The man is an innocent; he is no danger to me or to anyone else if he is removed from Lady Charlotte's influence. He has a gift for healing; he can work on the stud farm and my men there will keep an eye on him. He can be useful there, Fee, and I think he will be happy.'

She eyed him doubtfully. 'If you are sure, Nathan…'

He nodded. 'I am sure.'

'Poor Lady Charlotte,' murmured Felicity. 'I wish you had explained. When you were so reserved, I thought you suspected me…'

'That was never my intention, but I could not tell anyone until I had confirmed my suspicions.' His grip on her hand became momentarily painful. 'I did not want to admit to you that my aunt, a blood relation…'

'You thought that I would think ill of you because of Lady Charlotte's illness? Oh, my dear, I could never do that!' She turned to hug him. 'Only think of my own uncle, eccentric enough to drag me to northern Spain and to spend every penny he had, trusting to God to provide!'

'Eccentric, yes, but not the same!'

'Not so very different, when you think he condemned me to the life of a missionary with no concern for my own wishes.' She caught his hands. 'It is *you* I love, Nathan, for the good, kind man that you are. I love you for your forgiving nature, and your forbearance, when I have been so foolish.'

He pulled her on to his lap. 'We have both been foolish, my love, but no more—let there be no more secrets between us.'

'No,' she whispered. 'None.'

Nathan's hold tightened as Felicity responded to his kiss. She filled his senses, he was drowning in the taste of her, the touch of her fingers on his skin fanned his desire and it was with difficulty that he resisted the temptation to tear away her silken gown and lose himself in the delectable flesh he knew lay beneath it. Reluctantly he eased away from her.

'Enough,' he muttered, breathing heavily. 'We should stop now while I am still able.'

Felicity sighed. 'I never want this to end, Nathan.'

She snuggled into him, her head against his chest and her curls tickling his chin. With admirable resolution he put her gently but firmly on to the seat beside him.

'A jolting carriage is not the place to make love to one's wife. Besides, we are already at York House.'

Felicity straightened her wrap and waited patiently while the carriage slowed to a halt outside the tall, imposing frontage of the hotel. Nathan jumped down and turned to help her out of the carriage, then with one hand possessively about her waist he swept her up the steps and into the building.

Sam was waiting at the door of his apartment.

'Bring some brandy, and wine—or perhaps ratafia for Lady Rosthorne, if you please, Sam,' said Nathan. 'Then you may leave us.'

There was a cheerful fire burning in the sitting room and Nathan helped Felicity to remove her voluminous cloak before drawing her down beside him on the sofa.

'Now,' he said, when they were alone, 'tell me what it was that made you come to Bath.'

'Your mother showed me the letter you had written to Adam before you marched out of Corunna.'

He kissed her neck. 'And what was so special about that?' he murmured.

She closed her eyes, enjoying the touch of his lips on her skin. 'You wrote that you…loved me.'

'Mmm.'

'You never said that to me.'

He raised his head. 'Did I not?'

'Never, until tonight.' She added shyly, 'I did not believe it could be so, until I read your letter.'

He pulled her on to his lap in a rustle of silk.

'How very remiss of me,' he murmured, his mouth against her ear. 'Because I *do* love you. To distraction.'

She slipped her arms about his neck. 'Oh, Nathan, that makes me so happy! I—'

He cut off her words with his mouth, kissing her ruthlessly. She melted beneath the onslaught, almost fainting with love and relief and the sheer bliss of being in his arms again.

At length he broke off, but he kept her on his lap, safely enclosed in his arms and for a while they sat in silence, listening to the crackling of the fire.

'One thing,' said Nathan. 'At the Hazelford Assembly—did anyone else see Serena kissing me?'

She nodded against his chest. 'Mr Elliston.'

'Hah! So that was why he has been so distant of late. Oh, Fee, you little idiot, why did you not challenge me at the time, or come up and slap my face for me? Come to think of it, why did Elliston not charge me with it?'

'B-because I begged him not to say anything.' Felicity dared not look up. 'Serena Ansell is so beautiful, so assured—all the gentlemen think her very desirable.'

'Not all of them, Fee.'

'I am so sorry I doubted you, Nathan,' she whispered.

His arms tightened around her. 'You are not wholly to blame. If I had been more open with you, perhaps you might not have believed her so readily. Hell and damnation, no wonder you have been so unhappy! Did you think I had installed my mistress in the neighbourhood? What a scoundrel I should be to do that! Fee, I should ring your neck for thinking me capable of such a thing!'

'I am sorry,' she said again. 'Sometimes my temper overwhelms me, and I find it impossible to think rationally.'

He kissed the top of her head. 'I'll make sure she does not hurt you again.'

She raised her head and looked into his eyes. 'She cannot hurt me, now I know the truth. Oh, Nathan, I was a fool not to trust you.'

'Let us put all that behind us now, love.'

In one swift, fluid movement he swept her up into his arms and carried her to the door.

'What are you doing?'

'Taking you to bed.'

She gave a little, shaky laugh and buried her head in his shoulder. 'Nathan, the servants! They will see us!'

'Let them. It is a tradition in my family to carry a bride to her bed.'

'It—it is?'

He looked down at her, a wicked glint in his eyes. 'It is now.'

Felicity said no more. He carried her into the bedchamber where a fire blazed merrily in the hearth and a few candles burned around the room. There was no sign of Sam, or Martha.

'I think they knew they would not be needed tonight,' grinned Nathan, gently setting her on her feet. 'Now turn around and let me undress you.'

Amid fevered kisses they began a breathless, undignified scrabble to shed their clothing. It involved many oaths on Nathan's part and much giggling from Felicity until the last stocking had been removed and Nathan scooped her up and placed her none too gently upon the huge bed.

A sudden stillness enveloped them. Felicity lay on her back, looking up at Nathan, his shape outlined blackly above her. In the near-darkness her other senses were heightened—she breathed in the smell of his skin, a mixture of spices and musk and brandy, but at the same time she was aware of the scents from the perfumed candles burning in the room and the hint of herbs coming from the freshly laundered sheets. It was like lying in a meadow on a summer's night.

She reached up and ran the tips of her fingers down Nathan's body, from his neck to his navel. A fierce joy filled her: this was where she belonged. With Nathan, as his partner, his wife.

'By heaven, but you are beautiful,' he muttered hoarsely.

He lowered his head to kiss the valley between her breasts. She held him close, her hands moving over his back while he covered her body with delicate kisses. She stretched beneath him, throwing back her head as she gave herself up to the sensations his touch was arousing. He did not hurry, devoting himself to each area of her body, caressing and kissing her until her senses took flight and she was writhing beneath him, crying his name while her fingers dug into his shoulders. With a wild abandon she gave herself to him, aware of his own growing excitement as their bodies met in a tangle of limbs and hot passionate kisses. Her senses climbed higher and ever higher until she was no longer in control. She clung to Nathan, their two bodies moved together, harder, faster, and they shared a brief moment of exultation before they collapsed, panting, on to the covers.

Felicity lay in the darkness, worn out by the force of her passion. She sighed, trembling, and

Nathan wrapped himself around her. Then, in the safe cocoon of Nathan's arms, she slept.

Nathan's first action the next morning, even before opening his eyes, was to reach for Felicity. She was not there. Quickly he looked around the room, his initial alarm fading when he saw her standing at the window.

It was quite dark, but the moonlight shining in through the window filtered through her thin nightgown, outlining every curve of her body. Desire stirred again. As if aware of his eyes she turned towards him.

'Fee? Is anything wrong?' She came across to stand beside the bed. He sat up. 'What is it, my love?'

She ignored his outstretched hand. 'We said no secrets, Nathan.'

Immediately he was on his guard. It was an effort to keep his voice neutral. 'Is there something you need to tell me?'

She nodded. 'I am going to have a baby.'

At first he thought he had misheard. Then in a bound he was out of bed and standing before her. 'Truly?' He took her hands. Even in the darkness he could tell she was smiling.

'Truly,' she said unsteadily. 'I suspected it some time ago; but now, I am sure.'

Nathan could not restrain himself. He gave a whoop of joy and caught her up in his arms, swinging her around even as he kissed her. Just as suddenly he put her down again.

'I should not have done that. You will need to lie down, to rest—'

'No, no.' Laughing, she put her hands against his chest. 'I am very well, I promise you.'

'But after the last time,' he said decisively, 'you must see a doctor.'

'And so I shall, as soon as we return to Rosthorne Hall.' Her voice softened as she realised the depth of his concern. 'Perhaps, since we are in Bath, I will take the waters. They are said to be most efficacious.'

'Perhaps.' He kissed her, wrapping his arms about her and holding her close. 'Listen.'

He lifted his head. Outside the window the church bells began to chime. 'It is the first day of the new year, my love.'

Felicity laid her head against his heart. 'The first day of our new life, Nathan.'

Epilogue

Notices: *Morning Post* and *St James's Chronicle*: 25th July 1815:

BIRTH
On Monday last, the Countess of Rosthorne, of a son and heir, at the Earl's seat in Hampshire. Lord Rosthorne, a hero of Waterloo, is reported to have returned to England two weeks before the birth. Mother and son are in a fair way.

A Supper and Fireworks held for workers and tenants of the Rosthorne Estate was hailed a great success.

* * * * *

HISTORICAL

Large Print

THE EARL'S RUNAWAY BRIDE
Sarah Mallory

Five years ago, Felicity's dashing husband disappeared into war-torn Spain. Discovering a dark secret, she had fled to England. Still haunted by memories of their passionate wedding night, Felicity is just about to come face to face with her commanding husband – back to claim his runaway bride!

THE WAYWARD DEBUTANTE
Sarah Elliott

Eleanor Sinclair loathes stuffy ballrooms packed with fretful mothers and husband-hunting girls. Craving escape, she dons a wig and disappears – *unchaperoned!* – to the theatre. There she catches the eye of James Bentley, a handsome devil. His game of seduction imperils Eleanor's disguise – and tempts her to forsake all honour…

THE LAIRD'S CAPTIVE WIFE
Joanna Fulford

Taken prisoner by Norman invaders, Lady Ashlynn's salvation takes an unexpected form. Scottish warlord Black Iain may be fierce, yet Ashlynn feels strangely safe in his arms… Iain wants only to be free of the rebellious, enticing Ashlynn. But then a decree from the King commands Iain to make his beautiful captive his *wife*!

MILLS & BOON

HISTORICAL

Large Print

RAKE BEYOND REDEMPTION
Anne O'Brien

Alexander Ellerdine is instantly captivated by Marie-Claude's dauntless spirit – but, as a smuggler, Zan has nothing to offer such a woman. Marie-Claude is determined to unravel the mystery of her brooding rescuer. The integrity in his eyes indicates he's a gentleman…but the secrets and rumours say that he's a rake beyond redemption…

A THOROUGHLY COMPROMISED LADY
Bronwyn Scott

Has Incomparable Dulci Wycroft finally met her match? Jack, Viscount Wainsbridge, is an irresistible mystery. His dangerous work leaves no space for love – yet Dulci's sinfully innocent curves are impossibly tempting. Then Dulci and Jack are thrown together on a journey far from Society's whispers – and free of all constraints…

IN THE MASTER'S BED
Blythe Gifford

To live the life of independence she craves, Jane de Weston disguises herself as a young man. When Duncan discovers the truth he knows he should send her away – but Jane brings light into the dark corners of his heart. Instead, he decides to teach his willing pupil the exquisite pleasures of being a woman…